FIT TO DIE

A Crime and Mystery Collection

RENDEZVOUS
PRESS

FIT TO DIE

A Crime and Mystery Collection

Edited by Joan Boswell and Sue Pike

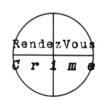

LE CONSEIL DES ARTS
DU CANADA
DEPUIS 1957

THE CANADA COUNCIL
FOR THE ARTS
SINCE 1957

We gratefully acknowledge the support of the Canada Council for the Arts
for our publishing program.

Napoleon Publishing/RendezVous Press
Toronto, Ontario, Canada

Printed in Canada

05 04 03 02 01   5 4 3 2 1

National Library of Canada Cataloguing in Publication Data

Main entry under title:
  Fit to die

Short stories by the Ladies Killing Circle.
ISBN 0-929141-87-3

        1. Detective and mystery stories, Canadian (English)
2. Canadian fiction (English)--21st century. I. Boswell, Joan
II. Pike, Sue, date- III. Ladies' Killing Circle.

PS8323.D4F58 2001   C813'.08720806   C2001-901968-8
PR9197.35.D48F58 2001

TABLE OF CONTENTS

FIT TO LIVE

AUDREY JESSUP

I could have strangled Merrilee Parker. In my role as
President of the Social Activities Club at Sunset Lodge
Seniors' Residence, I had just announced that we would be
holding tai chi classes every Monday and Thursday morning
starting the next week.

"Tai chi?" Merrilee squawked. "That Chinese thing where
people stand around like statues in the park? I don't think so.
What use will that be to us, Eileen? Some of us hardly seem to
be moving as it is."

Louise Martin's face clouded, and she looked down at the
walker she was obliged to use when her arthritis flared up.

"It promotes balance," I said, "and some of us certainly
don't seem to have much of that, mentally anyway. I took it
many years ago, and I found it very helpful. But you don't
have to sign up if you don't think you can handle it, Merrilee."

Of course, I knew she would turn up on Monday. She
always wanted to know what was going on, and she would
certainly want to prove she could do tai chi. But she was never
in favour of something suggested by somebody else,
particularly if that somebody was me. She had been President
until I was elected nine months ago, and our ideas of
worthwhile activities were like sugar and pickles. Her idea of

interesting events had been a fashion show and a cosmetics demonstration, but the dress shop she selected thought Velcro was a dirty word, and the cosmeticians left us with a discouraged feeling and a bagful of makeup which we never touched again.

I knew between now and Monday she would be dropping sarcastic remarks to the other residents about the new program I was introducing, and I thought it was really important to keep the mind and body active, not just well-covered. I was therefore very keen on getting as many as possible signed up. I was quite proud of the programs we had introduced in the past months. I had visited other homes where they didn't seem to do anything except sit in front of a television set, and I certainly didn't want that to happen to us.

A few of the residents, friends of Merrilee, complained. "You've got too many activities going on, Eileen," they said. "We like to watch the soaps in the afternoon." But I noticed when they heard someone yell "Bingo" or caught the sound of the sing-along round the piano, they would gradually creep in and get a card or a song sheet. No, I didn't think Merrilee would opt out of the tai chi program. She would come if only to say "I told you so" if it didn't work out.

The person I was concerned about was Nora Barton. She had been at the Lodge three weeks but had been quite reclusive. I had made a point of sitting with her at lunch the day she arrived, and although I had to work at it, I did find out she was the widow of Herb Barton of Barton's Berry Farms.

"That must have been an interesting life," I said.

She looked at me as if I were crazy. "Interesting?" she repeated. "It was backbreaking and heartbreaking work. As I'm sure the new owners are finding out."

"But at least you could get away in the winter."

"We had animals, and we couldn't leave."

I thought it was time to change the subject. "And what made you choose Sunset Lodge?" I asked.

"I didn't choose it. My son did. He sold the farm out from under me and made me come here."

"Well," I said, as cheerfully as I could, "I know it's a big change for you. We've all gone through it. But you'll soon find lots to do. As a matter of fact, I've brought you a list of the various activities. I'm sure you'll find something you like."

As these places go, Sunset Lodge is very nice. Well, except for the name. Why don't they realize we don't need to be reminded at every turn that we're getting old and coming to the end of our days? There are three levels of care here, according to a resident's capabilities. The owners call them Pavilions A, B and C. The residents call them Sunset, Twilight and Goodnight. In Pavilion A, we're all more or less able-bodied. At least we can take care of our personal needs, even if we might be a bit slow about it.

My aim is to help us all fend off the further deteriorations of old age, physical and mental. The other four members of the Social Committee are not always as enthusiastic about the new programs as I am, and sometimes it takes all my efforts to convince them. I always manage it in the end, though.

Nora didn't come down for dinner that first day, and she didn't sign up for any more meals in the dining room. In Pavilion A, each resident has a small apartment with a kitchenette, but meals are available for a reasonable price in the dining room. Most of us sign up for at least one meal a day. Nora was probably living on grilled cheese sandwiches from the toaster oven provided in each apartment. I didn't think it could be a matter of cost. They must have been paid a pretty penny for the farm.

3

For three weeks, the only time I could catch her was when she came down to check her mail, change her library book or use the washing machines. I tried to tempt her with something every time I saw her. "We're doing calligraphy this afternoon. Why don't you give it a try?" "There's a sing-song tonight after dinner. Why don't you drop in?" "We've got *Casablanca* for the movie tonight. You should come down. Starts at seven." She always gave me a polite but firm "No, thank you."

I couldn't figure out what she did with herself all day in her little apartment. I can't stand people sitting in a corner and sulking because life has taken a new, unwanted path. One must get up and at it and try to enjoy where one has landed. So I took her aside one day. "You know, Nora," I said, "we're all in the same boat here. And when somebody is really unsociable, it makes the rest of us feel very uncomfortable. Why don't you at least come to the tai chi classes? You don't have to talk to people, and you could use the exercise. It's not good to sit in your room all day." She finally agreed to try a class, which I considered a personal victory.

As she had only been given the most cursory introduction to most of the other residents, I invited her to come down to dinner on Saturday night as my guest. She could hardly refuse. Dinner on Saturdays was always a buffet, and that week there was either chicken pot pie or baked ham (which meant we'd be getting pea soup and ham croquettes next week) and for dessert lemon meringue cake or apple pie. As we were leaving the buffet table with our loaded trays, Merrilee came swishing in behind us. She always changed for dinner, but tonight she had outdone herself with a long embroidered cream skirt and a rose-coloured blouse.

"Oh, Merrilee," I said, "I don't think you've met Nora Barton from Apartment 203. Nora's husband owned Barton

Berry Farm over near Manotick." I turned to Nora. "Merrilee is our resident expert on fashion and decorating." At least she was always commenting on what people wore and the colour of the cushions in the lounge. I thought it would make her more gracious to Nora if I buttered her up a bit. It didn't work. She looked sharply at Nora's black polyester skirt and flowered cotton blouse, and without actually curling her lip, managed to convey disdain in her cool "I'm pleased to meet you."

Nora, poor naïve soul, thought Merrilee really was pleased to meet her and tried to fumble her tray onto one side so she could shake hands. As she extended her right hand, the tray began to tilt and the chicken pot pie started its fatal slide down Merrilee's skirt, followed by the lemon meringue cake, which landed with a soft plop on her shoe.

Nora was frozen to the spot, her eyes wide and her mouth open. She started to babble. "I'm so sorry, oh dear, I'm so sorry." She bent down to gather up the debris at Merrilee's feet.

"Don't touch me," shrieked Merrilee, jumping backwards. "Look at my new skirt. And it came from the French Salon. I'll have to change." With that, she gathered up the edge of the garment and stalked off, stopping at her cronies' table, where she loudly said something about farmers.

"I'll pay for it to be cleaned," Nora said to her back.

"You certainly will," said Merrilee without turning around.

The kitchen staff had come out by this time and were cleaning up the spill and handing Nora another tray. Louise came forward and took it, saying "Come and sit with me. Your accident did my heart good. I've wanted to throw my dinner at Merrilee Parker many times."

Nora and Louise hit it off very well. Everybody gets along with Louise. She's a kind soul and usually very even-tempered despite the arthritis, but Merrilee often tried even her patience. "Has she been here long?" Nora asked.

"About six years. Her husband was a dental surgeon. He had a heart attack about eight years ago, right in the middle of a root canal. Her sons were both married with children and Merrilee went to live with each of them in turn, but from what I heard, she just wanted the whole house to revolve around her and the daughters-in-law couldn't take it." Louise frowned. "It probably won't be long before you hear about her husband."

Merrilee never missed an opportunity to remind us of his important, and well-paid, profession. Nearly all of us were widows, in varying stages of the grief process and financial comfort, but if you tried to mention your own husband, Merrilee always found a way to turn the conversation back to hers. The general irritation with Merrilee was such that most of the people who had witnessed Nora's mishap with the tray stopped at our table to say a few words of welcome to her. Percy and Janet Lowther even sat with us for a while and reminisced about the many happy times they had spent picking berries at Barton's Farm with their children and grandchildren. So, all in all, the evening accomplished everything I had hoped for.

• • •

It was no surprise when Merrilee started her usual tactics at the tai chi class. The notice had suggested that we wear flat shoes or slippers, but Merrilee turned up in sandals with one-inch heels.

"They're the lowest things I own," she stated. "Flat shoes make me look so…"

"Short?" suggested Mr. Lowther, his eyes twinkling. His wife gave him a dig in the ribs, and Louise covered her laugh with a mock sneeze when Merrilee shot her a glance.

"Oh, you," cooed Merrilee, batting her eyelashes, "you're always teasing me." Had the comment come from one of the women, her reaction would not have been one of amusement. Merrilee had been Miss Buttermilk in the 1945 Renfrew Fair, and she had never gotten over it. She was still a pretty woman, petite and dainty, but she had made no concessions to her seventy-two years. She still dyed her hair blonde and wore it in an outdated page boy style. She bought clothes for her size rather than her age, and many of her outfits were meant for someone younger. Today she was wearing peach slacks with "Lauren" embroidered in black down the left leg and a matching top saying "Number One". She must have gone out to buy them on Saturday, because I had never seen her in that outfit before.

Mrs. Yee, our diminutive Chinese instructor, had brought a bag of those black cloth Chinese shoes, and she offered to lend Merrilee a pair for the first lesson until she got something suitable.

Merrilee was horrified. "Wear shoes worn by someone else?" She recoiled as if she had been physically struck. "I won't have any trouble in my own. I used to be a dancer, you know."

Mrs. Yee looked at her and nodded before addressing us all. "Merrilee right to mention dance. Tai chi not dance but like dance, movements are graceful and smooth. But done very slowly. Thing to remember is all movements circular. And don't forget—breathe!"

She told us she was going to teach us the eight-minute version of tai chi, which only has twenty-seven forms in three groups. She thought this would suit us better than the classical long program which has 108 movements. I thought we'd do well if we could remember seven, let alone twenty-seven, but we'd see how it went. Merrilee, of course, seemed to master the moves quite easily, but Nora was in trouble almost at once. The opening move was fine, because you stayed in one place. It was when we got to the second form, "Parting the Wild Horse's Mane", that the trouble surfaced. It quickly became obvious that Nora couldn't distinguish her left from her right, and she got completely turned around. Mrs. Yee was patience itself. She repeated the sequence several times, and she stood with Nora and guided her arms and feet. In the end she paired her with Merrilee, telling Nora to follow her movements. Poor Nora got mixed up again, though, and ended up crashing into Merrilee, who flounced off saying loudly that at this rate we'd be lucky if we ever got beyond Lesson One.

"I won't come again," said Nora. "It's not going to work."

Louise came to the rescue. Despite her physical limitations, she had made a good attempt at the movements, and she wasn't going to let Nora quit so easily.

"You aren't going to let Miss Margarine of 1935 make you give up, are you?" she said. "You're only like the rest of us: a bit overweight and a lot out of practice."

"Now, Nora," I said, "you come from a farm, and you know all about setbacks. Did you give up every time your crops failed because of bad weather? Just think of Merrilee as a big wind, but in her case she can only do damage if you let her. Don't give up. Practise in your room."

The second lesson was no better. When we arrived, Merrilee, who had, I noticed, bought herself some black satin ballet slippers, seemed to be arguing with Mrs. Yee. I heard her saying something about two groups, but Mrs. Yee just said: "We see. We see. Too soon."

The class started with a repetition of the moves from the first session. Nora was only marginally less awkward and frequently got turned around. "I've been practising," she told me, "but there's not much room."

Merrilee snickered. "Everybody else is parting the horse's mane. Nora seems to be working on the tail."

While we learned the two new moves, "White Stork Cools Its Wings" and "Brush Knee", Louise and I took our places on Nora's right and left, but even so, we lost her a couple of times when she started to go north while we were all going south.

Nora found the session very stressful, but fortunately, Mrs. Yee always finished with a period of meditation during which we all cooled down mentally and physically. Before we left, Mrs. Yee gave me a book on tai chi showing the exercises. "You help Nora," she said.

"I don't care about the book," Nora said. "I'm not going back."

"Why don't we give it another week?" Louise said soothingly. "Now Eileen has the book, we can take our time. We won't have to keep up with anyone."

Nora reluctantly agreed to Louise's proposal, but Louise herself was having doubts. "I've been wondering," she said to me later, "whether we're right to persuade her to continue. It's quite upsetting for her."

"But it's the only activity I've managed to interest her in," I said, "and she needs to do something. If she gives it up, she'll just go back to moping in her room. I think we should press on for a few more lessons, anyway. It's still very early." Louise looked sceptical. "You know, on the third floor there's quite a large space at the end of the corridor to the right of the elevator, where the stairs come up," I said. "You and I could help Nora practise there, and we'd be out of the way."

On Friday we took Nora up to the third floor. She protested that she would never be any good at it, and she might just as well give up right now, but I managed to convince her to keep on with us helping her. We tied red bows to her right wrist and ankle and green ones on her left wrist and ankle. I held a large red rosette and Louise held a green one.

We started with the easy opening exercise, staying in place and lifting and lowering our arms. The book said that during this exercise, you're supposed to concentrate your spirit and empty your mind of disturbing and extraneous matters. Nora could raise and lower her arms all right, but it was obvious her spirit was only concentrating on the ordeal of the next movement. Still, we persevered. For the next movement, I asked her if she had ever watched a baseball game.

She looked at me in amazement. "Yes, of course."

"Well, think of the batter's body when he's going to hit the ball. First his body swings a bit to the right as he prepares to hit and then it swings over to the left as he follows through. The start of "Parting the Horse's Mane" is a bit like that but much, much slower, and you have to imagine you're holding a large beach ball. Now, swing your body from the waist a little to the right, putting your weight on your right leg, and bring your right arm up and your left arm down as if you've got this giant ball between them." Nora gingerly followed instructions. "Bravo, Nora. That's it. Let's try just that bit again, so we don't even have to think about which hand is on top of the ball."

Louise took over for the next part, in which Nora had to swing to the left, stepping forward on the left leg and reversing the arm positions holding the ball. This took quite a few tries before Louise was satisfied.

Then we had the job of trying to unite these two parts into a smooth-flowing whole. With me calling "Over to red" and Louise shouting "Come to green, baby", we managed to get the bits cobbled together into a reasonably acceptable form.

We finished by having Nora try it on her own without our coaching from each side, and the look of surprised delight on her face when she did it was worth all the effort.

Louise and I burst into that song from *My Fair Lady*, "I think she's got it, I think she's got it", and I invited them both down to my room for a glass of sherry to celebrate. This was another first for Nora. Actually, it was a first and a second, because she knocked the first one back so quickly I had to pour her another.

"Sherry's like tai chi, Nora. It should be taken slowly," Louise said with a grin.

On Saturday morning, we thought we'd be able to plunge right into the "White Stork Cooling its Wings", but unfortunately we had to backtrack, as Nora seemed to have forgotten quite a lot of yesterday's lesson. Still, we kept at it, and eventually she had it again. I suggested we have a break for lunch, and again we went to my apartment for a glass of sherry, which seemed to give us all fresh heart.

In the afternoon, we tackled "White Stork Cools its Wings", but it didn't go too well. We were all a bit stressed out when we finished, and I thought both Louise and Nora were going to suggest giving up. Before they could open their mouths, however, I jollied them along by reminding Nora how well she'd done "Parting the Horse's Mane" and said I was sure we'd get it after another lesson with Mrs. Yee, and in the meantime, let's all go for a glass of sherry. Nora didn't come down for the buffet that night.

It was on Sunday afternoon, while I was checking the magazine rack for the latest issue of *Crafts for Every Day* in case there was something new we could introduce, that I overheard Merrilee giggling with her cronies.

"I understand she and Louise are giving her secret lessons,

trying to turn a sow's ear into a silk purse. Talk about the blind leading the blind. Eileen's about as graceful as a cart horse, and Louise can't even stretch her arms out properly. It must be like a performance by the Three Stooges." And out came that irritating tinkling laugh. "Mark my words, this tai chi business won't last more than another week. Everybody thinks Mrs. Yee spends too much time on Nora and that it's time wasted."

I was furious. Not about her aspersions about me and Louise, though they were aggravating enough, but if it killed me I was going to prove that Nora *could* and *would* master the tai chi moves. We'd just have to step up the practice program.

That Monday's lesson was not too bad. Because most of the class was not too sure about the "White Stork", a fact which Louise and I found very reassuring, Mrs. Yee only introduced one new move, "Playing the Harp".

"You see, Nora," I said afterwards, "lots of people have difficulty learning the moves. You're not the only one. Maybe we should have a little session this afternoon while the 'White Stork' is still fresh in our minds."

This time it was Louise who complained. "I need to have a rest this afternoon, Eileen," she said. "My arthritis is acting up."

"I'll tell you what," I said, "we'll all have a rest. Then Nora and I will meet at four o'clock for a little session before dinner, and if you're feeling okay, Louise, you join us. Nora really needs the two of us."

"Perhaps we could leave it till tomorrow," suggested Nora rather timidly.

"No, no," I said. "We must strike while the iron's hot, and that stork still needs to cool its wings."

Louise and Nora went off together, and I had the

impression that Nora was pleading with Louise to be there.

In the meantime, I nipped out and bought two more bottles of sherry. After all, we still had three more forms to learn.

Louise did come at four o'clock, but she had her walker, and she looked rather pale. We had been coaching Nora for about forty minutes, when she was totally thrown off balance by Merrilee suddenly appearing in the stairwell opening. We hadn't heard her coming up, and it gave us all a shock, I must admit.

"Oh, dear," she said, "did I startle you? I had no idea you were practising here. I sometimes walk up and down the stairs to keep myself limber, you know. You should all try it." She gave her tinkling laugh and started down the stairs. I thought Louise was going to throw her walker after her.

Anyway, that finished practice for that session, and we retired for a sherry to restore our equilibrium.

The next day I could sense more rebellion in the ranks, and I had to exhort both Nora and Louise to stick with it. "We've already done five of the forms, and there are only eight in the first set. There's just 'Needle at the Bottom of the Sea', 'Wave Hands Like Clouds' and 'Repulse the Monkey'. So we're almost through, and then it's only a matter of repeating them until they become second nature."

"I'm not sure I want a Chinese second nature," muttered Nora. "I was all right with my Canadian one."

They both declined the sherry that day, so I knew things were serious. I later saw them both coming out of Nora's room. I wondered what they had been discussing without me.

That evening I read right to the end of Mrs. Yee's book, and I discovered there was a form of tai chi which involved using a stick. Well, actually, it was supposed to be a sword, but I figured a stick would do quite well, and I thought the change might spark their interest again. I got a yardstick and coloured one end green and the other red.

When I showed it to Nora the next day, I went back to the baseball simile. "If the batter is right-handed, as you are, Nora, when he draws the bat back, his left arm is down and close to the body but when he hits and follows through, his left elbow comes up, and his right arm is close to the body. If he only held the bat in one hand, his right hand would drop below his left arm. It's a nice circular motion, all from the waist. Let's try it with the stick and see if it helps give you that feeling of drawing a circle."

The stick helped for some of the forms, but at one point it clattered out of Nora's hand and bounced into the stairwell. Nora burst into tears. I had to go down a flight and a half to retrieve it, and I was a bit breathless when I got back.

"I think I'll just stand here, ready to stop it in case it takes flight again," I said, still puffing. I decided to ignore the tears. "Right, now let's try 'Playing the Harp' once more. You're not concentrating, Nora, and I think you called her to the wrong side, Louise, and your walker got in the way. Okay, let's go. Play the harp, Nora."

Nora glared at me. "Stuff your stupid harp," she hissed, and she ran straight at me with the yardstick pointed at my chest like a sword. I involuntarily took a step backwards, and the next thing I knew, I was tumbling head over heels down the stairs.

I heard a shout, "How's that for 'Needle to the Bottom of the Sea'?"

• • •

From my room in Pavilion C when they wheel me over to the

window, I can watch the group doing tai chi on the lawn. Merrilee is out in front, but I don't see Louise and Nora anywhere.

AUDREY JESSUP'S *aversion to exercise changed when she read of a Manchester University study claiming that the body cannot distinguish between actually doing an exercise and thinking about doing it. So if you catch her with glazed eyes contemplating her navel she is, in fact, thinking herself into svelte perfection.*

RACE

VICKI CAMERON

I change Michael Calendri's right front tire. That's my job. They told me crewing on an Indy race car team would make me popular with the girls, but it doesn't generate much conversation, changing the right front tire. I work less than thirty seconds over the course of a race. That's my whole job, thirty seconds.

It's an important job, precise and speed-driven. I have ten seconds to change that tire. One second to get myself and my air gun in place. Seven seconds for the tire. Two seconds to get back to the wall with the gun, swinging its hose clear. I can't have a bad day, ever. I can't be off my beat and take a second too long. I can't take a half step in the wrong direction and get in the way of Jerry changing the left front tire. I have to be a sprinter, too, and dart in front of the car when I've changed my tire before the driver screams back toward the track. Other right-front guys on other teams have been run over by their drivers. Hit and run by their own man. Michael has never hit his right-front guy. I've never given him a reason to shake a fist at me. Our crew is finished four tires and fuel in twelve seconds.

My goal is to be the first tire changer finished every time. Right now I am half a second behind Jerry, on left front, but he doesn't have to sprint in front of the car. I watch the other right-front guys on the other teams, looking for ways to shave off a nanosecond.

The crew next to us today is the upstart Lavatin team, one car, one driver, a hodge-podge of sponsors and Ray on right front. Ray is good. I've been watching his footwork over the season, his explosive start from the pit, his finesse with the pneumatic air gun. He whips that hose in an arc behind him so it's precisely in the right spot to unscrew the wheel nut. He has that used tire off and a new one on in one and a third seconds better than my best time.

The entire Lavatin crew is speed obsessed. Even more than the rest of us. The driver, Kurt, sits in the cockpit with eyes blazing right through his visor. His hands are clenched on the steering wheel, and you can see his anger at every pit stop. I hear he resents pit stops and the twelve seconds it takes to refit his car for the next set of laps. I hear he isn't much of a team player, just wants to get out there and win.

All that focus and raw talent has put him in the lead today. He's a lap and a half ahead of Michael, and we're sweating in the pit, pumping ourselves up for speed, more speed. I've piled the old tires further back than usual, to give everyone more room to work. I scope out the Lavatin pit, and their tires are not as precisely piled as ours. They keep their old tires up front, forming a privacy screen between them and the next crew. Their new pile is closer to the wall. I measure my stride and pile our new tires four inches closer to the wall. I practise and shave a quarter second off my takeoff.

Kurt is coming into the pits on the next lap. That Ray, he's braced to leap the wall. I have two more laps to wait, so I give Ray my full attention.

Ray's sloppy tire pile is to blame. He reaches his right front on time, but the hose catches on the tire pile, and he has to give it an extra yank to get it in position. Costs him a quarter second. Throws him right off his game, and he's a half-second slower changing the tire. Kurt's eyes are pinpricks of fire. Ray finishes and explodes into his sprint.

Kurt hits the gas and roars out of there an eighth of a second before Ray clears the car. Runs right over Ray's ankle. Ray hits the pavement in agony and comes up in a white heat. I don't know if it's anger or pain. He says he's fine, wraps an icepack around his ankle, pops a handful of pills and starts flinging the tires around, clearing his hose path. I watch him for signs of slowing down. If he's feeling any pain, he doesn't show it.

Michael hits the pits and I spring over the wall, using Ray's finesse with the hose. It works. I shave three-quarters of a second off my time. I see Michael grinning as I sprint past him.

Kurt holds the lead. Next Lavatin pit stop, Ray shucks the icepack and is over that wall in a blur, changing that tire in the best time I've seen. Motivation, that's the key. Somehow I've become so obsessed with time and precision and style that I've lost sight of the real reason we are all here—to win.

Ray leaps back over the wall and lands funny on his ankle. The rest of the crew huddles around him and carries him to the doctor in less time than their pit stop. A mechanic takes his place and starts warming up.

Two laps later Kurt hits the wall on the third curve and explodes in a ball of metal and flame. The television crews go nuts. The Lavatin team become zombies, white faces and jerky movements. We don't have time to worry about it in our pit. Focus, focus, focus on winning. All the drivers hit the pits under the yellow flag. We do everything but floss Michael's teeth.

With the Lavatin car out of the lead, Michael has a clear shot. He drives like he does when the finish line is only ten laps away. Flies right past them all into the straightaway, picks up the checkered flag, the trophy and the fat envelope.

We're all going to Kurt's funeral in his home town. His sponsors are already searching for a new driver. Word is Ray has three broken bones in his ankle from being hit by the car. They were holding together until his last leap over the wall.

I figure I owe Ray a lot. I learned new pit techniques by watching him. Mostly, I learned to put the fire back in my job, to remember the desire to win.

I don't have much patience for drivers who mow down their own crew.

I change Michael Calendri's right front tire. It doesn't generate much conversation. So nobody asked me about Ray. I never had to tell anyone I had seen him put an old tire on the right front of Kurt's car.

VICKI CAMERON *writes fiction and non-fiction, long and short, ranging from dog training* (From Heel To Finish: The System Of Ghent For The Nineties) *to UFOs* (Don't Tell Anyone, But…UFO Experiences In Canada). *She is the co-editor of and contributor to* The Ladies' Killing Circle, Cottage Country Killers *and* Menopause is Murder. *Her first young adult novel,* That Kind of Money, *was nominated for an Edgar Award by the Mystery Writers of America, and an Arthur Ellis Award by the Crime Writers of Canada. She lives and plots near Ottawa.*

WRITER'S CRAMP

I sat down to write you a poem 'bout fitness;
'Bout murdering victims without any witness;
'Bout barbells, and skip ropes, and good things for killing
With violence and grimness and every scene chilling.

I thought about weights coming down with a crash
For reasons like jealousy, revenge and cash.
I thought about drugs that induced heart attacks
In people on treadmills pushed up to the max.

I thought about diving and some broken necks.
I thought about poisons and causing car wrecks.
I thought about joggers who fell over cliffs,
And how muscle builders look better as stiffs.

So I sat in my chair and I thought quite a bit
About how many people would die to be fit.
My muscle was hurting; I pushed much too deep.
Never wrote you that poem—my brain fell asleep.

JOY HEWITT MANN *has been published coast to coast. In 2001, she placed first in poetry from the Cambridge Writer's Collective. In 2000, she was the winner of the Acorn-Rukheyser Award for her chapbook* Grass. *Her first short story collection,* Clinging to Water, *was published in 2000, and her first full-length poetry collection,* Bone on Bone, *is scheduled for publication in 2003. She also has a novel,* Lacrima Christi, *coming out in 2002.*

DOWN IN THE PLUMPS

VICTORIA MAFFINI

The last straw was at the 7-Eleven. With an already opened bag of Doritos in the crook of my arm, I flipped to the "Do's and Don'ts" on the back page of *Glamour* magazine. I was snickering at the too-short skirts and noticeable panty lines when a chubby figure under the caption "Anyone for a sausage roll?" sent a flicker of recognition through my brain. *I have a skirt like that, but it looks much better on...*the little black strip over the face had served its purpose until that point. My stomach dropped into my shoes. The chunky girl billowing out over the waistband of her skirt, squeezed into a tank top, was me walking in Soho with my uncle. I'd gone to visit him in New York for a week. He looked fabulous. I, however, seemed to be both bending and twisting, creating a sea of fat waves and three extra chins.

Panic.

I scrambled to snatch up all the copies left in the 7-Eleven. Sweat stung my forehead. I tried to keep my voice from quavering. "I'll take these." I plunked down the half-eaten bag of chips and twelve magazines.

"These are all the same, you know," the petite blonde girl behind the counter chirped.

I swiped at the sweat on my face with a grungy sleeve. *She*

21

knows it's me. She's read the magazine. I became acutely aware of the fact her thighs and my upper arms were the same size.

"Yeah, my friend is in one of the fashion shoots." Any attempt at flippancy was sabotaged by the three-octave hike in my voice.

For what seemed an eternity, the girl, whose nametag labelled her Cheri, snapped her gum and stared at me. "Whatever."

Half an hour later I slumped onto my couch, exhausted. The sheer terror of anyone seeing this magazine had led me to buy up all the copies at every store in my neighborhood. I examined my trembling fingers. They *were* fatter than before. When did that happen?

I reopened the glossy back cover. Did they use a wide-angle lens on the camera? Were there support groups for the people who have appeared in "Glamour Don'ts"? Could I sue for mental anguish and get enough money to hire a personal trainer?

I crawled to my bed with a pair of scissors, a pint of ice cream, a two-litre bottle of Pepsi and a pack of cigarettes. I wept into my Häagen-Dazs, chain-smoking and cutting the rolls off my hideous magazine debut.

• • •

Two days later, I discovered that when you have prescriptions delivered, the pharmacy will also send smokes and chocolate. Before the delivery arrived, I'd begun to glue my fat cuttings onto my uncle. I envied the lady wearing too many animal prints; at least she only looked genetically spliced. I looked like Jabba the Hut in platform sandals.

The door chimed. Usually, I change several times before

22

finding the perfect outfit in which to answer the door. At that moment, I only cared that there were no M & M's stuck in my teeth.

The lanky, greasy-haired delivery guy, wearing a faded Black Sabbath T-shirt, stifled a gasp when I opened the door. I was unable to find the energy to be insulted. It *had* been days since I'd changed my clothes. I envisioned stink lines rising from me.

"That'll be, uh, $38.98." He looked at the small bag quizzically and checked the receipt. "Whoa, I didn't realize they could sell you *that* much Valium at once."

He made my change, slowly. It was at this point that I noticed the commotion outside. A moving van was emptying its contents into the condo across the street. The relative silence of our upscale Toronto condo-complex was shattered by a very thin woman yelling orders. Under her arm was a Dachshund wearing a mauve sweater. In her hand she held the largest martini glass I'd ever seen.

The woman seemed concerned the movers might ding the Mercedes that was parked at a jaunty angle on the sidewalk.

I retreated inside and watched her from my sofa. She spent most of the morning motioning wildly with her drink and sloshing gin on the grass. I fell asleep watching her dog poop in my parking spot.

•   •   •

Monday held nothing in the way of joy. My answering machine blinked incessantly. I feared messages regarding my sausage attire and chose to ignore it. Instead I submerged myself in work: decorating for the aesthetically challenged.

After an hour of staring at the snapshots I'd taken of my

latest client's home, I was thoroughly disgusted. They should have decorating Do's and Don'ts. My client's bedroom was whorehouse pink. Her comforter looked as though it had been caught in a tornado in Las Vegas. A rose-smattered valance with lilac sheers accosted the window, and her wallpaper had stripes and paisley and kittens. My sugar-ravaged body suppressed a retch at the sight of the gold-smoked mirrors in the hall. The task at hand began to overwhelm me. She loved the work I'd done with warm neutrals and stark minimalist furnishings in a mutual friend's apartment. How did someone who could appreciate the sleek lines of Corbusier go so drastically wrong when left to her own devices? Where the hell was her husband when these atrocities were being purchased? I studied the pictures further. He could have been in the shots. Had his wife dressed him he would have blended right in with the rest of the chaos. Perhaps my client was afflicted with the same illness that allowed me to walk through one of the most stylish areas of New York looking like a small water mammal in drag.

Frustrated with the enormity of the project, I gave up and headed for the shower. Green tea shower gel soothed my bruised spirit. I had nearly relaxed when the doorbell started ringing with frightening repetition. By the time I flung open the door, I'd assumed it was stuck or someone was on fire.

The martini lady and her dog greeted me. "Hello, Chloë dear." She looked me up and down, carefully.

"Ah..." I managed, while cinching my towel and raising my hand self-consciously to my suds-covered head.

"*I* am Ms. Leopold. *This* is Mr. Oodles. We are your new neighbours." Leading with her martini glass, she pushed past me into my living room.

I stood frozen in my empty doorway. The Mercedes was now nestled against the mailbox.

Hearing tuts and hmms from the living room, I closed the door and joined Ms. Leopold.

"I must say you do have quite an interesting touch, darling."

"This really isn't a good time, I…"

"Go put on a robe, darling." She swivelled, leaving an arc of gin on my footstool. "We must chat about what can be done with my condo. You wouldn't believe what they did with the bathroom, dear. I know you were just fabulous with Bunny, and let's face it, it couldn't have been easy with Edgar, the pompous old goat, breathing down your neck."

Bunny Birk had been a client the previous year. A woman with more money than God, Bunny also possessed the same surgically enhanced ageless quality I saw on Ms. Leopold's tight face.

"Well, I…I…" Then the shopaholic deep inside me remembered Bolt Grenfrew was opening a new store, and I was almost entirely broke. "I'll be right back."

I returned in a robe with a towel for my hair. Mr. Oodles hopped effortlessly onto my leather love seat. He was wearing a pastel blue Pashmina wrap.

"You're a friend of Mrs. Birk?" Opening my portfolio, I tried to seem professional. "I hope she's well."

Ms. Leopold's eyebrow arched impossibly, nearly disappearing into her hairline. "I should say so. Her new pool boy is named Miguel, and he's an aspiring gymnast." A sly, crimson smile followed. "I'd say Bunny is behaving quite like her namesake these days."

Pushing Bunny and her flexible Latino lover from my mind took some effort. I felt another shower was in order. "Would you like to see my other work, Ms. Leopold? I have a variety of…"

"No, no, no. I like what I've seen already. Bunny simply raves on and on about you. And, although you could obviously use a maid, your home speaks for itself."

I'd almost missed the last part, being more concerned about Mr. Oodles, who was licking himself on my Calvin Klein throw.

"We'll have lunch together at the Château Poivre." Ms. Leopold scooped her dog up, anointing him with martini. "Here you are, dear." A cheque was pressed into my hand. $5,000.

"I'm afraid I don't understand." Not to look a gift horse in the mouth, but I hadn't even shown her a fabric swatch.

"Working for me, darling, is a package deal. My men must be rich and foreign, my dog must be purebred, my hair stylist must be gay and my decorator must be well dressed."

As I'd only been wearing bath linens during her entire visit, I began to protest. "Tut, tut." She silenced me with a gloved finger to my lips. "I'm a faithful reader of *Glamour*, dear."

I struggled through the rest of the afternoon. Why hadn't I ripped up the cheque and thrown it in her pickled face? The sad realization that I could be bought was only softened by the idea of a spree at Emporio Armani. Besides, how much of a pain in the ass could a stewed prune like Ms. Leopold be?

You have to dress like a runway-model when you go to haute-couture stores, otherwise nobody will look at you except the security guards. I brought out the big guns today and was horrified at how snug my cream Jones New York ankle-length blazer had become. I left it open with a simple white tee and yellow silk trousers. I put on my grandmother's diamond studs and pulled back my fire-red hair. Armed with my Fendi bag, a gift from Bunny upon completion of her en suite bath, I made a bee-line to town.

Fearing recognition, I chose my largest tortoise shell sunglasses to disguise myself until I was safely in Damon's Department Store.

I fondled the butter-soft Gucci shoes before skipping to Women's Wear. A pair of hot pink capris caught my eye.

"Hello." The sales woman crept up stealthily behind me.

"Hi." I said, polite but dismissive. I like to see everything before I commit to a change room.

"Pink is this year's black."

"Ah." *What the hell does that mean?*

Noting I was ignoring her, she began to retreat. "You may want to rethink the colour, though."

I turned to her quizzically.

"Lighter colors can make you seem…" her eyes focussed in on my yellow-clad thighs, "bottom-heavy." She was wearing white linen pants. She had been born without thighs.

I was speechless.

In a singsong voice she added, "Well, you just let me know if I can help you find anything in a larger size."

"Larger than what?"

"We mostly only carry up to a 10 in-store, but we can order as high as 14 in most of these lines. Of course, the prices can go a bit higher, because they use so much more fabric." Her face wore a condescending smirk. It clashed with the frown lines etched into her chin. "We here at Damon's are sensitive to our 'plus-sized' customers' needs."

Black dots swam into my line of vision. A knot tightened in my throat. I rifled through the contents of my purse, produced my Damon's Preferred Customer card and thrust it up to her face. "There is a special place in hell for people like you," I managed and ran from the store.

When did sizes 12 and 14 become "plus sizes"? I was so

shocked I couldn't drive. I was a 16. What did they categorize that under? *"Jumbo-size"*? *"Manatee-size"*? *"I'm sorry we have nothing but tents in your size"*, size? Not much can divert me from shopping, especially with $5,000 of someone else's money, but the waspish sales bitch did it. I headed for cheesecake.

I'm not proud of this, but when pushed hard enough, I can eat cheesecake, smoke and drive a stick shift simultaneously. Arriving home, I was less than thrilled to see Ms. Leopold. I contemplated speeding off but hadn't the energy. I'd tell Ms. Leopold to stick her martini up her butt and head for my bed.

Instead, I broke down on my doorstep. My story about the evil sales hag at Damon's, the *Glamour* magazine fiasco and my too-tight jacket came blubbering out of my cake-covered lips. Mr. Oodles licked icing off my pant leg sympathetically. All the while Ms. Leopold sipped her drink with a face of stone. I finished with a whimper. There was a long silence.

"Come, darling." She tentatively patted my elbow.

"Where are we going?" I sniveled.

"*You* need a spa." She expertly rolled the olive around the rim of her empty glass. "And I need a drink."

•   •   •

"Fatso."

The call had awakened me from a fitful sleep. "What?"

"Heifer," a raspy voice taunted. "Tub of lard."

"Who the hell is this?"

"Bitch."

Click.

Before I could pry my fingernails from my mattress, it rang again.

"Buffalo-butt. Cow."

"I've got *69. I can find out who you are!"

Nothing.

I listened to the even breathing on the line.

"What are you going to do, come *sit* on me?"

"No! I'm going to send my boyfriend over there to kick your ass!" Juvenile, yes, but what do you want at three a.m.?

"Well, I'm looking forward to meeting *Colonel Sanders.*"

Click.

*69 informed me the calls came from a phone booth. Usually, I am not bothered by crank-calls, but this one left me feeling uneasy. The *Glamour* magazine fiasco was still fresh in my mind. I sat up the rest of the night watching Richard Simmons info-mercials. By five I'd ordered the Deluxe Deal a Meal Plan and a Pocket Fisherman.

I used my sleepless night as an excuse to keep the spa at bay for two days. At first the thought of a pampering appealed, then I realized I would have to be naked with strangers.

I caved on Thursday morning. Ms. Leopold summoned me at ten-thirty. Mr. Oodles, sporting a leather vest with fur trim, was basking in the morning sun on my welcome mat. My neighbor, Mr. Balducci, was swearing at Mr. Oodles and waving a plastic bag with dubious contents.

"*Cara* Chloë, please-a tell me that is not-a your dog."

"No, he belongs to Ms. Leopold. She moved in this week."

Dino Balducci began to swear in Italian. "Where I come-a from, that-a sausage would be make into a nice-a stew, not dressed up-a like a Barbie doll!" He stormed away muttering about dog-based recipes.

• • •

"So glad you found him, darling. He just slips out sometimes, heaven knows how."

We pulled up to the River Grand Country Club and Spa and were whisked inside. Three people fawned over Ms. Leopold, and by virtue of having arrived in the same car, I was at the receiving end of some strange attention as well.

"Wheat grass juice?"

"Do you need a kelp wrap?"

"Our sugar detox advisor can fit you in at noon, is that okay?"

"Would you prefer endurance or strength spinning?"

My day was spent being poked, rubbed, stretched, steamed, waxed and tortured on various machines that insisted on knowing my weight before they would work. Ms. Leopold watched from behind soundproof glass in an indoor tropical paradise with drink service.

My nap on the ride home came to a screeching halt. Mr. Balducci's garbage can was wedged neatly into the rear wheel-well of the Mercedes.

"Shall we go to Damon's tomorrow?" Ms. Leopold inquired.

I scrunched my face with displeasure.

"Oh, don't worry, dear. I think you'll find the situation has been rectified."

Too tired to ask for clarification, I said goodnight, then limped to my door. I nearly missed the envelope peeking out from my mail-slot. It wasn't labelled. I tore into it while flopping onto my bed. Inside was a photocopy of my last grocery bill. I'd been in the clutches of a bingeing spree and purchased more than a few items containing double-chocolate fudge. Underneath was a simple sentence. *This little piggy went to market.* Nausea washed over me. I came to the creepy realization that it had not been a crank phone call the other night. I ran through my house, closing blinds and locking windows.

How did someone get my grocery bill? And why? It must have been left in one of the numerous plastic bags I'd put out for recycling. I struggled with the strange events.

My sleep was littered with nightmares of being chased by the "Fat Police". I barely managed to settle my nerves with several cups of camomile tea. When I went for the paper, any internal calm was sucked out of me by Ms. Leopold's shrieking. She was standing on her doorstep, wrapped in plum chiffon and feathers, waving at me desperately.

"They've snatched my Oodles!"

Mr. Oodles had escaped the night before. He was inclined to do so after a stressful day. Ms. Leopold assumed he'd be back by morning. But instead she'd found his ascot with a note.

"Kiss your wiener goodbye." It was penned in smeared red lipstick.

Mr. Balducci watched from his balcony. He wore an apron proclaiming him to be a "naughty gnocchi".

I settled Ms. Leopold into her bed with a box of Kleenex, camomile tea and a 40-ounce bottle of Bombay Sapphire. Then I phoned the police.

In fifteen minutes three cruisers arrived, lights and sirens on. Apparently, Ms. Leopold played bridge with the chief of police.

That evening I was posting "Missing Oodles" fliers after visiting the liquor store for Ms. Leopold. I slipped into Low-Mart for new workout attire. I didn't want to spend a bundle on clothes. I knew from experience they would not get much wear. I was led to the fitting-room by a pinched-faced woman in a blue smock. She must have overheard my grunts as I forced the waistband of the medium stretch pants.

"Another size, perhaps?" She called from just outside the stall.

"Maybe a large would be more comfortable."

Moments later, the loudspeaker announced the store would be closing. A flowered housedress was flung over my stall door. I eyed the 28XXXL tag.

"Oh, I don't think that's for me."

"I think it will do perfectly."

The store lights dimmed.

"The men will be *swooning* over you. You see, spandex is not your friend. It shows off all your rolls and dimples."

That condescending, nasal voice! I'd been thrown off by the smock, but it was the sales lady from Damon's. *That bitch!* Wanting nothing more than to throttle the snotty woman, I stuffed myself into my clothes, but found the change room door was locked.

"Hey!" I banged hard against the door. "Let me out!"

"Perhaps *Colonel Sanders* will come to your rescue. Although he may be hurt to find you're having an intimate relationship with *Mr. Christie* and *Joe Louis* as well."

The lights were completely out in the store. I strained to listen for signs of life over my pounding heart. A Muzak version of "La Bamba" accompanied my cries for help.

I slumped to the floor to ponder my predicament. It was hard to believe someone with such a high calibre of snobbery would be caught dead in Low-Mart. Why would she have traded her Donna Karan suits for a blue smock and grey polyester slacks? She had obviously been going through my recycle bin. The references to the Colonel were no coincidence. I'd perched a greasy red and white cardboard tub on top of my green box.

In the hours I had to think, I figured out where Mr. Oodles was being held. The threatening note was written in the same shade of Revlon Red that coated the thin lips of my captor. I'd never thought to connect my harassment with the disappearance of Ms. Leopold's treasured pooch. I replayed the conversation I'd had with Ms. Leopold about the situation at Damon's being "rectified" and shuddered to think what she'd done to defend my chubby honour.

The security guard found me in the morning asleep under the muu muu. The police had been searching all night. Ms. Leopold had contacted them when I hadn't returned home with her vermouth.

Two hours later they arrested Mrs. Bretton, aka sales bitch, on one count of unlawful confinement and one count of dognapping. Mrs. Bretton was fired from Low-Mart, just as she had been from Damon's. As I suspected, Ms. Leopold had called the manager at Damon's to air her disgust over my shabby treatment. Being a member of the pleasantly plump club himself, the manager had dismissed Mrs. Bretton immediately.

We were returned safely to our homes, Mr. Oodles swaddled in a police blanket and myself with a $700 gift certificate from Low-Mart.

•   •   •

I sipped my Pina Colada poolside at the River Grand Country Club. Ms. Leopold was holding a chintz fabric swatch to Mr. Oodles.

"I do enjoy the red, dear, but it's just not his colour." A couple in the hot tub caught her eye. "Well, well."

"Who are they?" I knew they must be important for Ms. Leopold to have stopped putting zinc on Mr. Oodles' nose.

"She is Dana Swan, the world's highest paid plus-sized model. She's on the cover of *Mode* and *In-Style* this month."

I peered around Ms. Leopolds's hat-*cum*-golf umbrella.

"And him?" I asked of the handsome silver-haired man fawning over his curvy companion.

"That, my dear, is Mr. Bretton."

I blinked at her. "As in married to Mrs. Bretton, psycho sales cow from hell?"

"The same." She fanned Mr. Oodles. "From what I understand, Dana worked at Dairy Dream before her modelling career took off. He always stopped in after his afternoon walk. Then one night, he went out for a scoop of butterscotch swirl, and never came back."

Dana Swan emerged from the hot tub. Her string bikini clung to her glistening size 16 frame. Mr. Bretton panted after her.

"Rumour has it the article in *Mode* is rather racy."

• • •

Later that week, I took great pleasure using my $700 Low-Mart certificate to buy 100 copies of *Mode* magazine. I sent them to Mrs. Bretton in care of the womens' correctional facility. I was careful to dog-ear the feature article: "Sizzling Sex with your Sixty-Something Sweetheart" by Dana Swan.

VICTORIA MAFFINI *Long known to customers at Prime Crime Books as Vic the Chic, Madame Maffini-Dirnberger now inhabits the dangerous world of educational publishing. She lives in Hull, Quebec, with her husband, her dachshund, a pair of squirrels, two lovebirds and a flock of cockatiels. "Down in the Plumps" is her first published short story.*

DOUBLE TROUBLE

BARBARA FRADKIN

If it hadn't been for my brand-new Discount Dan's hiking boots, I'd never even have met Patrick. I'd spent a long, wet day trying to hitch a ride into the mountains, and I was covered in mud and sweat. No one wanted to pick up a guy who looked like he was on the run from a chain gang, so I had to hoof it about eight kilometres to the next little Welsh town, whose name resembled a bad hand of Scrabble. When I finally hit civilization, it was dark, and I limped to the nearest pub to knock back something cold while I rethought my plans. My feet weren't going to take me any farther that day.

Wales was supposed to be a hiker's paradise, crisscrossed with trails along sea cliffs and over mountaintops steeped in the lore of ancient wars. A far cry from the flat, featureless city of strip-malls I'd left behind in southern Ontario. But it wasn't turning out quite as I'd planned. Prices were astronomical, and I had wasted half my money before I even got out of London.

I entered the Trewern Arms and dumped my gear by the bar. The pub owner took his eyes off the rugby match long enough to flick a question at me. I pointed to the nearest draft, hoping it wasn't that awful tar the Brits drink. Smooth amber liquid foamed into the mug, and I downed half without even taking a breath.

"Do you know a—" I almost said "cheap", but stopped myself "—a reasonable place I can stay the night?"

The pub owner shook his head without missing a second of play. So much for country hospitality. Dead tired, I dropped into a chair in the corner and leaned over to pry my feet out of my boots. I felt, more than heard, a presence above me, glanced up, and there he was. It was almost like looking at myself. Same blonde brush cut, same blue eyes and hatchet face, same six-foot, string-bean body.

"I don't mean to intrude," he said in an accent that sounded like Boston, "but I heard you were looking for a place. I'm just about to go to this small B&B up the road. You're welcome to come and see if they have any rooms."

I took a few seconds to size the guy up, because he was wearing a fancy shirt and Britain seemed to be full of fags. Either that or I was giving off the wrong signals for this side of the ocean.

The guy's smile faded, and he backed away. "Just trying to be friendly."

I didn't want to seem too eager, but my feet weren't up to much hotel hunting. Besides, I'd been in Britain nearly a week without talking to a friendly soul, so I accepted.

His smile returned. "Do you want to check it out now, or grab a bite to eat first?"

I didn't want to admit this place was probably too steep for my budget, so I scanned the blackboard over the bar and saw fish and chips. How expensive could that be?

He pulled a chair over and stuck out his hand. "I'm Patrick Johannsen."

My jaw dropped. "Hello, Patrick Johannsen. I'm Patrick O'Shea."

Over fish and chips washed down by the half dozen beers

he insisted on buying, we laughed at the coincidence.

"I was born on St. Patrick's Day, that's my only claim to the name," he said, then nodded to my backpack. "Are you here for the hiking?"

"If I ever get there."

"Where are you headed?"

"The Brecon Beacons, mountains north of here, with all those ruined Roman castles. What about you?"

He smiled and inspected his hands, like he was embarrassed. "I'm just going. I don't know where. I finished university, hopped a plane, bought a car and headed out of London this morning. This is where I was when I got tired."

"You've got a car!" I thought of my own pathetic stash of pounds. I'd been such an idiot to think three thousand bucks was enough. Of course, if I'd taken any more, my stepfather would have noticed, and this time the bastard would have pressed charges. "I guess you're in a different league from me."

He shrugged. "Depends what you're measuring. At least you know where you're going." He paused to study his hands again. "Maybe we could team up for a while."

He seemed a bit nerdy, but it would only be for a few days, and he had a car. So what the hell. We cemented the agreement with a couple more beers, then stumbled out the door, me barefoot with my boots in my hand. Patrick led me over to a silver sports car. I remembered this car; it had passed me in a cloud of spray earlier in the day.

"This is not just a car! You must have some major bucks," I exclaimed as I climbed in. The leather felt like a baby's skin beneath my hand. Things were looking up.

"I guess." Patrick shrugged, and I thought, oh-oh, not one of those gloomy drunks. But then he started the car and revved the engine like he was gathering strength. "Okay, to the beginning of a new adventure."

"This is going to be fun," I said. "The two of us walk in the door looking enough alike to be brothers—hello, I'm Patrick and this is Patrick."

Patrick chuckled. "We could even switch last names and really confuse them."

The little B&B was squeezed in tight among the trees, and as we turned in, Patrick eyed the narrow, cobbled drive worriedly.

"Here, you sign us in while I make sure I get the car parked safely."

I took his wallet and passport and hauled our backpacks out of the car. A doubtful-looking woman greeted me as I hobbled in the door. The house smelled like old socks, but it looked clean. I could see the woman wasn't impressed with me.

"Have you got a room for two? My friend's just parking the Jaguar around back."

Her frown cleared like magic, and she stepped brightly over to her desk. "Names?"

Amazing what the smell of money does, I thought, as I handed over our passports and introduced myself.

•   •   •

Old socks or not, the little inn was too pricey for my wallet, but before I could open my mouth, Patrick paid for three nights in full.

"As I said, money's the one thing I do have." He bent over to heft my backpack over his shoulder. "You've been lugging this thing around all day. Christ, what's in it?"

"This trip was a spur of the moment thing, and I just threw everything I owned into a bag." Plus quite a few things my stepdad owned, but I wasn't going to add that. This guy probably wouldn't know about deadbeat dads and resentful stepfathers, and about not having a thing to call your own. Anyway, I figured my stepfather would consider the empty safe and the maxed-out credit cards a small price to pay for getting me out of the house.

Patrick stopped halfway up the stairs. "You mean you're never going back?"

"Not if I can help it." I tried to sound cool, like it was my way of breaking free, but I was thinking of the warrant my stepfather had probably sworn out for my arrest.

Patrick unlocked the door to a converted attic with two beds and a bathroom the size of a closet. He dropped my bag on the larger bed, then collapsed onto the cot. I was about to protest, because he was paying for the room, but he silenced me with that shrug that was becoming his trademark. Like he was trying to get the world off his shoulders.

"Don't you have any family? Any parents?" he asked.

"Yeah," I said. "But it was time I left."

"You won't miss them?"

I thought briefly of my half-sisters, who'd always relied on me to lead them in their minor mutinies against Adolf. I'd miss my sisters. I'd even miss my mother, although she'd made it clear where her loyalties lay when she'd dragged me kicking and screaming into that control freak's life. I'm still young, Patrick, she'd said. I need a life. Needed sex, she meant, although at ten I was too young to know that. Well, I hope the sex was good, because she sure paid for it. Mom called my stepdad Andrew, but Adolf suited me fine. Was I going to miss Adolf?

In a pig's eye.

"I'm twenty-one," I said as if that were answer enough. "Do you miss your family?"

He shook his head, then shoved himself off the bed and disappeared into the bathroom. Touchy, I thought. Morose and touchy. Maybe this wasn't going to work out after all, despite the fancy car and the wallet full of cash.

•   •   •

But the next morning he jumped out of bed, grinning from ear to ear, and announced he was ready to hike a hundred miles. I was trying to cram my feet into my boots and accepted his hiking sandals without protest. Rockports. My blistered skin barely felt the leather.

The inn boasted what they called a traditional Welsh breakfast, which was the same as the Canadian breakfast my mother served before the Führer took command and instituted a regime of All Bran and brown toast.

"I've been studying my trail map," Patrick said as our food arrived. "We could pick up a fabulous trail in the Brecon Beacons that goes up over the moors to some Roman ruins. Or there's this heritage trail that runs all along the southwest coast. We could drive down to the Marloes Peninsula—that's a wildlife sanctuary for wild ponies and migrant birds—and we could hike around the cliff tops."

"Cliff tops?" I stopped with a forkful of scrambled egg halfway to my mouth. "How high?"

"It varies. Some of them are two hundred feet. The pictures look amazing. Sheer drops down to the foaming surf."

I'm not keen on heights. Actually, I turn to jelly when I'm five feet off the ground, but I wasn't going to admit that to Patrick. Gentle mountain slopes were about all I was ready for. "Well, I really came to Wales for the mountains."

"All right, the Beacons it is."

The sun had been shining when we woke up, but halfway up into the mountains, a thick white fog rolled in, slicking the windshield and blocking the views I had come to see. Patrick slowed the Jag to a crawl.

"We're going to get soaked," he muttered as we reached the trailhead. "I didn't bring rain gear."

I reached into my backpack and pulled out a windbreaker. "You can wear this; I brought a poncho too."

Patrick accepted it with a surly grunt, but once we'd stepped out onto the open moor, he pulled it around himself tightly. We scrabbled up the mossy slope, dodging sheep turds and bowing our heads against the damp. Beyond us, pale mist swallowed everything. I could see Patrick trudging up ahead, and occasionally a sheep appeared out of the fog, but mostly we were in a cocoon. Nothing, not even sound, penetrated. But despite the cold and wet, it felt magical.

Patrick stopped suddenly, gasping for breath. "O'Shea," he said, "why are we doing this? We can't see a damn thing."

"It might clear," I said. "I read the weather changes every hour."

"But there's not another human being for miles, and I'm freezing."

I unzipped my backpack and pulled out a sweatshirt which Patrick took with a grudging smile.

"Do you have two of everything?" he asked.

"Training from my stepfather. Be prepared, the Führer always told us."

He sat down on a rock to put the sweatshirt on. "You don't like him much, do you?"

"He had a way of making you feel you were always failing some test."

"What about your real Dad?"

"Well, he did fail every test, including fatherhood," I said. "Couldn't get his priorities straight, my mother said. I haven't seen him in ten years."

Patrick unscrewed his water canteen and offered it to me. "It must feel pretty shitty to matter so little to someone."

"I went through a stage of that," I said, wondering why on this gray, empty moor, I was telling a perfect stranger about the part of me that still hurt when touched. "But Dads are highly overrated anyway."

"Mine's dead."

He said it so quietly I hardly heard him through the fog. I sat still a moment, wondering what to say. I didn't want to ask how he died, because I wasn't keen to stir up Patrick's gloom.

"Sorry," was all I could come up with. "I guess your mother does double duty then."

"She's dead too."

I cringed inside. I thought of my own mother, whose favourite saying was "Patrick, don't make waves." I'd always thought her worse than useless, even accused her of driving Dad away, but I'd never wanted her dead. The magic of the moor vanished, leaving only bleak, bone-chilling damp. I knew I had to say something helpful now. I couldn't make a joke or pretend it was no big deal. "That's rough. Was it an accident?"

He turned his face away. "Car accident. I might've been killed too, if I hadn't decided to stay on campus a day longer to pack up my things."

"How'd you manage?"

He slitted his eyes against the mist. "After the affairs were settled, I packed all the things I wanted, bought a plane ticket and took off."

"Wow." I fell silent, thinking about what it would be like to have no one. No one telling you it's time to grow up, no one whining that you should finish university. Or get a job.

Freedom. Complete, utter freedom.

"I guess your parents left you pretty well off, eh?"

"That doesn't make up for it."

"I didn't mean that, but you can do pretty much anything you want."

"I could." He hunched down into his shoulders. "It just takes time to figure out what that is."

"Still, I'm sure you've got friends to visit."

"I don't have friends, Patrick. I have drinking buddies and good-time boys who haven't shown their faces since the funeral."

I was failing miserably at yet another test, that of cheering the guy up, so in time-honoured, male-bonding tradition, I reached into my backpack to pull out a couple of beers. Hardly Adolf's idea of hiking equipment, but they came through in a pinch.

"Well, my friend," I said, tapping my beer against his. "Here's to a new start for both of us."

Patrick's hatchet face worked a moment, then a slow smile transformed it. "Agreed. And tomorrow we're going to the Pembrokeshire coast to hike along the cliffs. In the sun."

Back inside the B&B, we peeled off our soggy clothes and hit the shower. Since my only pants and sweatshirts were soaked, Patrick offered some of his. I marvelled at the rich materials and expensive labels. Adolf shopped only at Discount Dan's. Anywhere else, he said, and you're just putting money in the pockets of the rich. I picked a pair of black Cartier jeans and a Hugo Boss sweatshirt with leather elbow patches. It felt good to be rich. By contrast, Patrick put on his most tattered jeans.

Again I marvelled at the effect money has. When we

returned to the Trewern Arms for dinner, the pub owner was all over me and the waitress who cleared tables was almost slipping in her own drool. With my string-bean physique and gawky lack of class, girls rarely gave me a second glance. This was a change I could get used to. Patrick grinned at my open delight but said it would wear off.

"I've had money all my life. After a while, you think people only like you because of it. No girl's ever wanted the real me, and my frat buddies liked me only when I was picking up the tab. It leaves you feeling empty."

"Well, no girl's ever wanted the real me either," I replied, ordering a new round of drafts with a flick of my finger. "At least this gets you something. And when you were growing up, I bet you had a swimming pool, the latest toys and vacations in Hawaii."

"All under the watchful eye of nanny. Or rather nannies, because Dad kept trying to screw them and Mom kept firing them."

"Better a gorgeous Swedish nanny than the beady eye of an ex-army sergeant with a fetish for All Bran. 'A cleansed body's a cleansed mind', my stepfather always said."

"At least he didn't raise you by proxy, like mine," Patrick countered. "Kind of like a wholly-owned subsidiary." He stopped himself just as a scowl was beginning to spread over his face and drained his beer with a quick toss.

"Okay, so Dads are shits the world over. We're out from under them now, right?"

But the scowl was still spreading. I tried again. "And at least you've got the money." Curiosity gripped me, for I was getting used to the feel of Boss leather against my skin. "Or is that still all tied up?"

With an effort, Patrick shook his head. "Dad had accounts

all over the world, which I can access if I need to." He paused, then patted his daypack beside him. "But I've got the entire life insurance policy in diamonds right here at my side."

I plunked my beer down with a jolt. "You've got to be kidding!"

He held his hands out, palms up, like a beggar. "I wanted the feel of it in my own hands. Not a little piece of plastic or a signature at the bank. I wanted something to hold on to, something to give me a good time. Two million dollars, right here in my hands—that's got to give me a good time." His eyes grew glassy. "Right?"

The exercise, the rich pub food and the four pints of Murphy's stout were taking their toll, and I figured I should get Patrick home before he started tossing hundred pound notes around. Later, I lay awake listening to his snoring and to the pounding of my heart. Two million dollars in diamonds lay in a bag only a metre from my feet. I could pack my stuff, steal half of them—I wouldn't leave him with nothing—and be back in London before he even woke up. Then I could deck myself in Boss leather and surround myself with drooling girls to my heart's content.

Oh, the temptation.

• • •

By some miracle, the next day dawned sunny and Patrick awoke in fine spirits again. It was the darkness that seemed to haunt him, and he emerged from the shower singing. He opened his suitcase and handed me a shirt. Raw silk with an Armani label.

"Here, I know you love this stuff. I'll trade it for your Our Lady Peace shirt."

45

I took the Armani without protest. I suspected he'd never even heard of the Canadian rock band and just wanted to slum it for a while, but I was quite happy to play king for another day.

To complete the image, I wore his Rockports again, and, with a chuckle, he donned my discount equivalent. Patrick had calculated that the hike along the coast would take us all day, so he sent me down to ask the landlady for a picnic lunch.

When I returned, Patrick had our daypacks ready and he dangled the Jag's keys in front of me. "Want to try it?"

I gaped. "On these roads? On the wrong side?"

"Where we're going, the roads are only one lane wide. Come on, I know you're dying to."

The car engine caught on the first try. My heart raced. I gave a jaunty wave to the landlady pruning her roses and accelerated down the highway. Beneath my hands, the car throbbed like a sexy woman. It was magic, as tempting as the diamonds sitting in the little bag by my side. Patrick didn't understand the seductive lure of his life.

He spread the map out and directed me through a maze of little roads, and when we finally broke through the hedgerows, we found ourselves in a field of parked cars. Ahead of us stretched a rugged expanse of red rock, heather and coarse scrub, cropped close by wandering sheep and ponies. In a jagged inlet, I could just glimpse the plunging drop and the jets of white foam below. My stomach lurched.

Patrick jumped out and pulled our daypacks from the car. The wind in his hair and the scent of roiling surf seemed to give him energy. Tossing his bag over his shoulder, he set off towards the cliff top, where I could just make out a narrow path meandering along the edge.

I gave the car one last pat, pocketed the keys, and went

after him. Once I'd found my feet on the rocky soil and learned to look ahead into the distance rather than over the edge, I relaxed enough to enjoy the hike. Gulls wheeled overhead, and Patrick enthusiastically pointed out the puffins and other shore birds perched on ledges in the cliff face. I could never tell one bird from another but accepted Patrick's word that we were witnessing a rare sight.

By noon, we had reached the tip of the peninsula, where we could see out over the water to a large island off the shore. The cliff top was rounded and fell away to outcroppings of rock further down. Patrick turned off the main path and called up to me.

"Come on, there's a natural ledge down here. We can eat our lunch and watch the birds."

I hesitated before beginning to pick my way down the slope. The grass was thick and held my sandals well, but even so, my heart was pounding by the time I reached the ledge. Patrick cracked open a beer and peered out over the ocean, which churned and seethed like something alive.

"Between here and the island, that's Jack Sound, one of the most treacherous stretches of water along the coast. The tides funnel into the narrows at great speed and suck everything in with them. Boats trying to get through are dashed against the rocks. God, look at the power of that water!"

His word was good enough for me. I wasn't anxious to look over the edge. But after lunch, Patrick studied the cliff below and began very slowly to pick his way down. Far below him, the black ocean threw itself against the rocks, shooting plumes of foam high into the air.

"Awesome!" Patrick shouted over the roar. "Come on! It gives you such a rush!"

"No thanks." I felt foolish, a prisoner of my fear. When I

was twelve, I'd stood on a high diving board, trembling and crying while Adolf taunted me from below. I'd backed down, but his word "pissypants" had rung in my ears for years. I studied the slope. Patrick stood on another ledge, safe and without fear. He was beckoning. Not taunting me, but eager to share his joy. Which was rare, I knew.

I left our packs on the ledge and began to inch my way down the slope. My hands clutched at passing sedge as stones slipped beneath my feet. My legs quivered from the strain, but gradually I drew nearer till I stood at his side. His eyes danced as he pointed along the cliff to our left.

"See that little cave? I think there's a bird's nest inside. If we go along this little ledge, I bet we can see inside."

"Along that ledge? Are you crazy?" The ledge was barely two feet wide and wet with spray from the surf below.

Patrick eyed me closely. "You're afraid of heights, aren't you?"

"No, I—I just don't go into orgasms over some old bird."

"Just follow me, and put your feet exactly where I do. I promise you'll be fine."

He set out before I could object, and I stood frozen, watching him pick his way slowly along the cliff, gripping the jagged rock with his hand to steady himself. My hands turned clammy, and the surf pounded in my ears.

Patrick turned. "It's a chough! And I think there may be eggs!"

In his excitement, his foot slipped on the wet ledge, and he fell to his knees. For an instant I thought he'd plunge to his death, but then he grabbed the cliff face and crouched motionless on the ledge.

"Patrick?" His voice was frail against the roar of the surf. "I twisted my ankle. Help."

Help! He had to be kidding. He was stuck on a flimsy ledge above a precipice, inches from death. What good would two of us be, inches from death? I'd have to go for help.

I thought of the diamonds and the Jag waiting above. Peered at the sea below...

"Help," came his voice again, even weaker. I looked down at his rigid frame, swore, and began to make my way down towards him. Sliding one foot at a time, testing each toehold, inching my hands over the rock face, wrapping my fingers around each tiny knob. I didn't look down. I didn't even look ahead to Patrick's face. I stared at the wall and pressed its rough surface against my cheek. After an eternity, I reached him.

"I just need to lean on your arm," he said. "Then I can walk without putting much weight on it."

I braced myself and extended my arm so he could pull himself up.

"Ready?" His voice was tense.

I risked a nod. Patrick grabbed my arm and pulled hard. Instantly I was thrown off balance, my foot slipped and I felt myself going over the edge. In that instant, I caught a glimpse of Patrick's face, alight with triumph as he tried to wrench himself free.

Shock jolted through me. On blind instinct I clutched at him, every inch of me fighting to survive. My free hand caught a jagged tooth of rock and my feet found a toehold on the wall beneath the ledge. I clutched Patrick's arm and pulled for my life. Suddenly his body shifted and slithered over the edge. Pain shot through my arm as he fell, held only by my hand clamped to his wrist.

He flailed about, vainly seeking a grip on the rock. His face, upturned to me, was white as death, and his eyes bulged.

"God, Patrick, help me!" he gasped.

I hung on despite the pain screaming through my fingers. Had he really tried to push me off? Had I really seen triumph in his eyes? Why? And if so, why should I save him? I could just open my fingers and let him plummet to certain death on the rocks below. It would be so easy.

No one knew he was here. No one even knew who he was. He was wearing my clothes, and I could throw my backpack over with him. Just some poor lonely Canuck who'd taken a wrong step along the top of the cliff.

And I would walk away with the identity of a millionaire, a car to die for, and two million dollars in untraceable gems in my bag.

Surely that had been triumph I'd seen in his eyes. He'd tried to play me for a sucker, and no one did that to me. Not ever again. "Help me, buddy," Patrick said, stretching up his free hand.

"Fuck you," I said. And I let him go.

• • •

The sun had nearly set over the distant hills by the time the Jag purred back up to the Bed and Breakfast. I'd considered not coming back. After all, I had Patrick's backpack with his diamonds, passport and papers. My own papers were in my backpack, now floating with his body out to sea.

But I had to make sure Patrick had left no telltale evidence at the inn. In the twilight I spotted the row of shiny cars parked along the edge of the house, but thought nothing of them. I climbed out of the Jag, slung Patrick's bag over my shoulder and headed for the front door. My legs felt like rubber and my heart thumped sickly in my chest. That's to be expected, I told myself. You've had a harrowing day, and it's not every day you let a man die. You'll get over it.

I crossed the threshold and caught sight of the landlady behind her desk. She wore a glare, not her usual smile at the sight of me.

"That's him," she said.

Four figures emerged from the shadows of the sitting room. Two uniforms, two dark suits. Four gold badges, glinting in the light from the desk.

"Patrick Johannsen?"

I turned, a denial stuck in my throat, but before I could form it, cuffs were snapped around my wrists. Incredulity rushed through my mind. How could they possibly know?

"What's going on?"

"You're under arrest for the murders of Richard and Beatrice Johannsen." The suit had the same Boston twang as Patrick. "It took us a while to track you down, son, but you should never have underestimated the power your father has, even from the grave."

BARBARA FRADKIN *works as a child psychologist during the day, which gives her plenty of inspiration for her favourite night-time activity, plotting murders. Her dark, compelling short stories have appeared in the previous Ladies' Killing Circle anthologies, as well as in several magazines, and her debut detective novel,* Do or Die, *featuring Police Inspector Michael Green, was published in 2000 by RendezVous Press. A sequel,* Once Upon a Time, *is due out in 2002.*

GRUDGE MATCH

THERESE GREENWOOD

O f course one feels for the late—though, let's face it, unlamented—Harry Pilgrim, but nothing beats a little armchair detecting. It makes a girl's heart thump." The girl in question, Miss Case Doyle, was in high spirits as she leaned across the bar towards Gunboat Merkley. He would not have been surprised to see her pull a magnifying glass and Sherlock Holmes hat out of the overstuffed little sack she called a purse.

"Think of it, Gunboat," she said. "Comfortably ensconced in her beloved watering hole, the beautiful but brainy sleuth mulls over the unsolved mystery with a dispassion brought on by the passage of time. Witnesses are gob-smacked as she reveals the now screamingly obvious pattern that left the local flatfoots flat-footed. There is absolutely nothing I would enjoy more, you can take that to the bank."

Gunboat would have put five to one this was not strictly true. Miss Doyle enjoyed a lot of things. Take that crazy jazz whooping out of the new Victrola the boss had brought back from Rochester, and that loopy hat with the scarlet feather that came from no bird he had ever seen, and the martini she was lapping up like a kitten at the cream pitcher. And the boss. She liked the boss. But Gunboat would not have laid odds on how much. She was a dark horse that way. Look at the handsome pill stringing her along now.

"It'd take a month of Sundays to sort through all the jokers who wanted to kill Pilgrim," said the pill, one Lester Ketcheson. He was so right about that. Harry Pilgrim was dead six years, but even tonight, you could swing a stick in the speakeasy and hit a half-dozen people who had wanted to do the chump in. It bothered Gunboat, though, that after all this time the boss was still the odds-on favourite. Oh well, he thought, at least the boys in the backroom kept Ketcheson steady at two-to-one.

"And here you are, Les," said Miss Doyle, "back at the scene of the crime after six years. You must have some vital but overlooked clue that once known will reveal all."

"Wish I could help," Ketcheson said agreeably. "But I had just popped in to conduct a little business and take the boat home before that crumb Pilgrim bought the farm." He was watching his language in front of a lady or he would have used a different word for crumb. But those years in stir had not turned Ketcheson crude. He was still a fine-looking, loose-jointed know-it-all, wearing his hat, if you called that lousy piece of felt a hat, indoors to hide the work of the prison barber. His jacket was a dog's breakfast, too, lopsided like it was buttoned wrong. Gunboat supposed he hadn't had time to get a snazzier one, given that he had only been sprung that morning.

"The most interesting part of the puzzle is the gunshot, of course," said Miss Doyle. "It's something right out of a melodrama. A pair of doomed lovers bursts into the room screaming blue murder about a body by the croquet hoops. And then the topper, a shot rings out. I hear the girl fainted, which must have been a lovely touch. It really happened that way, didn't it, Gunboat? It isn't a bit of embroidery stitched on over the years?"

It wasn't. It had been a helluva scene, the room more or less quiet with the orchestra taking a break. Then Pilgrim's son and the young housemaid Harry Jr. was so nuts about ran screaming in. The pair had just calmed down enough to gasp out something about a murder when the gunshot blasted outside.

"You couldn't touch that for dramatic effect," Miss Doyle said with satisfaction. "A gunshot after the body is discovered. As a plot twist it is second to none."

"Somebody was just making sure the old crumb was really dead," said Ketcheson, tugging at the frayed collar of his open-necked shirt. "Harry Pilgrim was an A-one louse. You'd have had to stand in line to do him in, and the line was pretty long that night."

True enough, Gunboat thought. It had been a big crowd, even for a Friday. Back then Pilgrim's Rest had been a high-class club for smug folk who wore badges on their coats. They'd thought a lot of Harry Pilgrim then because he did not smoke, drink, bet, chew gum or talk loudly. It didn't matter he was mean as cat's piss. They came in the dozens, sailing pricey boats up to the dock, liking that the hotel was on an island in the St. Lawrence River, for the exclusive use of rich people fishing a little, shooting a little and gossiping a lot.

Things had changed after the War, but the private locale was an even bigger draw now Prohibition had turned it into a gin joint. They still came in the dozens, still sailing pricey boats, but now they wanted to smoke, drink, gamble and brush up against wickedness. Now the smug folks thought a lot of the boss because he never boasted, never flirted with a man's wife, never took a drink from his own bar and was suspected of killing the previous owner. Tonight, with the Dempsey fight to come on the radio, they came because they thought the boss had once fixed a big-time heavyweight scrap.

The boss, as always, looked like the rumours had never laid a glove on him. There was a fresh nosegay in the narrow lapel of his fitted double-breasted jacket, his pants were creased and cuffed in the smartish way he had worn even before the Prince of Wales made it the rage, and his shirt was a brilliant, crisp white. He seemed almost merry as he walked up to Stevie Pounder, the serious-looking lad donning the radio's ear pieces and twiddling the dials on the fat wooden box as if his life depended on bringing in the fight. The boss put Stevie at ease with one of the Cuban cigars special-ordered four to a box labelled "Reginald Ashe". Gunboat noticed the boss had lit his third stogie tonight, and that he was in no hurry to talk to Ketcheson.

Ketcheson had been cooling his heels for half an hour, although a nice half-hour inching his stool closer to Miss Doyle, pretending to look at her newspaper for the poop on the Dempsey fight. Not that they did much reading. She was a born talker, going on about a new pair of boots she had ordered, about learning to shoot at her papa's knee, about Dempsey's right hand, and about the night Harry Pilgrim bought the farm. She had made what she called "a tableau of the crime scene" with now-empty martini glasses standing for the folks Gunboat had seen that night when he went down to the boathouse to fetch a twelve-bottle case of real French champagne.

"The night air must have been especially invigorating," Miss Doyle was saying, as she gave her funny tableau the once over. "Everyone and his brother was out for a stroll. The band was taking a break by this bottle of vermouth. Darling Reggie had slipped behind the soda siphon. Stevie Pounder's father was out by the ashtray helping the boatman tie up the launch. Harry Junior and that girl he was so mad about were stealing a minute somewhere around the Beefeater, although I guess they don't have to steal any more. I heard they got married on the proceeds when Reggie bought this joint."

Ketcheson sniggered. "They had to, I suppose, after everyone got a look at the grass stains on the back of that pretty red dress of hers. They weren't playing croquet that night."

"Tsk, tsk," said Miss Doyle, but Gunboat figured she was more ticked off at Ketcheson than the pretty housemaid. Miss Doyle felt certain allowances ought to be made for pretty girls, likely because she was very pretty herself. Tonight she looked like a flower, more like a rose than a girl. Her pink, freckled cheeks made her look younger than the twenty-three he knew she was, and her gold eyes had an agreeable way of sizing up a fellow. Gunboat liked, too, that she showed off her first-rate gams with a paper-thin, slinky number that quit just below the knee. Though he didn't like Ketcheson's hand, rock-hard from the hoosegow quarry, resting just above the hemline on her first-rate knee.

The boss wouldn't like it either. But he was busy making with the friendly, chatting up the Wall Street big shot and the son of the man who owned the Waldorf-Astoria, and keeping a fatherly eye on Stevie Pounder, who suddenly stood up halfway, before the wire on the radio ear pieces jerked him back.

"Hot dog! There's the Polo Grounds!" Stevie cried. "The fighters are going to their corners."

"Holy Mike, is it fight time already?" Miss Doyle said. "I've just got time to plunk down a few smackeroos on the champ."

She clicked open the glittery crystal clasp on the cloth purse no bigger than Gunboat's fist. When the pencil and notepad came out it reminded him of clowns coming out of a paper car at a vaudeville show he had seen at the Winter Garden when he and the boss were on the road. He kept a poker face as the tiny pearl handle of a gun peeked out of the bag, too. As long as she didn't point it at the boss, it was none of his business, and a girl who went to speakeasies and talked to jailbirds and bet on prize-fights couldn't be too careful.

"You're throwing your money away on Dempsey," said Ketcheson, stabbing a calloused finger at the scandalsheet still spread across the bar. "Says right here, the champ doesn't want it like he used to. It's more fun fighting to the top of the hill than standing up there and defending it."

"I suppose I'm not the best judge," Miss Doyle said, crossing her legs beneath the satin and giving the brush-off to Ketcheson's long-fingered paw. "I only get halfway up a hill when I think, cripes, why I am bothering with this stupid hill? What do you think, Gunboat, has the tattlesheet got it right?"

Her silver charm bracelet jingled as she started to slide him the newspaper, but the boss slipped in and took it, brushing against her in a way that said he would like to brush up against more than that. He must have seen the offending hand get the bum's rush from the first-rate knee, and another man would have said something cutting. Not the boss. He was one of nature's gentlemen.

"It's right about the challenger, Case, darling." The boss pointed to a line of ink halfway down the page. "No one knows what Luis Firpo will do in the ring if he's hurt, because no one has ever hurt him. He lets other fighters come to him and takes what they dish out. Then he bangs away until they collapse."

"Dempsey is an overrated chump," Ketcheson said. "They always say whoever holds the title is the greatest fighter of all time. Bunk and twaddle of the worst kind. Dempsey's never been up against anything but slow-moving, slow-thinking bums."

"You don't say," said the boss. If there was a note of warning in his voice, Miss Doyle didn't hear it. Or maybe she did.

"Gunboat went a few rounds with the champ before the War," she said stoutly. "The only knockout of your career, wasn't it, Gunboat?"

"So they tell me," said Gunboat.

"I remember all right," said Ketcheson. "They said you telegraphed your best punch." He acted it out, drawing back his right and lifting his butt, thin in the pants that had fit him before prison, an inch from the barstool.

"I heard Gunboat punched like a charging elephant," Miss Doyle said. "A telegraph from a charging elephant doesn't do much good." Ketcheson had got Miss Doyle's Irish up. "Gunboat, give me one hundred smackers on Dempsey."

She clicked shut the twinkling clasp, tossed the bag down as if she were packing nothing heavier than face powder and handed him a scribbled note he could not read. "You know, there's nothing I like better than a grudge match. Two fellows going toe-to-toe to knock the chips from each others' broad shoulders." She fashioned her right into a tiny fist that would not have given a mosquito trouble and floated a powder puff that melted before it got halfway across the bar towards Gunboat.

"Can I set you up, Lester?" the boss asked, waving towards the bottles lined up in front of the bar's mirror.

"Very open-handed of you. But I'm after more than a watered-down drink."

"Feel free to buy me one," said Miss Doyle.

The boss smiled and nodded, and Gunboat took the solid silver cocktail shaker from the shelf over the mirror behind the bar. In the mirror he saw Ketcheson's dark eyes glued to his back. "As soon as I collect the money owed to me," the jailbird said agreeably, "I'll buy a round for the house."

"There's the bell!" Stevie Pounder was too loud, as if the

sounds coming though the radio and into his ears filled him up with noise. It beat Gunboat how something in New York City could fly through the air and into those skinny pieces of wire. He thought it almost sinful, but everyone else, everyone but Miss Doyle, was bunched about the boy, hanging on his every word.

"What money?" Miss Doyle was asking. Gunboat didn't like the interested look on her pretty face.

"My cut from the Dempsey fight."

Stevie squeaked again. "Dempsey rushed in with a right, but Firpo beat him to the punch! The champ is down on one knee!"

"You have a pretty swelled head, Les," said Miss Doyle, those gold eyes narrowing. "The fight has barely started, and here you are collecting your winnings."

"Not this fight," laughed Ketcheson. "The one before I got sent up, the one where Gunboat took a dive."

Whatever the boss was going to say, he couldn't beat Miss Doyle to the punch. "That's loopy," she said, waving away the words with a flick of her bangled wrist. "Gunboat makes the finest martinis in the Thousand Islands and is as stand-up as they come. It's not in his nature to take a dive."

The crowd around the radio lowered their noise to a dull roar to hear Stevie's next report. "The champ is back on his feet, throwing like a crazy man, and Firpo is down!"

"Lester," the boss said, "watch yourself."

Gunboat took the top off the silver bucket and saw the ice had melted into a solid block. He took the ice pick in his large, hard fist and splintered it with one short stab.

"The last thing I want to do is get Gunboat's blood boiling," Ketcheson said with a wink. "But we both know he took a fall. It was me that told him to."

The boss looked around to see who else had heard, but Stevie's words had the suckers in a spell. "Firpo is up with a big swinging right and bam, he knocks the champ right out of the ring! Dempsey's gone head over heels over the rope into front row!"

"You see, Miss Doyle, Pilgrim wasn't crazy," Ketcheson went on like he was teaching a pouty kid her ABCs. "If he laid down a bet against his own fighter, everyone would know the fix was in."

"You don't say," she said, like she really wished he hadn't said. She turned her back to the bar, and Gunboat saw the back of her dress dipped scandalously low beneath her shoulder blades, a fact he forced himself to ignore.

"But he wouldn't go face-to-face with Gunboat, either. He had me do his dirty work there. I couldn't bring myself to spit it out, not looking at those fists, why, they're like hammers. I don't mind telling you, my own hands shook when I gave Gunboat the marker and said it was a message from his boss. But Gunboat's a gent. When he saw how much was riding against him, he just gave me one of those shrugs and handed the paper back like he was handing a mother cat a kitten."

"Ah," said Miss Doyle, "the plot thickens." Gunboat had never heard her voice so small or so soft.

"It was my fault," said the boss. He was looking at Miss Doyle, but talking to Gunboat. "We were flat broke, but if we made good against Dempsey, we'd be set. So I sold most of my stake to Pilgrim." There was a slump in his shoulders that hit Gunboat like Dempsey's right. "I wish to God I hadn't, but he was the only one with that kind of cabbage."

"My God," young Stevie croaked, "the champ is back in the ring! The swells in the first row pushed him over the ropes!"

"Why didn't you collect before, Les?" Miss Doyle's voice was stronger now, Gunboat thought, like she had made her mind up about something. She had twirled her stool back towards Ketcheson, but she wasn't looking at anybody. Her eyes were on her lap and she was playing with the clasp of her little bag.

"It was one of those crazy things. A few days after the fight, I was celebrating and got in a little spat with a lady's husband. Could've happened to anyone." A spat, thought Gunboat. The hard-done-by husband was shot in the leg and nearly bled to death, and Ketcheson's payday was a ticket to Kingston Pen.

"But you said you were here doing business that night," said Miss Doyle. "So if you didn't get your money, Harry Pilgrim must have tried to stiff you. That would be your motive for killing him."

"Now wait a minute," Ketcheson said, leaning back on his stool. "There's no need for crazy talk. I just want what's coming to me."

"You'll get what's coming—" Miss Doyle said "—if the cops ever find out you were still here when Harry died."

"I lit out long before the old crumb got topped," said Ketcheson. "The boatman backed me up on that."

"Then how did you know the housemaid had grass stains on the back of her dress? Surely it's not the kind of gossip you hear around the chain gang. No, you must have collected already. That's how you could pay the boatman to say he took you home earlier. Clearly you had the dosh to go out on the jag that ended you up in the slammer."

"Now slow down, honey," Ketcheson said. "Okay, I was on the back porch finishing my smoke when that girl and her lover boy charged right past me and into the house. But it was

Fancypants here," he pointed a calloused finger at the boss, "who took off out the back door like a bat out of hell."

"To investigate the screams," said the boss smoothly.

"With a shotgun?" Ketcheson said.

"Ah, so that's the pay-off you're after tonight," said Miss Doyle. "Reggie pays the piper and you won't play a little tune in Mr. Policeman's ear."

Stevie's voice cut in, yipping like one of those pug-dogs well-off American wives carted about. "Dempsey hit Firpo so hard that he lifted him in the air! Boom, Firpo's hit the canvas!"

"Things have changed while you were up the river, and Reggie would be nuts to pay you," Miss Doyle said cheerfully and began ticking off the reasons on her little fingers. "First, he's a big-time bootlegger, he's got cops on the payroll now. Second, the suckers up from Syracuse love that murder bit, it brings them in by the boatload. And third, you saw Reggie leave the house after the dead body was found. Why, Reggie has a better alibi than you do. Maybe you killed Pilgrim that night and kept all the dough."

"Your logic astounds, my dear," said the boss. "Like your charm, it bowls one over like a careening motor car."

"You rat, Ashe!" cried Ketcheson, his work-hard hand snaking towards his baggy pocket. "Put the frame on me, will you?"

Gunboat felt things slow down, like when he was in the ring, and his left foot travelled forward in a long falling step. As his weight shifted, his half-opened left hand came straight out from his shoulder, chin high across the top of the bar, and his fingers began to close with a mad clutch, his knuckles lining up like soldiers.

"No, Gunboat!" the boss barked.

The boss could not stop him, no one could stop him, no one but Miss Doyle, who leaned in to plant her little gun in Ketcheson's side. Gunboat lurched to the left, and a punch that could have killed her breezed past, catching the tip of her silly hat and knocking it a little off kilter.

"Reach for the sky, pardner," Miss Doyle said. "I always wanted to say that, like one of those Zane Grey posses arriving in the nick."

"You won't shoot," Ketcheson hissed, careful not to move an inch.

"Don't bet on it," said the boss. Gunboat agreed. Miss Doyle was not the goofy dame she made herself out to be, but then Gunboat had suspected as much. The boss did not go in for goofy dames. He liked his women like his steak and his whiskey, a little on the rare side.

"If you do Reggie in, Gunboat will go on a rampage and you'll shoot him. Then where will I find another bartender who makes the perfect martini?" Her hand was steady as the boss reached into the jailbird's lop-sided jacket, took out something heavy and dropped it in his own pocket.

"Usually, I don't have to pull a gun to get a fellow's attention," Miss Doyle said, putting her peashooter back in her little bag. "But let me give you a tip. See how Reggie's pocket sags? If you're going to cart around a concealed gun, don't let it pull your coat to one side and, for goodness sake, don't keep brushing up against someone wearing a sheer little number like mine. Cold metal leaves little to the imagination." Checking her reflection in the mirror behind Gunboat, she straightened her hat.

The boss kept one hand in his pocket. With the other he brought out some banknotes and thumbed a few bills on the bar in front of Ketcheson. "Here's a few bucks for a guy down on his luck, Lester. But that's all she wrote. Don't come looking for more."

Ketcheson grabbed the bills and gave a halfways grin that made it clear he had thrown in the towel. "Win some, lose some," he said, as Gunboat made to come out from behind the bar.

"No, Gunboat, I'll see Lester out," said the boss. "Miss Doyle has earned another perfect martini and, while you're at it, tear up her bar tab."

Miss Doyle was the only one watching as the two men left. Stevie was rhyming off a ten count that reminded Gunboat of when Dempsey knocked him out, the numbers coming through layers of wool. The gang at the radio picked it up, chanting till he couldn't hear the lad, and when the count finished, they went nutty, carrying on like gangbusters because one man licked another, and money from the side bets started changing hands.

"Gunboat, would you please look at that marker I gave you." He looked up at Miss Doyle, surprised, although people did the damnedest things at pay-off time. He poked his big fingers into his shirt pocket and fished out the paper.

"Read it to me," she said.

He could smell her perfume on it, like no flower he had ever smelled, but soft and fresh and suiting her. He wanted to hold it up to his nose, but instead he unfolded it and looked at the words she had written. Then, he couldn't help himself, he shrugged.

She reached over, took the note, and read. "One hundred dollars on Jack Dempsey to beat Luis Firpo, and another fifty dollars here and now if you can read this note."

Gunboat stood there dumb. A good word for him, dumb. He could not read a lick, but somehow she had read his secrets, maybe on his big dumb face.

"When I handed you that newspaper tonight, Reggie went for it like a stick of dynamite," she said. "He was trying to sidetrack me and that stuck in my craw, so I slipped this dirty little trick in." She tossed the marker down on the bar.

"That's why you killed Harry Pilgrim. Because you can't read. When Ketcheson handed you those markers, you weren't going to let him know you had a glass jaw in the written word department. So you pretended to look it over, shrugged your old shrug, then climbed in the ring and Dempsey licked you fair and square."

Gunboat looked at his fists, like boulders, which had failed him the one time he had needed them.

"Pilgrim sent you for champagne, and you found out what he was celebrating. The dive you didn't take," Miss Doyle said. "Then you knew he'd done what no one could do in the ring. He made you a bum."

"It was just one punch," Gunboat said. But it was like a cannon going off, a perfect right uppercut driving the base of Pilgrim's jaw into his brain. If he'd had that punch with Dempsey, they'd be listening to him on the radio now.

"You found Reggie and came clean, but before he could get rid of the body, those lovebirds stumbled over it. Reggie was running out of time, so he used the shotgun to disguise the weapon only one man around here had."

They both looked down at his big clenched fist, and she reached out and took it in her two hands.

"I didn't like it," Gunboat said. If it weren't for the boss, he'd still be fighting for hooch in some two-bit joint. Or dead.

"But Reggie insisted," she said. "He's one of a kind, isn't he? Carrying on, a ray of sunshine, knowing everyone thinks he's a murdering skunk while he's the truest of pals. It's the kind of thing that makes me think I ought to marry him."

"Marriage is a fine institution," said Gunboat, although he wasn't too sure.

Neither, it seemed, was she. "Can you picture me living in an institution? And come to think of it, I'd get myself banned from this fine institution if Reggie knew what I've been spinning to you. So why don't we keep mum? I don't want to gamble with my supply of martinis, and say, how's that one coming along?"

Gunboat was reaching for the honest-to-God Beefeater, not the bathtub rotgut they used for the saps, when Stevie Pounder bounded up. "The champ is some man! Helps Firpo to his feet after the big knockout. What a class act!"

Speaking of class acts, Gunboat thought, and looked at the marker face down on the bar. "You just made two hundred shekels, Miss Doyle."

"I knew the champ would come through. Anyone who knocks out Gunboat Merkley is the world's toughest hombre. But forget the bet." She picked up the marker and began tearing it into strips. "I've lost my taste for grudge matches. In fact, I've gone off gambling altogether."

Too bad, Gunboat thought. He was sure his money would be safe if he bet on her really liking the boss.

THERESE GREENWOOD *lives and writes in Kingston, Ontario. She was a finalist for the Crime Writers of Canada Arthur Ellis 1999 Award for best short story and winner of the Bloody Words 2000 short story contest.*

IT'S A DIRTY JOG, BUT SOMEONE HAS TO DO IT

I have to keep up this facade.
I have to run each day.
I have to look real womanly.
It's like I'm in a play.

I have to wear an itchy wig.
I have to wear spandex.
I have to wave at all the men
Leaning from their decks.

I have to shave my hairy legs.
I have to wax my face.
I wish that I had taken off,
Instead, I took her place.

I have to run five miles a day
And make the neighbours see
This sweaty, gritty, jogging jock's
A she and not a he.

I have to keep up this facade
Because I took her life.
And no one will suspect me while
I'm running for my wife.

JOY HEWITT MANN

SIGN OF THE TIMES

MARY JANE MAFFINI

She's going to kill me. It's just a matter of time until she gets it right. All I can do is putter about my garden and check over my shoulders for the next sneak attack.

Don't think I'm imagining it. The woman is capable of anything.

Consider her flawless organization of "Citizens Against Community Homes". Didn't that just keep those pesky halfway types out of the neighbourhood? People still speak in hushed voices about her crusade against dogs in the park. Her campaign to wipe out street parking was as organized as any militia, though perhaps a bit more bloodthirsty. So, you see, I don't have a hope in hell. Now is that a fair outcome for someone with a bypass for every artery and seventy-eight years of peaceful living?

Once, I was a painter. Now I use flowers to colour my life. As far as I can pinpoint, more than ten years have passed since I retired to the privacy of my garden, alone but not lonely. A garden can have that effect. I have grown scrawny where once I was lean, bedraggled instead of fashionably bohemian. I have decided I prefer myself this way, like my flowers, just a bit out of control.

The days pass quite nicely when your mind is busy with where to plant the bachelors' buttons and how to keep the phlox from creeping into the lilies.

I would be happy if only she weren't closing in daily. This morning, while admiring the gentle pink of peonies in the early sun, I hear her triple-glazed patio door open and then the smart, sharp clicks of stilettos on the cedar deck that shadows my small garden. My heart rate soars in a symphony of agitation. I shrink back behind my French lilacs and hope not to be seen. Why can't I make anyone understand what she is doing?

"Miss Ainslie," she bellows, rather like Wellington lining up the brigade at Waterloo, "you will have to do something about that dog."

Now what? How can my dog be a problem? In the five weeks since I brought Silent Sam home from the Humane Society, he's been nothing but a huge, heaving bundle of gratitude. Loving and loveable. Shambling and confused. I have always placed a high value on randomness, a low value on boundaries. So Silent Sam suits me. Mrs. Sybil Sharpe doesn't.

"I don't have a problem." I infuse my voice with false confidence, but I am glad to be out of reach of her two-inch fuschia nails.

"Well, I do. That dog is driving people crazy. If you have no consideration, and I am already fully aware of that, then you will find the city ordinances are firmly on my side."

I fail to see how Silent Sam can bother anyone.

"The city ordinances can be firmly up your backside as far as I care," I say, but the sound is muffled by the lilacs.

•   •   •

My doctor pats my hand. "You've had a bad couple of months. The key thing is not to get upset and to stick with your regimen: strength, flexibility, cardio."

"Got it," I say.

He does not believe my next-door neighbour is a serious health hazard. I have explained she is deadlier than a random clot, more insidious than a ticking embolism, more determined than a clump of blue cancer. I should know, I've held them all at bay, but only Mrs. Sybil Sharpe causes me to gasp awake every night at three, heart twisting with fear.

"She sent Social Services around. Remember? She said I wasn't fit to live alone."

"And are you still living alone?"

"So far."

"My money's on you in this contest. I figure you're far more tenacious than any difficult neighbour. And speaking of tenacious, let's talk about your resistance exercises. How many repetitions?"

"Twenty of each with the five-pound weights." I take a sideways peek at him to see if he's falling for it. Those weights would probably be a piece of cake compared to the clean-and-jerk with the bags of sheep manure I needed for my spring maintenance. It seems a fair substitute to me, but I keep the details to myself.

"Excellent. What about the flexibility regime?"

"Fifteen minutes of stretching, twice a day." It seems prudent not to mention this takes the form of reaching to prune, deadhead and transplant. Bend, reach, bend.

"Great. And cardio?"

"Got myself a pooch from the Humane Society. Brisk walks twice a day." This is not the highest form of truth, since I fail to mention Silent Sam is down to three legs and blind as a mole. Getting him to the nearest fire hydrant feels more like resistance work than cardio.

He chuckles and shakes his head. "Wouldn't surprise me to

see you in the 10K race one of these days."

Once again, I've failed to convince him of the danger presented by Mrs. Sybil Sharpe. That's the problem when your doctor remembers you as his childhood art teacher. He'll go through life thinking you are inclined to colour things to suit your own purposes.

"My money's always on you, Miss Ainslie. Always." He is smiling. I am not, since I have lost another round. *Mrs. Sybil Sharpe: 1, Miss Callista Ainslie: Zip.*

He calls out as I near the clinic door, "You'll live to a hundred."

Not likely. And I won't even rate an inquest, I'm sure. Pretty straightforward for the coroner. Seventy-eight-year-old woman, recovering from quadruple bypass and with a whopping melanoma in remission, pitches into the day lilies following a stroke. A kindly neighbour's attempts to get help are unfortunately too late. Mrs. Sybil Sharpe's broad face would blanket the City section of the paper bemoaning the slow response time of paramedics in our community. I can see it all now.

• • •

The animal control officer takes me by surprise. I am concentrating on finding just the right spot to relocate the rosemary, now that Mrs. Sybil Sharpe's shadowy deck has stolen the sun from the west side of the garden.

"Sorry to disturb," he says, "but we've had a complaint about your dog here."

"This dog? Are you sure?"

"I think so, Ma'am."

"What kind of complaint?"

"Excessive barking."

I laugh merrily. "You must be mistaken."

He wrinkles his brow. "Are you Miss Callista Ainslie?"

"Yes."

"And would this be your dog?"

"That's right. Meet Silent Sam."

Silent Sam takes a shine to the animal control officer right away, and it's hard to hear ourselves with the thumping of that tail. I fill in my side of the story, being careful to insinuate that Mrs. Sybil Sharpe is as crazy as a polecat and twice as mean. Besides the innuendo, I have a key fact on my side.

The animal control officer is impressed. "A barkless dog? Can't say I've ever heard of one."

"Feel free to check my story with the Humane Society. According to his rap sheet, Sam had debarking surgery some years ago."

He bends over to scratch Silent Sam behind the ears. "Nice old fella. With a tail like that, who needs to bark?"

I relax a bit. "Better than any alarm system."

The animal control officer looks around. "Nice neighbourhood."

"Used to be," I say.

"You have a wonderful garden."

A close call, but I am not foolish enough to believe this minor victory will divert Mrs. Sybil Sharpe for long.

• • •

There was a time when I could have turned to my neighbours for support. But the old ones are in Florida or mildewing in some hole of a nursing home. The few remaining are caving in to the relentless ring of the developers. The new ones have a tendency to scuttle through their front doors the second they see me. Their expressions suggest Mrs. Sybil Sharpe has put out the word I'm some elderly female version of the Antichrist, accessorized with the Baskerville hound.

I have tried in vain to pinpoint the moment when everything changed. All I know is the neighbourhood is going fast. Post-war bungalows and fifties-style duplexes have been flattened by spreading brick homes, gangling town houses and something called lofts. Where children played jump rope and street hockey, now huge, lumpish vehicles cut off the view. Instead of laughter across fences, now I hear the swish of leather cases and the beeping of small phones.

Gentrification, they call it. Real estate agents ogle our remaining properties with dollar signs in their eyes.

I can take that. It's only Mrs. Sybil Sharpe who pushes things beyond endurance. She has the light of battle in her eye tonight as she rages on about the spread of weeds, as she calls them, from my garden. It was naughty of me to plant mint so close to the boundary of our property, but I have derived a certain amount of pleasure watching it sneak onto her manicured Kentucky blue. I enjoy the resulting puce mottling on her neck when she spots the latest clump.

• • •

The woman from the developer sports a pair of python boots. How fitting. She feigns sympathy for the plight of the elderly abandoned in the increasingly dangerous and hostile urban jungle. That would be me. Her hooded eyes give her away. Doesn't fool me. I know whose prey I am.

She would like to help, she says. To take me away from this. Set me up with enough cash to fund a retirement residence. She has brochures conveniently on hand. No worries. Round the clock attention. Nurses. Communal dining. Bingo. Naturally, a suitable family could be found for Silent Sam. I am fascinated by the way her tongue flicks in and out as she spins her tale. She makes coy references to the amount I could be offered for my small war-torn property. I am expected to feel lucky.

"What led you to me?" I ask, all innocence.

"It's a booming market. We keep our eyes open."

"There's an excellent property next door," I point to the pristine expanse of Mrs. Sybil Sharpe's house. "A fine view of the river from the upper stories. I would think your buyer would find that of interest."

The heavy lids close and open again. What does that mean? Could the so-called developer be none other than my enemy next door?

"I'm more interested in yours."

"What company did you say this was again?"

"It's a numbered company. I am not at liberty to say."

"Really?"

"It's not significant. Guess what they choose to offer," she hisses.

"An apple?"

$$\bullet \quad \bullet \quad \bullet$$

Certainly the randomness of my garden outrages Mrs. Sybil Sharpe. But logic tells me it is the house that causes her eyes to bulge out so dramatically. She's not one to appreciate the sexy curl of the roof tiles, the holes in the screens that beckon to adventurous bats and the lovely weathered grey shingles under the peeled paint. I will not be able to afford to paint properly for two years. There may not be any shingles left by then. They seem to have more health problems than I do.

If only I'd spent my working life like a sensible person instead of hopping overseas for a year or two whenever my savings built up to the price of a ticket. A sensible person would have a full teacher's pension. And wouldn't have to choose now between a cluster of new climbing roses and paint for the house. It wouldn't come down to repairs to the roof or a pond on the east side. A new lock for the back door or a new dog at my side. But then if I'd been sensible, I wouldn't have been me. Now I'm hoping I can continue to be me just a little bit longer.

I keep checking the price of paint at Decker's. There are other regulars there, including dangerous looking young men who hang out in front of the Krylon display.

I am standing in the garden considering whether to take advantage of fine bargains on leftover custom-mixed paint at Decker's. No two colours are even remotely alike. Some you would think couldn't possibly belong to the same spectrum. I like that. I think the entire effect would be rather like Joseph's coat.

I have half convinced myself that climbing my old wooden ladder could be classed as a flexibility work, and a heavy enough paintbrush would be an improvement on my prescribed routine with handheld weights.

I can't do it, of course, because the exuberant colours would overwhelm the subtle shades of the hosta and astilbe on the east side and provide unfair competition to the purple coneflower and hollyhock on the west.

• • •

Of course, she's nice enough when she wants something. You would think I was her favourite aunt at the community meeting she organized to combat graffiti. She hit the combat trail at the first swish from a spray can. Tolerance of graffiti is the sign of a community in decline, she says, and she will wipe it out if it kills somebody. I wouldn't want to be one of the junior expressionists if she comes upon him. Mrs. Sybil Sharpe takes no prisoners.

A young police officer has been assigned to explain the phenomenon of graffiti to us. We learn a lot from the meeting. Graffiti is not meaningless. It consists of territorial messages and threats of bodily harm. We learn that it flourishes where young people are outlyers, lacking positive outlets for their time. I immediately think of street hockey.

He tells us some of the city's graffiti artists are just creative kids in competition with each other. I hear a sharp snort from you-know-who on this. But as a former art teacher, I would grade some of the samples he shows us quite highly. We learn a lot about "tags", which are signatures, and "bomb", which means to cover an area with your work, and "burn", which means to beat the competition with your style. The teacher in me is impressed with many of the designs.

Mrs. Sybil Sharpe clearly has the young officer in a panic. He loosens his collar and explains for the third time why we can't call 911 every time we see a swirl on a mailbox. He keeps trying to edge away. I could tell him it's not easy to do.

Mrs. Sybil Sharpe intends to petition our Member of Parliament to have it dealt with seriously. The police officer clears his throat and explains that vandalism is already well covered in the Criminal Code. If I were a legislator, I would start looking over my shoulder.

I have nothing to lose, really, so I put up my hand. "Does a bit of graffiti really matter? Can't we just paint over it and get on with life?"

Mrs. Sybil Sharpe shoots out of her seat. Her face is the

colour of my clematis. While purple is attractive in a flowering vine, it can't be healthy in a human. "*Does it matter*? It is the slippery slope to the teeming, drug-infested slums. It is nothing less than the rape of our neighbourhood. I, myself, feel violated by every instance of it. We have our investments to consider. The next thing you know we will be surrounded by hovels." The look she gives me tells the world who the subject of the next community public meeting will probably be.

"Oh, well then," I say.

•   •   •

What next? I should have been expecting the property standards by-law enforcement officer. I had not realized that broken windows were within their purview. Of course, I hadn't realized I had a broken window. But there it was. The small one high up. What would have been called a piano window in my day. How could it get broken? There wasn't even a branch near by. No children play with balls in my garden where Mrs. Sybil Sharpe could pounce on them. No one can even see it. I look up. Well, it is within sight of her vast deck. Something else is even more interesting. Anyone pussyfooting through my garden with the intent of doing a bit of damage is completely hidden. She could destroy my garden and the back of my home and no one would be the wiser.

I feel my aorta lurching. Not even the scent of viburnum is enough to calm me.

The enforcement officer doesn't really think my home comes under the heading of derelict properties, even if the hinge on the gate is a bit on the loose side. He trusts me to fix the window. He does not believe my herbs qualify as noxious weeds. Still, this visit has upset me. *Score: one all.*

Of course, I should have been more vigilant. I take my own share of the blame.

How did she set Silent Sam free? Perhaps she used sirloin to lure him away, and he was too blind and befuddled to find his way back to his new home? And unable to make his voice heard. I am filled with black thoughts. Seventy-eight years without a dog, and now I can scarcely cope for a few hours. Perhaps it isn't worth it to stay in this house.

. . .

I am looking for Silent Sam many blocks from home when it happens. The sidewalk has seen better days in this neighbourhood, which is still on the before side of gentrification. The sun has set when I become aware of someone following me. Someone large and fast. This would never happen if Silent Sam were there. Mrs. Sybil Sharpe will get her way if some mugger kills me.

He is even with me now, walking fast, his head down. Will he push me into a bush? Dump me into the alley ahead?

I have nothing to lose by standing my ground.

"You'll find I put up a pretty good fight," I say. "For that I thank the weight training."

"What?" It's just a boy, this mugger, still rangy, hands and feet waiting for his body to grow to meet them. He has so many rings in his face. But he doesn't seem any happier to see me than I am to see him. Maybe it's my Antichrist look.

"What?" he says again.

"I'm searching for my dog," I say. "He's playfully hiding behind some of those bushes and I need to get him to the vet quickly because I believe he has rabies."

This seems to startle the boy, and he drops a can. It rattles and rolls along the sidewalk, running out of energy near my foot. I am flexible enough to bend and pick up.

"Just leave it," he says.

By this time, he is shuffling from foot to foot. He is exhaling guilt. I remember the look well from my years in the classroom. He's done something. I look behind him. Sure enough.

The swirl of a black design.

"What dog are you looking for? The same one you had in the paint store?"

The paint store? Of course, that's where I've seen him before. Picking out the tools of his trade. "Yes. The same one."

"I saw him two streets over. He looked lost."

I find Sam where the graffiti boy suggests he might be. If I don't die of joy at the moment, perhaps I'll live forever.

• • •

Sam noses me awake even before the fire engines arrive. My little house is full of smoke. I am choking and hacking as we hurtle through the front door into the street. The neighbours begin to spill from their townhouses for the festival of sound and light.

I am having quite a bit of trouble breathing. The paramedics have oxygen for me. They wish to take me to the emergency ward. I have had more than enough trips in speeding ambulances. I am not willing to leave my dog. "That will kill me," I say. "My estate will sue you, seriously."

They are polite but firm. Like all the control officers, they are just doing their jobs.

Yes, ambulance. No, dog.

I spot Mrs. Sybil Sharpe, her shining housecoat wrapped around her expansive middle. She is watching the whole procedure from her front doorstep. Behind the mask of the concerned neighbour, I suspect a smirk is lurking. I wonder how she started the fire.

Perhaps I am just imagining the hiss and slither.

We are at an impasse, the paramedics and I, until one of the firemen whispers he will take Sam until I am home again. It's against the rules, so it has to be our little secret. There's something familiar about him. He looks a lot like one of the boys I taught. A Kevin perhaps? Another troublemaker. The right spirit for fighting fires. But I taught so many boys. Who is to say?

•   •   •

A pot left on the stove, the young fireman tells me, when he returns my dog. Lucky the harm was confined to smoke damage. Another couple of minutes and who's to say.

"Interesting," I said. "I never touch the stove. Do you think it was a self-cooking pot?"

He gives my hand a pat. "Maybe you need a bit of help around here." He said. I read the unspoken message. Forgetful. A danger to herself and others.

I smile compliantly. "I am fine on my own. I have just purchased an excellent new alarm system. If I even get hot under the collar, it will sound the alert." I don't trouble him with talk of Mrs. Sybil Sharpe, the snake woman, or the side door that never quite locked. I have fixed it now, anyway.

I know what I really need.

"What doesn't kill us, makes us strong," I explain to Silent Sam as he gets a nice bit of ground round for a reward. He looks at me as if to say, so what will it be?

It is my best effort ever. Reminiscent of my glory days when I could really toss paint on a canvas. And what a canvas it is. A vast, welcoming field of cream. I use every graffiti symbol I can remember. Probably overdo it a bit with the clouds. The resulting work is full of fury, threats and imagery. It takes me nearly all night, but it is worth it. Who would have realized how all that gardening helped me? The strength of the arms holding the cans of paint, the quick scampering up and down the ladder to scoop up new cans of colour, the ability to arch my body and take advantage of the grand sweep of the wall.

"I call it Joseph's coat," I say to Silent Sam. He thumps in approval.

Despite my exhaustion, I feel so much better when I'm finished. I can understand why those boys do it. Euphoria is addictive.

In the morning, I rise late. All I have to do is admire my handiwork. I make myself a wonderful pot of Red Zinger and settle comfortably in the old Muskoka chair to enjoy the sunshine and wait for the fireworks.

Perhaps it is Silent Sam's thumping tail that draws Mrs. Sybil Sharpe through the patio door. Perhaps she just wants to stare down at my little house and garden and plot her next strategy.

"Good morning," I call up. "I believe you are right about the violation of the neighbourhood."

"What are you talking about?" she says.

"Look behind you. I believe there must be a new gang in town."

She grabs her throat as the full enormity of Joseph's coat sinks in.

"I see what you mean by rape," I add.

Mrs. Sybil Sharpe appears to be in the midst of a little dance. Most unlike her. I sip my Red Zinger and watch. But what's happening? She's clutching her chest and making gurgling noises. She's slipping onto the deck. Her foot is drumming strangely on the cedar boards. Am I the only one who hears? So it seems.

I finish my tea and turn my attention to the Siberian iris, which are reaching their peak. I move on to plan where I might split the daylilies and get a bit more of a ruffled look to the bald spot near the fence. The bird feeders need to be filled. The impatiens wants water. I could split and replant those clumps of snow-on-the-mountain.

It all takes time.

The drumming seems to go on forever. Then it is quiet on the deck.

Artists: 2, Snakes: 1.

"Well," I say to Silent Sam after we have staked the morning glory, "we are neighbours, after all. Perhaps we should call for help."

Speak Ill of the Dead, MARY JANE MAFFINI's *first mystery novel for RendezVous Press, was nominated for a Crime Writers of Canada Arthur Ellis award, as was her short story "Kicking the Habit", in* Menopause is Murder. *She scooped the Ellis for Best Short Story in 1995. Now watch out for her chilly new novel,* The Icing on the Corpse.

GRAND SLAM

LEA TASSIE

"S even spades."

"Double."

"Pass."

"Pass."

"Redouble!" A smug smile accompanied Laurene Jones' triumphant bid. It was clear she thought making seven spades would be a snap.

A grand slam, doubled, redoubled and vulnerable. If Laurene made her contract, she and Marion would win the rubber and be up 3,140 points. That was as many points in one hand as I usually made in a whole afternoon of bridge.

My partner, Emily, stared at her cards as if wondering why she'd ever had the temerity to double Laurene's bid, then gazed out my living room window at the log booms in the rain-lashed inlet and beyond to the Coast Range. The view of forested mountains apparently offered no inspiration, for she sighed and examined her cards again.

Laurene was always full of herself, but when she made a doubled contract, she crowed so much that I wanted to take a dull knife to her tongue. There can be grace in winning as well as losing, but Laurene's grace was restricted to her perfectly coiffed blonde hair, her perfectly matched ensembles and her perfectly kept house. Oh yes, and her expertly brewed coffee and exquisitely baked brownies.

"It's your lead, Emily," I said. "And don't worry. We're not playing for money."

Emily led the deuce of hearts. Marion laid out the dummy's hand, shoved her chair back and rose.

"Where are you going?" Laurene demanded.

"Bathroom break." Marion's smile was strained. She hated listening to Laurene brag as much as Emily and I, but she usually managed to be gracious.

"Come and see what I have in my hand," Laurene said, "and watch how I handle the play. You need to learn more about strategy."

Marion, the youngest at forty, pushed her red hair back over her shoulders, smoothed her silk shirt over the hips of her Levis and went dutifully to stand behind her partner's chair, too gracious even to thumb her nose at the back of Laurene's head.

Laurene paused after each trick, whispering to Marion about the clever play she'd just made and the even cleverer play she intended to make next. Emily and I knew because she'd done the same thing to us, more times than we wanted to remember. The hand seemed to go on forever.

"If you've got all the tricks, why don't you lay your hand down and claim?" I asked.

"That would be a waste of a good teaching hand, dear. I want to play it right through to the end, so Marion can see how to do a squeeze play."

In fact, she simply wanted to torture us. We all knew how to do a squeeze play, a simple matter of playing all your winners and forcing the defence to discard until they could no longer protect their good cards and had to discard those as well.

Laurene made the grand slam, of course. Her bridge was

impeccable, like her life. She wrote the 3,140 points on her score pad, beaming as though she'd won a lottery, and said to Emily, "What on earth possessed you to double me?"

"The bidding indicated that you could be missing an ace and I thought Barbara might have it." Emily, at seventy-three, was the senior member of our foursome, her speech as precise as her tweed suit and severe chignon of grey hair. A true lady, my husband often said.

"And you had nothing in your own hand that could take a trick? Really, Emily! You must base your bids on logic, not wishful thinking." Laurene rose. "Barbara, do you want help in the kitchen?"

"No, no," I said hastily, "everything is ready." The last place I wanted her was in my messy kitchen, finding out I'd purchased the dessert from a bakery. Emily is a lady, Marion is gracious, I am a slob.

I brought the tray of coffee and brownies, and we moved to easy chairs to nibble and rehash the three rubbers we'd played.

As usual, Laurene took centre stage. She swallowed a delicate bite of her brownie, wiped her mouth carefully so as not to smudge the rose pink lipstick that matched her pant suit and said, "Ladies, I've said this before but it bears repeating. To play bridge properly, you must keep your minds fit, just as you should exercise and diet to keep your bodies fit." She glanced at me. "Barbara, have you started that diet I gave you?"

"No chance. We've had company all week." To tell the truth, I'd ripped it up and tossed it in the fire as soon as I came home from our last bridge session.

"You'll never reach your ideal weight if you allow yourself to be distracted, Barbara. It's like playing bridge. You must concentrate on your goal."

"I've always thought of bridge as a game," Emily said. "A challenging game, to be sure, but fun to play. I'm afraid I don't wish to regard it with the same seriousness as conducting a war."

Laurene reached for another brownie. "Barbara, these are quite good, but they do need a little something. Perhaps each one topped with a maraschino cherry?"

I have always hated maraschino cherries, but not as much as I hated Laurene at that moment. "I'll try that next time."

Laurene demolished the rest of the brownie without dropping so much as a crumb. "The goal in bridge is to win the most points. If you don't play to win, why bother playing?"

"I do play to win," I said, "but I make mistakes, like everyone else."

"You wouldn't if you dismissed every thought from your mind except the hand being played." Laurene returned her serviette to its original folds and put it on her plate. "Barbara, when I have time, I'll show you how to fold serviettes into marvellous shapes. Such touches add so much elegance to formal dinners."

"Thank you," I said, gritting my teeth. Elegance in my house consists of using serviettes rather than paper towels. In Marion's house it means sitting at the table to eat rather than in front of the television. In Emily's, a three-course meal rather than a sandwich.

"You played that grand slam very well," Emily said. Conversation about anything other than bridge, books or bird-watching usually bores her, but I was surprised at her giving Laurene another chance to show off.

"Thank you. By focusing on the hand, I realized I could make it by doing a squeeze play, thus avoiding the need to finesse for the diamond queen. All three of you would play so much better if you focussed properly."

"Well, of course, we're not perfect," Marion said with a straight face, kicking her shoes off and curling her jeans-clad legs under her in the corner armchair.

"But you could be," Laurene went on. "You could learn to bid and play as well as I do. Why don't you come to my bridge classes at the church hall on Tuesday evenings?"

"My book club meets on Tuesdays." Emily crumpled her serviette. "I couldn't possibly miss that."

"You could get the day changed if you learned to use psychology," Laurene said. "That's what is needed for bridge, too. With practice, you can train yourself to interpret facial expression, tone of voice and even hesitations in bidding and play."

Laurene rose and paced the room as though she were lecturing her class. "Now, Emily, try to get your book club to change its meeting night. Next week I'll be teaching strategy. Playing the right card at the right time is essential to winning."

I was itching to toss my cold coffee in her face and wreck her flawless makeup, but Emily and Marion were being such exemplars of politeness and forbearance that I felt ashamed of my impulse.

Laurene glanced at her watch and gave a tidy little shriek. "Oh, dear, I must be going. I'm teaching a class on cake decorating at four." She buttoned and belted her rain coat and added, "I just love living in little towns like this. There's so much one can do to improve life in them."

After the front door closed behind her, the three of us looked at each other. "I'll go get the coffee pot," Marion said. "We've all been out of school a long time and I, for one, don't feel like going back. We have to do something about that woman."

"But what can we do that won't jeopardize our husbands'

jobs?" I trotted into the kitchen after her to fetch the pan of brownies.

"The unfortunate part of living in a company town in a remote logging area," Emily said, when we were settled with fresh coffee, "is that one's social life is so limited. I'm lucky my husband is retired. I can offend anyone I please."

Marion and I couldn't. Both our husbands were in shaky management positions, reporting directly to the new superintendent, Laurene's husband. It was well known that Winston Jones intended to make drastic cuts to management. Winston and Laurene had been in town barely three months, and already Laurene haunted our nightmares as much as Winston haunted the men's.

"Remember how much fun we had playing bridge when Sally was the fourth?" Marion bit into another brownie. Sally was the previous super's wife, and Laurene had bulldozed her way into Sally's social life right down the line.

"It was wonderful," I said. "She never snickered or bragged when she trumped somebody's ace."

"Let's not waste time with regrets," Emily said, sitting up straighter than ever in her chair. "We must find a way to deal Laurene out of our bridge life so we can find a fourth who enjoys the game and doesn't have to be right all the time. Is there any chance Winston will be transferred?"

"Harvey overheard Winston say he'd rather be in head office in Vancouver," Marion said, "but that it probably wouldn't happen."

"Well, you know Laurene," I said. "She wants to be a big toad in a small puddle, and she probably runs Winston's life, too."

Emily pursed her lips. "I'd suggest her as chairperson of the library committee and the PTA in order to keep her too busy for bridge, but I'd hate to subject my old friends to such a horrible fate."

"It wouldn't work anyway," Marion said. "She'd never quit our foursome; every week she gets to win points against three imperfect victims. And I don't mean just bridge points." She picked up one shoe and hurled it across the room. It landed on a pile of newspapers and knocked them over. "When Laurene's finished one of her lectures about how I should have played the hand, I want to say to her, 'Laurene, please break wind again. I love the smell of roses.'"

"I want to do more than that," I said. "When she leans over and pats me on the shoulder and smirks while she's telling me what I did wrong, I'd like to kill her."

Marion and Emily looked at each other, then at me. Marion got up and headed for the liquor cabinet. She pulled out a bottle and turned to hold it up. My best scotch. Emily went to the kitchen and brought back three glasses and a tray of ice cubes.

"All right, let's focus on psychology." Marion poured a generous splash of scotch into each glass. "And let's not forget concentration and perfect strategy and perhaps even a squeeze play or two."

• • •

The following week, Marion and I arrived at Emily's house fifteen minutes early for our bridge session. We put our trays of brownies beside Emily's on the kitchen counter. In each of the three pans, one brownie sported a maraschino cherry nestled in thick chocolate icing.

"Did you phone Laurene?" I asked.

"Yesterday." Emily smiled as she prepared the coffee-maker.

"She's thrilled about the contest. She said she'd have no problem judging which brownie is best."

"Thrilled to death, I hope," Marion said. "I don't know how I'm going to get through three rubbers of bridge with the state my mind's in."

"You must learn to concentrate on the game, my dear," I said, mimicking Laurene's tone and accidentally knocking a knife off the counter.

Emily took my hands in hers. "I would suggest you take a couple of aspirins, Barbara. That might stop your hands trembling."

"Could I have a shot of scotch instead? And some fresh mint to chew afterwards?"

Before Emily could get the scotch, the doorbell rang. Laurene opened the door, ushered herself into the living room and sat at the bridge table. "Ready to play, girls?" she trilled, sweeping the cards into a perfect semi-circle so that we could cut for deal.

I was amazed at how smoothly we cut the cards and took seats opposite our partners. Mine was Emily for the first rubber, and it comforted me to see her calm face across the table. My nervousness receded, curling itself into a twitching, aching lump in my stomach.

Naturally, Laurene drew the highest card and dealt the first hand. "It's a shame you all missed my Tuesday class," she said, snapping the cards down with the precision of a drill sergeant. "I discussed strategy. For example, you may use any legal ploy to mislead your opponents, such as false discards, or looking worried when you know perfectly well how to play the hand."

"I think I'll practise looking worried today," I said. Marion kicked my foot.

Marion, who was Laurene's partner, opened the bidding

with one heart. Laurene raised it to four hearts and promptly got up to lean over Marion's shoulder and supervise her play after I led the ace of spades. Marion looked grim, but she made an overtrick.

"You should have led another spade for Emily to trump," Laurene said to me. "Weren't you counting the cards? You could have prevented us taking the overtrick."

"I forgot to count anything but trumps."

Laurene shook her head, a sorrowful look on her face.

It took less than two hours to stumble through our usual three rubbers and, to no one's surprise, Laurene garnered the most points. "I was at the top of my form today," she said. "I'm certainly ready for the brownie contest."

Emily carried in the three maraschino-topped brownies on three delicate china plates of different design and put them on the end table beside Laurene's chair. Marion served coffee. I sat twiddling with my cup and wishing I were somewhere else. Anywhere else.

"These look lovely," Laurene said. "Did you all use the same recipe?"

"No," Emily replied. "We thought it would be more interesting if we each tried something different."

"Ah, but that will make them more difficult to judge. You should have thought of duplicate bridge, where all the partnerships play exactly the same hands. It's an excellent approach because no luck is involved, only skill. Winston and I adored playing duplicate when we lived in Vancouver. I have almost a thousand master points, you know."

We knew.

Laurene picked up the brownie from the plate with pink roses and took a bite. She chewed slowly, raising her gaze to the ceiling as if communing with her taste buds by long distance. I tried to go on breathing; it was my brownie she was eating.

"Hmm. Tasty, though perhaps a little dry." She dabbed at her lips with a serviette and sipped coffee before attacking the brownie on the bluebell plate. Marion shifted restlessly in her chair.

When the second brownie had disappeared down Laurene's throat, she said: "Acceptably moist, but the chocolate was rather overshadowed by peppermint. The use of artificial flavouring requires a light touch, girls."

The third brownie was on a daffodil plate. Laurene tasted it, frowned, tasted it again. My palms were sweating. "At first I thought there was far too much sugar in this one, but there is an underlying bitter tang. Perhaps unsweetened chocolate? Interesting, though." She finished the brownie and held out her cup as a hint she was ready for a refill.

"So give us the word," Marion said. "Which brownie takes the prize?"

Laurene smiled. "Definitely the second one. It had the proper moist texture and the right chocolate smoothness. Go easy on the peppermint next time, though."

"Congratulations, Marion," Emily said, pouring second coffees for all of us.

Marion rose, gave a mock curtsey and took a brownie from the plate Emily had placed beside the cream and sugar on the coffee table.

"Oh, but girls," Laurene said, "where are your maraschino cherries? Those brownies are plain."

Emily's face went pale. I said quickly, "No one likes them but you, Laurene. We put them on yours as a special treat. As a reward for judging, you might say."

"Well, aren't you sweet," she said. "They do look delicious, even without the cherries. But I'll pass. Winston and I are guests of honour at the Rotary Club dinner tonight. I mustn't ruin my appetite."

Twenty excruciating minutes later, Laurene finally put her coat on.

"I should leave, too," Marion said. "Harvey and I are going to the movies tonight. *American Beauty* is on. The one that won all the Academy Awards, remember?"

Laurene stood in the open doorway, smiling. "You'll love the movie. And you'll never guess the ending. Kevin Spacey's character gets shot." She left, and Emily waved at her from the front window as she drove away.

Marion, face red, slammed her fist on the coffee table, bouncing the brownies on their plate. "Not only did she ruin the movie for me, but now I'll have to sit through it while Harvey watches." She shoved a brownie in her mouth and bit down as if it was Laurene's neck. "And to think that for a moment there I was regretting this brownie caper."

We retreated to the kitchen to help Emily wash cups and plates. "Barbara, what did you put in your brownie?" Marion asked, drying the same cup for the third time.

"Amanita mushroom. The death angel."

"I used methanol and a lot of peppermint essence to cover the taste. What about you, Emily?"

"Mashed ripe privet berries. And a great deal of sugar to hide the bitterness." Emily polished the sink. "I was so afraid she'd catch on when she asked about the cherries. Thank you for your quick thinking, Barbara."

"I was terrified she'd eat a fourth piece and find out it tasted different yet again from the others," Marion said. "For sure she'd have wanted to know why."

"It doesn't matter," Emily said. "Now we just have to wait.

Two of those poisons take several hours to work."

"A grand slam," I said, "doubled and redoubled, if all three work. Will you pour me a scotch, Emily? Waiting will be the worst of all. What if she finds out? What if the police find out?"

•   •   •

By ten the following morning, I was such a wreck that I invited myself to Emily's for coffee and moral support. Marion arrived a few minutes later.

"I'd put some Drambuie in the coffee," Emily said, "but if anyone comes asking questions, it won't look good if we're all drunk before noon."

We settled into our usual soft chairs, drank the rocket fuel that Emily calls coffee and gazed out the window at the clear-cut scarred mountain. There seemed to be nothing to say. Twenty minutes later, the phone rang.

Marion and I listened as Emily murmured, "Oh, dear," and "I'm so sorry," not once, but several times. When she hung up, she said, "Our grand slam didn't work."

The blood drained from my face and the starch from my knees. "What do you mean, it didn't work?"

Emily patted my hand. "It's all right, Barbara. Laurene was killed on the way home from her cake decorating class yesterday afternoon. A logging truck rammed her car into that stone wall the other side of the bridge. The car was crushed almost flat and, fortunately, she died instantly. Then the car burst into flames, and the firemen had a terrible time putting it out. Laurene's body was virtually destroyed."

"Oh my God, we're in the clear," Marion said, a trace of hysteria in her voice.

"Yes," said Emily thoughtfully. "Apparently Winston is going to lay criminal charges before he goes back to Vancouver."

Marion's face paled to ghastly grey, and her voice quavered. "Why? Who? Emily, what are you saying?"

Emily smiled. "Winston is going to charge the truck driver. The man said Laurene was weaving all over the road and driving on the wrong side."

"That would be the privet berries." I clutched my coffee mug in shaking fingers. "They're supposed to take a couple of hours or less."

Emily nodded. "Winston is sure the man is lying; he says Laurene was always in the right."

LEA TASSIE *grew up on a northern British Columbia homestead. One of her short stories, "Guardians", won* Storyteller*'s 1999 Great Canadian Short Story contest.* Tour Into Danger*, a suspense novel, is due out in 2001. She's working on two novels, one serious and one a romp with two crazy cats.*

SEEING RED

LINDA WIKEN

She couldn't run any faster. There was no escape. She tried to lengthen her stride, but it kept pace. She stumbled and almost pitched into the darkness. *Get up. Run.* The house. She had to reach the house and mommy. She needed her mommy. Keep going. Don't look back. Almost there. The house. With locked door. It wouldn't open. She pounded. She cried out for her mommy. Don't leave me. And then woke to the sound.

Hannah Price jerked bolt upright in bed, gasping to reach total consciousness. Trying to shake off the dream. Her heart was pounding too fast in her chest. *It's only a dream.* She tried deep breathing. It helped. She glanced at the bedside clock, 5:30 a.m. A shard of sunlight cut across her bed. Time to run. Shake off the night and the dream.

She groaned and rolled out of bed, jerking to a stop as a pain shot through her left hip. Running had brought that on again. She'd known it would happen. But she needed the high, needed to escape the horror of what was happening, if only for an hour.

As she pulled on a grey cotton T-shirt and nylon shorts, she listened for sounds from the next room. Carrying her Rykas, she crept along the hall and opened the door to her mother's room. She heard the same raspy breathing she'd heard last time she'd checked, a couple of hours ago. She longed to go to her mother, crawl into bed beside her, wrap her arms around her and make everything all right. *Why her, God?*

Once outside the house, Hannah went through her routine of stretches while sorting a mental list of tasks for later in the day. Then she started down the gravel driveway at a medium lope, waiting until she reached the main road before going all out. She didn't expect much traffic at this hour. Maybe on the way back, the occasional car would be transporting its load of office workers into Victoria for the day.

Hannah had no idea if that included the neighbours who were only a mailbox at the road's edge about fifty metres along. They were new to the area, moved in long after Hannah had left home for the promised land of Vancouver. Her monthly visits home were filled with her mother. There was no need to look for others to socialize with. And now that she'd come back to nurse her mom, she didn't want anyone else intruding. She wanted this time alone with her, to stretch out every moment of their final days together as long as possible.

Nobody loves you like your mom.

Ain't that the truth, thought Hannah, especially when there's no one else in your life to love you. And soon there wouldn't even be Mom.

No-body-loves-you-like-your-mom. It fit her stride. No-body-loves-you-like-your-mom. Her mantra for today. Block out all other thoughts. The ones she couldn't cope with.

•　•　•

"So what's it to be for lunch today, a decadent chicken broth or an exotic pea soup?" Hannah tried not to stare at her mother as she straightened the bedding.

Five months of fighting ovarian cancer had reduced her to

a body with sharply angled bones stretching a covering of translucent skin, a sharp contrast to the bright red and yellow scarf tied around her head. Her days were spent entirely in bed, mainly sleeping. Her short waking periods were filled with Hannah reading to her and, each afternoon, a visit from a home care worker.

"I don't know, Hannah. Surprise me." Her lips slid apart in a strained smile.

Death warmed over. The phrase, unbidden, leapt into Hannah's brain. She swallowed hard to allow an answer through the massive knot blocking her throat.

"O.K., Mom—a surprise it is."

She tried to think of some variation from the bland items that had become the daily food fare as she cranked up the volume on the Graco monitor in the kitchen. She'd had it installed last month, a convenience that allowed her to eavesdrop on her mom's bodily noises. Nothing was private any more. There's very little dignity in a painful death, thought Hannah. Her eyes filled with tears, and she quickly poured herself a glass of water from the ceramic rooster pitcher kept in the fridge. Hannah ran both hands along its orange and yellow contours, a link to her childhood, a happy time with just the two of them and the assortment of four-legged creatures that were a part of the family unit from time to time. None of the pets had survived, and soon there'd be only Hannah. *She can't leave me. I still need her.*

She shook her head and finished drinking the water, then opened a can of broth, adding some fresh mint and rosemary once it started heating, sniffing the aroma. A comfort food from a happier time. The doorbell startled her. She glanced at the aging round clock that hung above the sink. Another childhood memory. She turned the element to simmer and went to open the front door.

She knew this face but couldn't quite place it. Something familiar. That smile, so damned sure of himself. It couldn't be. *No. The son-of-a-bitch was back.* "What the hell do you want?" She stared at Dan O'Connor, debating whether to slam the door in his face.

As if he read her thoughts, he stuck his foot in the door and held out his right hand in appeal. "Hannah? It is you, isn't it? You're all grown up. Please, Hannah. Can't we call a truce? I'd like to see Carolyn. I do still love her, you know."

Hannah couldn't look him in the eyes. She'd never been able to, even as a kid. She concentrated instead on the mass of wrinkles etched on his tanned face and the greying hair. He'd aged in the seventeen years since she'd last seen him. The night of her twelfth birthday party. The night he'd walked out of their lives; one of the happiest nights she'd known in the five years he'd lived with them. The worst part was she knew her Mother still thought about him. She refused to believe it was love. But her Mother would want to see him.

Hannah pulled the door open wide. "She's in her bedroom. I'm just making her lunch." She turned her back on him and went to dish out the soup.

How dare he? He thinks he can just waltz back into our lives. The bastard.

She rushed pouring the soup into a mug, spilling some onto the counter and floor. She threw the dishrag on the largest puddle and plunked the soup mug on the tray, spilling some more. *Damn him.* When she joined them in the bedroom, Dan was sitting on the edge of the bed, holding Carolyn's hand. Hannah flinched and bit back an acerbic comment.

"You'll need to move, Dan." *That's my place.*

"Of course." He leaned over and kissed Carolyn on the

cheek. "I'll just go and put away my things. I'm in the guest room, I presume?"

"Yes, my dear." Carolyn patted his hand then looked at Hannah. "So, what's my surprise to be?"

The guest room? Hannah busied herself helping her Mom sit up, and with setting up the bed tray, wanting Dan to be out of the room before she spoke.

"Did you know about this?" she asked, guiding spoonfuls of the liquid to her mother's mouth.

Carolyn nodded. "Yes, he called the other day while you were out. I should have told you." She paused, struggling to catch her breath. "I wanted to see him. Please, Hannah, try to understand."

"All I understand is that life was hell when he was living with us. He was always butting in."

"He was your father."

"No. He was your husband. And the two of you were always arguing. Then he ups and walks out. And I thought that was great, but you were miserable for a long time after. And now, after all these years, he turns up in our lives again and you welcome him in. That I don't understand."

Carolyn closed her eyes. "I thought you'd grown up."

The words stung. Hannah blinked back the tears. Here he was, dividing them again, now when her mom was dying. *The bastard.*

"O.K. Mom, I'll be civil to him." *Just don't be mad at me.*

"Thank you, dear." Carolyn reached for her hand, but Hannah barely felt the weak squeeze.

Dan returned as Hannah prepared to take the tray away. Time to be nice. "I usually read to Mom a while after lunch. Would you like to do that?"

"Yes, I would. Thank you, Hannah."

She left as Dan sat down and stroked the side of Carolyn's face, left before her anger erupted.

She closed the door to her room and stripped, changing into shorts and sports bra. She had to get out of there, run off some of the tension. The temperature had risen, making it too balmy for late September. Indian summer. A last chance for the heat of summer. But there'd be no last chance for her mom. On her way out she stopped at the open bedroom door. Dan had made himself very comfortable.

"I'm going out for a run. Won't be long."

She didn't wait for an answer. She had to get out of there. She hit the laneway at top speed and didn't slow down until she'd done half her route, down the road, up a dirt trail through the woods and over to the cliff.

Her foot caught the tip of a stick and she stumbled, pitching towards the edge. She grabbed a low-hanging branch to stop her fall. Her whole body shook, her heart pounded in her ears. It was a long way down to the shoreline. She bent over from the waist, breathing hard.

She couldn't catch her breath. She never ran out of breath. Hadn't since her early days of running. She straightened, avoiding looking straight down, and did some leg stretches, then sat on a log well back from the edge, staring out at the ocean. *Breathe slowly. Relax.* She used to love coming here to sit and watch, sometimes to dream about sailing across that open expanse of water to whatever was beyond. Maybe all the way to Japan. *Just relax.*

Of course, in those days, she'd fantasized about a special guy going along with her. Well, guess what, he'd never materialized. Lots of false tries but never Mr. Right. One analyst had said it was because no one could compare to her father, the father she never knew, a memory she'd assembled from bits and pieces of other men. The warm laugh of a friend's father. The dark, haunting looks of a magazine model. The togetherness of television's Walton family. She didn't know anything about him; her mother had always refused to discuss him. She didn't even know his name, but that was okay, he was always "my daddy". She'd woven a rich fantasy life for the three of them. Before Dan had come along.

He couldn't compare to her daddy. And she had refused to call him that. He had pushed his way into their lives, taking up all her mother's time, and driving her daddy further away from her thoughts. Hannah had hated him for five long years. Until he had left. And her daddy was able to return, to be with her. And she was happy.

• • •

"Hannah, do you think we could have a talk?" Dan asked as he cleared the dinner dishes from the table. It had been a quiet meal, just the two of them, eating a nuked frozen lasagna and fresh green salad she'd tossed together with makings from the garden.

"I don't think we have anything to talk about." She ran the dishwater to drown out his words.

He went back to sit with Carolyn while Hannah fumed. Her mom. She was the one who should be sitting with her, not cleaning up after *him*. She finished the dishes then went in to get her mom ready for sleeping. Dan disappeared until later that evening, when Hannah sat reading in the living room.

"You can't avoid me for the entire time I'm here, Hannah." Dan sat down beside her on the couch before she had time to object. "I know you think I didn't belong in your lives, but I did love you both, you know."

Hannah closed her book and turned to face him. "No, I don't know and it doesn't make any difference anyway. You're here to visit with Mom. Let's leave it at that. I do appreciate having my privacy, if you don't mind." She heard the chill in her voice and was glad of it.

Dan shook his head. "Okay. Okay." He stood slowly and retreated down the hall. She waited until she heard the door to his room open and shut, then she opened her book and stared at the pages. An hour later, she closed it, not having progressed from that single page, and went to bed.

• • •

Hannah dreamed again that night but could recall only bits and pieces of it in the morning. She'd been with her mom, somewhere. Just the two of them walking along the river.

Her head throbbed. Another tension headache in full control. Run. She needed to run. Dan's door was closed as she crept down the hall. Her mom slept noisily but soundly. Her Rykas crunched loudly on the gravel laneway, drowning out the sound of the nuthatches as she jogged over to the road. After ten minutes of full out running, she cut back to a medium paced walk for one minute, then another ten minutes at full speed. By the time she reached the cliff, her breathing was measured, her mantra keeping her pace. *No-body-loves-you-like-your-Mom.* Run for ten minutes, walk for one, then…she stopped at the sight of Dan sitting on her log, staring out at the water.

Her heart battered the walls of her chest making it hard to breathe. Her log. Her mom. Nobody loves you like your mom.

She ran straight at Dan and pushed. He pitched forward, his yell becoming more faint as he plummeted the hundred metres to the rocks below. She bent over from the waist and gulped air. After a few minutes, she sat on the log and stared across the ocean. The silence surrounded her. No birds chirping. No waves intruding. No thoughts invading her head. She eventually roused herself and headed back to the house.

• • •

Hannah sat on the edge of her mom's bed and held her hand. The funeral had been held that morning, and Carolyn had insisted on attending. It had drained all of her strength, even on a gurney with an ambulance transporting her.

"I can't believe it." Carolyn sobbed, gasping for air. Hannah grabbed the mask from the portable oxygen unit and placed it over her mom's nose and mouth until her breathing became less laboured. After a few minutes, Carolyn pulled the mask aside.

"I had so hoped you two would get to know each other again."

"Please, don't try to talk. Just rest, Mom." Hannah reached for the mask, but Carolyn grasped her hand.

"I have to talk. To tell you."

"It can wait, Mom. Just lie quiet now."

"No. I have to tell you, now. Hannah, don't hate me, baby. Please. I did it for you." Her fingers actually dug into Hannah's hand, and her voice sounded stronger. "You'd built up such an image of your father. Of what you thought he was like. Except…Dan and I. We…we'd been lovers. My husband found out. Dan left. He was in the military. They sent him away to Cyprus on a peacekeeping mission. And my husband left because I was pregnant."

What are you saying? It can't be true. My daddy wouldn't leave me! He died. He wouldn't leave.

Tears rolled down Carolyn's face as she reached out her right hand to touch Hannah's face. "Dan didn't know I was pregnant. When he came back, he found me, us, and then we got married. We'd hoped it would work out. He tried to be a father to you, but you never—" she coughed and took a few minutes to get her breath back "—never let him get close to you. We couldn't make a life together knowing you were so miserable. So he left, too."

No. My daddy was dead!

"We should have told you. But I didn't want you to know what we'd done. At least, not till you were older." She shook her head. "But we should have told you."

"Told me what?" *I don't want to know.*

"Hannah, baby, Dan was your father."

LINDA WIKEN *is owner of Prime Crime Books in Ottawa. She's written for radio, newspaper and magazines, and has published a number of non-fiction books. Her short stories have appeared in the anthologies* The Ladies' Killing Circle, Cottage Country Killers *and* Menopause is Murder, Murderous Intent *magazine, and her mystery novel is in search of a publishing date. She also writes articles for the Ottawa Police and adds her voice to their choir.*

FIT TO DIE

The detective looked at the splattered gore
On the walls, the windows, and the floor.
There wasn't much left of the late Mr. Horner
Except for his wife alone in a corner.
"I confess to the deed," Ms. Horner lamented.
"He did nothing but exercise. He was demented.
He was a fitness freak in a fitness fog.
All night he'd lift weights; all day he would jog.
He'd rather score on the court than score with me,
So I put nitroglycerine in his last herbal tea."

The detective looked round and then said with a wink,
"Guess that was a pretty dynamic Power Drink."

JOY HEWITT MANN

LAS FLACAS

VIOLETTE MALAN

O h, no," Carlotta's laugh tinkled musically, "I do not need to lose weight. I need a place to exercise. The toning of the muscles, the flexibility. These things are important for a woman, you know." The look on the younger woman's face quite amused Carlotta. It was well known that everyone in North America was obsessed by his or her weight. At home in Spain they couldn't understand it. Everyone here was much too skinny. Why, Rodrigo even refused to watch television, especially that lawyer's show that Carlotta found so funny. "It hurts me to look at those women," he would say to her in Spanish. "They are starving. *Las flacas*," he would call them. The skinnies.

"Oh, but you'll want to sign up for our Super Weight Loss Special," the young blonde woman insisted in the chirpy voice Carlotta was beginning to associate with North American working girls. She seemed to have far too many teeth. "Twenty pounds for twenty dollars. It starts tomorrow, so you're just in time." The young women held out a clipboard and offered Carlotta a pen.

"No, no," Carlotta said, her own smile becoming just a little forced. "Exercise is so much more important for a woman of my age." At first Carlotta couldn't understand why the girl raised her eyebrows in that unattractive fashion. But then she realized. Of course! The poor girl was only twenty—perhaps twenty-two at the most. She thought she was always going to be flat in the right places. She thought that older women were rounder because they were fat. Carlotta smiled more easily. Poor child. She would learn soon enough.

And there were so many wonderful things about not being twenty any longer, though that was also something they seemed to have wrong here in North America. She shook her head. Strange people. After all, with age come status and dignity. Maturity and understanding. Carlotta thought of herself at twenty-two, still in the university, living with her aunt Emilia in Madrid, which was exactly the same as living with her parents. Never enough hours in the day for study, for friends, for romance.

And Carlotta considered herself now, almost thirty years later, a partner in the first all-female law firm in Barcelona, her daughter Antonia studying to be an architect like her father, and Emilio—well, Carlotta didn't understand why her son wanted to breed dogs, but at least he made enough money to support himself, which was more than the sons of many of Carlotta's friends could say. And, according to some of those same friends, maturity could also bring you younger lovers, who appreciated women who knew a thing or two.

Not that Carlotta had time for that, herself. Her own husband, her Rodrigo, was still very attentive, very attentive indeed, Carlotta thought with a satisfied smile. When the needs of her firm had required her to move to the Canadian capital of Ottawa for several months, Rodrigo had packed his briefcase, his AutoCad programs, his computer disks and moved his architecture business to Canada with her. Rather than do without her for what he had described as "an eternity".

Ridiculous to suppose that she was fat!

Later that night, as she and Rodrigo were having dinner, she amused him by telling him of her day.

Rodrigo shook his head. "Watch out for that girl," he said. "She sounds like my mother." Carlotta knew exactly what he meant. Rodrigo's mother was one of those made stupid by the force of their own certainty. Who always thought they were right, and never for one moment considered the feelings of others. A woman to be avoided. Carlotta shook her head. She wondered if people had already begun to avoid the little blonde. Poor child.

That first week, several other lithe young persons in spandex suits that looked hideously uncomfortable mentioned the weight loss class to Carlotta. Clearly these people were obsessed. It was somewhat annoying at first—the obsessions of others so often are—but most of the staff at the gym learned to just smile and nod at her as Carlotta came in every day at one o'clock. Perhaps, after all, she thought, they were not to blame. Victimized by their unpleasant advertising and browbeaten by their fashion industry.

But that first young woman—Tiffany her name seemed to be—she was different. Still chirpy, her blonde ponytails always bouncing, her gold earrings swinging, even when she was standing still.

"Oooo, hurry, you're going to miss your 'weigh in'," she would say, very loudly and slowly, as Carlotta walked into the fitness centre in plenty of time for her Nautilus class. At first Carlotta would smile and remind the girl that she wasn't signed up for the weight loss class, that, her accent notwithstanding, she spoke and understood the English language perfectly well. There was no need to speak in those exaggerated tones.

But as time passed and the girl Tiffany did not change her behaviour, it became harder and harder to keep smiling.

One day Carlotta spoke to the manager, just casually, remarking that on occasion Tiffany appeared to be abrasively aggressive. The manager nodded and smiled very brightly, pointing out that it was the girl's job to be concerned for the clients. And so many people resisted the idea that they needed to lose weight. So many were in denial. Didn't Carlotta agree?

Well, no. Carlotta didn't agree. She thought the manager unnecessarily obtuse. She went back to her office that afternoon and asked several of her Canadian colleagues about other fitness studios, but, as she had feared, this centre was closest to her building. There was nowhere else she could go at lunch and return to her office in time for the afternoon meetings.

As well, Carlotta thought, there was the yoga instructor whom she liked so much. A woman of her own age, comfortable, strong and with what flexibility! Ah, if only Carlotta had the time to apply herself, she too could achieve that divine level!

• • •

In the weeks after Christmas things became, if anything, worse. The suggestion, it seemed to Carlotta, was that everyone had behaved like starving wolves gorging on a carcass for the entire month of December, and now required drastic work in order to be returned to their normal size. Or perhaps even thinner. To be ready for the February cruises, and to get what they called a "jump start" on the summer bathing-suit season. Well, Carlotta thought, to be fair, it is true that more food than usual seemed to be eaten at the holiday season. She had noticed this herself. Perhaps they had some reason to be concerned.

One day, Carlotta saw the little Tiffany standing to one side in the yoga class, watching. Later, as Carlotta was soaking in the whirlpool, the girl stopped beside the water.

"You know what would really help you get flexible?" the girl said brightly, her blonde ponytails swinging, her earrings glinting in the light. "I think you'd find that if you lost a few pounds, that would really help. Of course, if you feel you don't need to…" and the girl shrugged.

Carlotta's mouth fell open, but no response came out. She could only watch as Tiffany smiled and bounced away. The girl stopped to talk to another woman who was just stepping out of the shower. Carlotta could not hear the words that passed, but she saw the naked woman nod and hang her head like a chastized child.

Carlotta told herself she was not at all disturbed by this. But from that evening onward, she no longer entertained Rodrigo with funny stories about the fitness centre.

• • •

A few weeks later, Carlotta overheard two women in her office talking about having to lose weight, "just a few pounds", and "look at how so-and-so has let herself go", and "just as she was doing so well". And the one who said she just needed to lose five more pounds—a senior administrator, a smart woman— she was actually a stick, an absolute stick. But then, most of the women looked fine to Carlotta. Why would they talk about themselves that way?

Later, as she walked to her car, Carlotta watched her own reflection in the glass front of her building. She examined her profile critically.

Could she really be certain that *she* wasn't too fat?

That night, when Carlotta was eating dinner with her husband, she found she had no appetite. When they were getting ready for bed she asked him. "Dear one," she said, "do you think I need to lose weight?"

"Let me look at you," he said from where he sat on the edge of the bed. She stood very still. He frowned. That meant he was thinking. Her husband was a very serious man, who would not dream of answering such a question with anything but the truth. The idea of what he might say to her made her very nervous. "Can you turn around, my dear?" She lifted her arms slightly and turned slowly, counter clockwise for luck. When she had finished turning and faced her husband once more, she was relieved to see him smiling.

But why didn't she feel happier?

The next day, Carlotta decided she was letting her imagination get the better of her. Of course she was fine. Nothing had changed. Everything was still the same as it had been four months ago when she first came to Canada. She must be working too hard to let these ideas take hold of her. Perhaps she and Rodrigo could get away for the weekend.

In celebration of her restored sanity, Carlotta decided to wear her favourite suit to the office. It was the one she had worn last year to the Business Woman's Conference in Seville. The one she had been wearing when she had shaken the hand of Her Majesty, Queen Sofia of Spain.

Carlotta chose her blouse carefully. Slipped into the skirt and pulled up the zipper. Shrugged into the jacket and did up the button. Then she undid the button again. She looked at herself in the mirror on the door of the old-fashioned wardrobe in her bedroom. Somehow, she remembered looking better in this suit. She turned sideways. She examined her bosoms and her hips. Surely, she thought, it is not possible that I have *gained* weight? She remembered that there was a photograph of her in this suit on her husband's desk. Quickly she rushed into his study and scrutinized the portrait-sized photograph. Her eyes narrowed.

Was it her imagination? Was there, even in this photo, a little tightness across the hips? A few horizontal wrinkles? Carlotta put her hand to her mouth and gnawed on the side of her finger, ruining her manicure.

Could it be true? Could she be fat? Could Rodrigo be wrong?

Carlotta clenched her teeth. Then she changed her suit.

• • •

Carlotta found that if she concentrated very hard, she could actually go whole hours and not think about her weight— while she was at work, or asleep. But every time she passed the scale at the fitness centre, with its evil red blinking numbers, it was all she could do not to step on. One day, when she was coming from her Nautilus class and feeling particularly forceful, Carlotta managed to walk right past it without looking. She went into the locker room, removed her sensible black leotard and stepped into the shower. When she came out, wrapped carefully in her silk shower robe, she found one of the other women in her yoga class weeping into her monogrammed towel.

"Oh, Carlotta," Hilda sobbed, "I've been working so hard. I've lost twenty-five pounds you know, the second twenty-five pounds, which let me tell you is a lot harder than the first twenty-five, and I was feeling so proud of myself and so pleased with my new look and then...and then she said...she said, oh, it's too horrible."

"Do not tell me," Carlotta put her arm around the woman. "It was the little one, the Tiffany." Carlotta really didn't need the other woman's nod. She'd known who it would be. She let Hilda cry on her shoulder. This cannot go on, Carlotta thought. But what can be done?

Carlotta watched as Hilda finally dressed and went home, dragging her feet and clearly unhappy with the new outfit that she had shown off so proudly only that morning. Carlotta rose stiffly to her feet, wondering if she had the strength to return to the office. She felt something at her back. She turned, knowing that…yes, it was the red, blinking eye of the electronic scale. Carlotta looked swiftly around. She was alone. Surely there could be no harm…she stepped onto the scale. She was just waiting for the electronic numbers to stop flashing and announce her weight when she heard a noise behind her.

It was the little blonde Tiffany. Her earrings swinging. Her teeth longer than natural. Her grin a little too triumphant as she continued into the pool room.

In that moment Carlotta realized what was happening, and her heart turned cold within her. Of course she was not fat. She was never fat in her life. And Hilda, and the lady who had hung her head after stepping out of the shower, and who knew how many others, were not fat. They were normal healthy women. This was all a virus spread by *las flacas*, the skinnies. Brainwashed by the silly advertising, the foolish fashion designers and the people who made money from the diets and the exercises and the many, many books that all told you over and over that you were unhappy, that you were not living up to your full potential and that beyond all else you were fat, fat, fat. A conspiracy to make all women feel sick about themselves. To make women spend so much time worrying about how they looked that they had no time to think.

And this girl. This girl in particular was one of the conspirators, the plotters. Her little remarks, her little looks, all calculated, all poisonous. Look at what she had almost done to Carlotta herself. This girl is killing us, Carlotta thought. She is killing our happiness, our contentment. Our selves.

She has to be dealt with.

Carlotta took her bathing suit out of her dressing case. She would relax in the whirlpool for a while. It would soothe her nerves and help her think. She followed the girl into the pool room.

The next day Carlotta came in at her usual time to find the fitness studio in chaos. She carefully expressed her astonishment when she learned that the little Tiffany had been found drowned in the whirlpool. She had evidently dropped one of her gold earrings as she had entered the water—one could see where it lay gleaming at the bottom of the pool—and when she had reached for it, the vigorous movement of the whirlpool had wrapped her blonde ponytail around the chrome ladder, where it was fastened to the wall. Accidental death, the policeman said. A petition was being circulated to replace the whirlpool.

"Poor child," Carlotta said as she signed in.

VIOLETTE MALAN *writes from Elgin, Ontario. Her published fiction crosses several genres, including mystery, romance, fantasy and erotica. Violette won the inaugural short story contest at the Bloody Words Crime Writer's Conference, and most recently she has sold a story to* Over My Dead Body *for their Canadian issue.*

SNAP JUDGEMENT

SUE PIKE

"Here. Have a look at this." The bald guy sitting next to me leaned across and waved a photograph in front of my nose.

It was a small snapshot, an old one judging from the wide border and all the folds and creases. The woman looking up at the camera had great bone structure, but she seemed to be hiding behind too much hair and black eyeliner. Mr. Jones, who leads our high school photography club, was teaching us all about bone structure.

I nodded and looked away, but the creep leaned closer and tapped the snapshot with a stubby finger.

"My wife." Tap. Tap. "She's dead."

He was way into my personal space. I shifted sideways in my chair as far as I could and looked around at the rest of the group, hoping someone more my own age might have come in while I wasn't looking. But the others seemed pretty old, and they were either crying or staring straight ahead like zombies.

Now he was leaning forward, peering at the stud in my nose.

"How d'ya blow your nose with that thing in there?"

I felt like asking how he tied his shoes with the big gut hanging over his belt, but I just shrugged and looked away.

"Hey! I'm talking to you." He reached over and clamped a

hand on my knee. Oh, please!

I jerked my knee away and scraped my chair a couple of inches to the other side.

The noise made the group leader look over. She cleared her throat. "Welcome everyone. Let's start by introducing ourselves." She smiled at each of the five of us in turn. "My name is Helen. I'm Program Coordinator here at Coping with Grief, and I'll be your facilitator this evening." She sat down and her voice went quiet. "My husband and daughter were killed eight years ago at a railway level crossing, so I've experienced something of what you're all going through."

"I seriously doubt that," the guy beside me said.

She looked a little surprised. "Mr. Simpson. Would you like to start?"

"Name's Russ Simpson. Career army. Retired." He laid the snapshot on the arm of his chair and stretched back, his fingers laced behind his neck. His shirt was one of those loud Hawaiian jobs with the first four buttons undone. I could see gold chains tangled up in a bird's nest of gray chest hair.

"Moved here from Calgary a month ago." He cracked some knuckles. "My wife, Debbie, was killed a while back."

Helen waited to be sure he was finished and then turned to me.

"I'm Jill," I said. "My mom died in March. Breast cancer."

That was all I felt like saying. My throat and chest had started to ache, and I could feel tears making rat tracks down my cheeks. I sure didn't want to be bawling in front of strangers.

"All of us are bound to cry at one time or another during these sessions. And that's okay. In fact it's more than O.K." Helen pushed the box of tissues on the coffee table closer to me, but I kept my eyes on the floor, and after a bit she turned to the woman on my other side.

"My name's Mary Anne."

I hadn't had a chance really to look at Mary Anne before because she'd been hunched over in her chair since I arrived. Now I could see she wasn't all that old, probably not more than thirty. She was pretty too, even with puffy eyes.

"My little girl died of leukemia. She—"

"Hey. Life's a bugger." Russ gave a low whistle.

"Go on." Helen said to Mary Anne, but she'd clamped her mouth shut and was staring down at the wet lump of tissues in her hand.

Helen waited then looked across the room at an old couple sitting close together and apart from the rest of us. The man had a tight grip on the woman's arm. "Our daughter and her husband died in a car accident last winter. They were on their way home from a ski trip. Left three kids—"

"Hoo boy. Gotta take it easy on those winter roads. Wonder there aren't more accidents. Eh?"

The old man straightened up and glared at Russ. "The wife and I are doing the best we can."

Helen spoke up. "Your names…?"

"I'm Bert. This is Doreen." He slumped back.

"I want to say something." Russ dropped his hands to his knees and shifted forward in his chair. "The wife here," he tapped the photo again, "she was a beautiful woman. Great cook and housekeeper, too. I get real mad when I think how some runner could just up and kill her and get away with it. I could kill…"

Helen frowned. "It's quite normal to feel anger—"

"Just walking home from the mall one day, minding her own business and this woman jogger runs past her and pushes her off the sidewalk and into traffic. Wham!" He slammed his right fist into his left palm.

"That's terrible—"

"Police never found the bitch who did it." He was breathing hard. "Sometimes I get this red, this blood-red light in front of my eyes. Can't see past it. Tried anger management, but they told me to come to this group."

Helen turned to Bert and Doreen. "Were you going to say more about how you're feeling?"

"Well, I get a little angry at Trish sometimes." Doreen's mouth was quivering. "I know it's not fair to her. She didn't choose to die." She looked at Bert. "But we already raised our family. We didn't expect to have to raise—"

"Kids. Nothing but trouble, you ask me." Russ seemed calmer now and was slapping his heels against the chair legs.

"The kids are okay. It's just they're teenagers, and teenagers are different today. More independent." Bert glanced over at me and I could see him sizing up the purple streak in my hair and my black leather jacket. I wondered if he might say something else, but he just shrugged.

"A certain amount of anger is—"

"You bet I'm angry. Police didn't even try to find Debbie's killer." Russ sat back and drummed on the photo with his fingers. "But I'll get the bitch. Believe you me."

"I don't think—"

"I can see her right here." He tapped his forehead with his finger. "And I got a pretty good idea where to find her."

He pulled cigarettes out of his pocket and held the pack out to me. I shook my head, and he leaned closer.

"She better watch her step, eh?" And then, I swear to God, he giggled.

Helen stood up. "I think we could take a short break now. Top up your coffee or juice. The bathrooms are just down the hall, and you can smoke outside on the front steps. See you back here at 8:15."

Russ must have left during break, because when I got back from trying to scrub the mascara off my cheeks, the discussion was starting again, and his seat was empty. We talked about a lot of things in the second half. We talked about the shock of not having the person around any more, and I said that even though my mom was sick for so long, I felt real empty when she was finally gone. And I told them how worried I was about my dad, who just played computer games all evening. Without Russ there to hog all the conversation, everybody else had a chance to talk, and I recognized a lot of my own feelings in what they were saying.

Nine-thirty came before I knew it. Helen did a final check on how we were doing so far, then said she hoped we'd all be back next week. I waited while the others got their stuff together and Helen was gathering up coffee cups and juice bottles.

"I know you've already spoken to my dad, but do you think you could try talking to him again about coming next week? He's driving me nuts. He never talks about his feelings, just tries to be cheerful all the time. I asked him to come tonight, but I think it would be better coming from someone his own age."

She laughed at that, and I realized I'd jumped to conclusions. It was hard to tell, but I thought she might be in her early forties. She had a nice smile, and I decided she might be just the one to get my dad away from solitaire.

"It would be better if you could make him see how important it is to you."

We agreed we'd both try to talk to him. As I was leaving the room, I noticed the snapshot of Debbie Simpson sitting on the arm of Russ's chair. I picked it up to have another look at it.

Helen frowned. "I hope Russ didn't upset you, Jill."

I shook my head and studied the snapshot. I sure liked the way the photographer had angled the light on her cheekbones.

Helen held out her hand. "Here. I'll give it to him next week"

"Could I borrow it? It's got good composition. I'd like to show it to Mr. Jones in my photography club."

Helen looked a little unsure, but then her briefcase started ringing, so I stuffed the photo in my backpack and left her rummaging around for her phone.

●　　●　　●

I showed the photo to Dad the next morning, pointing out the lighting and how the camera had captured her bone structure. I could tell he wasn't really listening, and that didn't surprise me. He'd been pretty spacey ever since Mom died.

What did surprise me was when he looked over and said, "How did you get a picture of her?"

"What do you mean? Have you seen her before?"

"I think so. I don't know her name, but she's often at the gym, and she takes part in most of the charity runs."

I guess my mouth was hanging open, because he tapped it shut with his finger and laughed, "What's this about, Jill?"

I told him about Russ Simpson and his dead wife.

He held the photo up to the light by the window and shook his head. "She looks older now, but I'm pretty sure it's her."

"But this woman is dead." My head was spinning.

He was looking at his watch. "I'm going to be late for work." He picked up his briefcase and keys and opened the door. "I've registered for the 10K race on Saturday. Why not come along and see if she's there."

● ● ●

I wasn't sure I'd be able to pick out the woman in the photo from a whole field of runners, and I realized Dad would see even less from inside the pack, so I called Helen to see if she'd go with me. I was pretty sure she'd been seriously spooked by Russ and would be curious to see the woman Dad thought resembled the one in the snapshot.

I stuffed my camera and tripod and some high-speed film into my backpack ready for Helen to pick me up at eight-thirty the next morning. Barriers were already up along the Parkway, so we left the car near the university and walked back through campus. We found the registration tent and grabbed a printout of runners' names and registration numbers. Then we pushed our way through the crowd to the starting line. There were already several hundred spectators on the sidelines and twice that number dressed in shorts and stringy tops with numbers pinned to them, stretching and jogging in place, waiting for the starter's pistol.

I looked for Dad and pointed him out to Helen. Then I scanned the front-seeded women. I looked at the photo again and stopped short on Number 36. She had short gray hair and her face was tanned and lined, but other than that, she was a ringer for the woman in the snapshot. I nudged Helen and she nodded, then ran her finger down the list and said: "Number 36. Amber Thompson."

I was studying the woman's profile when I heard Helen gasp.

"Look!" She was pointing at a man climbing up a grassy slope near the bicycle path that runs alongside the Parkway. He was dressed in a bright yellow rain suit, rubber boots and work gloves and he was holding a glass mason jar out in front of him.

It was Russ Simpson. He lifted his head, and I saw the weirdest look on his face. I turned to see what he was staring at and sure enough, there was Amber Thompson, right in the cross hairs.

I dropped my backpack to the ground, scooped the tripod out of it and took off running as fast as I could, trying to cover the distance between Russ and me before he got to the top of the hill. The grass was still slick with dew, and I almost slipped, but I got to him just before he made it to the road. I came up on his right side, crouched down and thrust the tripod in front of his ankle. It snared the plastic pant leg, and he went down with the whooshing sound of air going out of a tire.

He twisted around and kicked out furiously, his boot catching me square on the nose. The bottle fell from his hand and bounced, splashing its contents over him and the grass. I got a couple of drops on my hand and they burned like mad, but that was nothing to what the stuff seemed to be doing to him.

I could hear him screaming as the fluid burned into his scalp and face. The grass around him sizzled and steamed, and I rolled away down the hill. Finally, I came to rest on my back, and by the time I got my bearings, Dad was leaning over me. He looked pretty worried, so I reached up and touched my nose with my hand. It came away covered with blood.

"You've lost your nose stud," Dad said, handing me a wad of tissues.

"No problem. It's time I lost it, anyway." I struggled to my feet and looked over to see the race officials trying to coax Russ into the First Aid Tent. He was still shrieking and flopping around on the grass. The exposed skin on his head and neck was turning a sickening red.

Helen came up beside me carrying a big plastic cup of water. I plunged my sore hand into it. It sure felt good. "So, I guess you two have met, eh?"

Dad shook Helen's hand. "Jill tells me I'll be coming to your grief session next week."

I grinned at Helen and she gave me a thumbs up.

I turned and looked up the hill then, to where Amber Thompson was standing stock still, staring at Russ. She caught my eye and walked stiffly over to where we were standing. I hoped she wasn't going to pass out.

"I want to thank you," she said, and her voice sounded wobbly and weak. "That acid was intended for me."

"I figured." I said. "Did you know he came to our bereavement group and he was carrying a picture of you?"

"Bereavement group?" She closed her eyes and sighed. "So he's still grieving for Debbie Simpson."

"Did you even know he was in town?"

"No. I had no idea he'd managed to track me down. It's been years since I got away, changed my name, my appearance, everything. I thought I was safe."

"I've been wondering," I said, "if you're the woman he told us about, the one he says killed Debbie Simpson."

She looked puzzled. "Is that what he said?" Then she nodded without waiting for my answer. "That would make some kind of sense, I guess."

"It would?"

"Absolutely. I did kill Debbie Simpson, and she deserved to die. She was a pathetic, frightened little girl, totally controlled by her abusive husband."

"I see," I lied.

There was a long pause. Then she held her hand out to me.

"I think I'd better introduce myself," Amber Thompson said. "I am Debbie Simpson."

SUE PIKE *doesn't own a camera but she greatly admires anyone able to capture mood and meaning in a single snapshot. She limits her hobbies to writing and has had stories in all of The Ladies' Killing Circle anthologies. "Widow's Weeds" from* Cottage Country Killers *won the Arthur Ellis Award for best short mystery story of 1997.*

RETURNING THE FAVOUR

JOAN BOSWELL

F inished with the day's training and back in my dorm, I flipped through my mail. Pizza Pizza—a two-for-one deal. VISA—a pitch for my business. A hand-addressed envelope— probably a machine-simulated charitable appeal.

I removed a single sheet of paper.

"Dear Anna. Because of what I read in an article about you and the Olympic rowing team, I realize I'm your mother. I left you in St. Michael's church when you were three months old. Just like the article said, your birthday is February 15 and you're 26. I saw in the picture that you still have the birth mark on your left shoulder."

Much larger printing and capital letters made the next sentence jump from the page. *"IF I SPILL THE BEANS, YOU WON'T GO.*

"You're not a citizen. I brought you to Canada from Holland. Your father emigrated first but didn't meet us. I couldn't look after you. I did you a BIG FAVOUR by giving you up and letting you have a good life. It's time to return the FAVOUR. Pay me $10,000 and I won't tell your secret. I'm in Cabin Ten at the Bide-A-While motel. If I don't hear from you by FRIDAY, I'll phone the Victoria paper."

I reread the letter. The shocking message remained the

same. My birth mother wanted to blackmail me. What kind of woman was she to even contemplate doing this? But she had one thing right. She had done me a favour—a huge favour. No one could have been luckier with her adoptive parents than I'd been.

If what she said was true, what should I do? Borrow $10,000 and pay her? But was she right? Would the circumstances of my birth bar me from the Olympics? The Children's Aid Society would know. I dialed and asked for the director.

"Ms. French is out of the office for the day. She'll be in tomorrow, but, if it's urgent, perhaps I can help you?"

Twenty-four hours to wait for the verdict. Should I warn Carol, my coach? Of course not. Why upset her about something that might not happen? I threw the envelope in the waste basket and shoved the letter in my desk drawer.

But I couldn't get it out of my mind. After a nearly sleepless night, I staggered out of bed. Exhausted, I debated whether to drive or walk to the lake for the first of our three daily rowing practices. I opted for the twenty-minute walk, hoping the exercise would untie the knot in my stomach. The grey clouds that blanketed the sky, promising rain, echoed my mood.

As we gathered on the dock, my team mates handed folded sheets of paper to Carol. Damn, I'd forgotten this morning was the deadline for returning one of the many forms our bureaucratic country required.

"Carol, I left it on my desk. Is it too late to run over at lunch?"

"It is. One of the guys from the office is coming to get them…" she checked her watch "in half an hour. They have to go out in this morning's mail."

"Dad could go," Bobbie Johnson said.

Most mornings, multimillionaire Marshall Johnson, a

rower on Canada's 1968 Olympic team, parked his Porsche at the far end of the lake and watched our practice.

Carol shook her head. "The girl at the desk in the residence wouldn't let him go up."

"My car's here," Bobbie said.

It always was. Her car, a dark-blue Porsche that matched her father's, seemed to be her security blanket, her reassurance that her daddy loved her enough to buy the very best. Poor Bobbie lived in fear she'd lose her place on the team and her father's approval. Marshall Johnson supported Olympic rowing financially. I suspected he'd withdraw his money if Bobbie lost her spot. This had to be the reason why Carol kept her when Marnie, the first alternative, was a better rower.

Bobbie curried Carol's favour in every possible way. "It won't take me a minute. I'll be back by the time everyone's warmed up."

Carol nodded.

I could offer to go with her, but why spoil her chance for brownie points? I thanked Bobbie and tossed her my room key.

We'd just finished our stretching exercises when, true to her word, Bobbie's Porsche peeled around the lake and screeched to a halt beside the dock. She delivered the paper to Carol and joined us as we lowered ourselves into our shell.

In the boat I forgot everything but the joy of moving through the mirror-calm lake. The oars dipped, dragged, lifted, flashed forward, turned and sliced. The creak of our seats as they slid back and forth, the rush of the bow as it cut through the water—every motion and sound was as familiar and comforting as my own heartbeat.

We followed the row with a two-hour run. Light rain coated the path with a film of moisture which made each footfall treacherous. Rain drizzling on our skin chilled us as we clocked the miles. Although I tried to empty my mind, to focus on breathing, to visualize molecules of fresh air entering my nostrils and filling my lungs—I failed. Instead, I fixated either on the possibility of not being on the Olympic team, or on my birth mother—her name, her appearance, her life.

Later, back in my room, mouth dry and heart clattering, I dialed the Children's Aid. After the opening pleasantries, I posed my question.

"Of course, you're a Canadian. Once your adoption became official, the province issued you a new birth certificate. The circumstances of your birth have no bearing on your citizenship."

Relief. I could forget the letter.

But could I? Could I ignore the presence of my birth mother waiting for me at the Bide-a-While cabins? I flopped on my bed and hauled the duvet over my head, but, no matter how I twisted and turned, I couldn't get comfortable. Finally, I faced two facts: I wasn't going to sleep until I set up a meeting, and I needed sleep before I faced her. I thumbed through the telephone book and, before I could change my mind, dialed the Bide-a-While cabins.

"Cabin Ten," I said.

"The cabins don't have no phones. You wanna leave a message?"

"Please tell her Anna called and will drop in later."

Exhaustion washed over me.

•   •   •

Four a.m. Should I go now, before morning training? It wasn't exactly a normal time to visit, but this wasn't a normal social call. Sure, I'd wake her, but, in case she turned nasty when I told her there wouldn't be any money, I'd have the advantage of being wide awake. Just to be on the safe side, in case there was trouble, I tucked my cell phone in the pocket of my track pants.

As I approached the cabins, the fluorescent Bide-a-While sign flickered a lurid welcome. At the last moment, my nerve failed. I drove by, slowed, made a U-turn and parked beside the highway, where I could watch the motel and argue with myself. This was crazy. Who but a burglar appeared at five in the morning? But, if I didn't do this now, I'd never have another chance.

I peered at the lopsided cabins sloping away from the road. Except for the fourth one, they were dark. While I surveyed the run-down collection of buildings, a car pulled out of the drive and sped past me. Only the first twittering of waking birds and the wailing of a baby broke the silence.

Crazy or not, I had to see her.

Cabin Ten carried its sixty or seventy years badly. The tiny front porch, trimmed with peeling dark green paint, listed slightly to the right. When I stepped inside the porch, it smelled of mildew and garbage. I opened the outer door with the torn screen and knocked gently. Nothing. I banged harder. Still nothing. She must be an exceptionally heavy sleeper. On impulse, I turned the knob and pushed. The door opened.

Inside, my eyes just had time to adjust to the light filtering through the flimsy curtains and to fix on the outline of a substantial woman lying on her back in bed before my nose told me something was wrong—very, very wrong. The place reeked of exhaust.

I rushed to the bed and grabbed the woman's shoulders.

"Wake up. Wake up." I shook her and felt her unresponsiveness.

Thanking God for the strength I'd gained during the months of training, I flipped the bedspread on the floor and hauled her heavy body off the bed. Quickly knotting the ends, I grabbed hold and dragged her outside.

She looked dead, but I didn't check for vitals. Instead I made sure her throat was clear and began CPR.

She was breathing.

I checked her pulse. Thin, irregular, but there. I reached for my cell phone and punched 911.

"It's Anna Marks. I'm calling because I've just found a woman nearly dead from carbon monoxide poisoning in Cabin Ten of the Bide-a-While motel on Highway 5."

God. This was awful. Where had the carbon monoxide come from?

I stared down at her. Blonde hair framed a broad face. My own heavy bone structure.

The ambulance, the firemen and the police arrived. Without seeming to rush, the paramedics clamped an oxygen mask on her face and bundled her into the ambulance, which then shrieked its way toward the hospital. An officer, Constable Stern, suggested I wait in his cruiser. When he joined me, I asked: "Will she live? Were the fumes from a space heater?"

"Hard to say. Why did you think it was a space heater?"

"Because there wasn't a car outside the cabin, and I've read that malfunctioning space heaters kill people. What was her name?"

He eyed me for what seemed like ten minutes before he said: "You don't know her name, yet you *dropped in* to see her at what time—five in the morning? Not the usual hour to visit a person you don't know."

Nothing for it, the story had to be told. "It's very weird, but here's what happened."

After I'd finished, he said, "Who else knew of this blackmail threat?"

"No one. The letter arrived yesterday and, except for talking to the director of the Children's Aid, I haven't told anyone." I couldn't wait any longer. "What is her name?"

"Her name? You really didn't know?"

"No. She didn't sign the letter."

"Wilhemina Groenveldt."

Wilhemina—like the Dutch royal family. Had my, my what, my biological grandmother named her after the queen, or was it a family name? And I was Julianna, the mother of Beatrix, today's Queen. Tears clogged my throat.

"Are you okay?"

I swallowed. "No. But, if you're finished, I should get back to training camp."

"We'll have more questions, but that's it for now.

I'd missed the first rowing session. Back at the university, I sprinted from the parking lot to the gym, grabbed what I needed and joined the pack of runners stretching and jogging-on-the-spot while they waited for the laggards. On the two-hour run, my mind returned again and again to Wilhemina Groenveldt's face. What if there hadn't been a space heater? If there hadn't, that meant that someone... I shook my head. Denial. It couldn't be, but what if it was? What if someone had tried to kill her?

The letter. Could it have been because of the threat to keep me out of the Olympics? But no one knew about the letter. My pace slowed. *I* hadn't told anyone except the director, but I'd given my keys to Bobbie. What if she'd snooped through my desk and found it? A surge of intense anger propelled me past other runners. As we traversed the edge of a steep ravine, I caught up with Bobbie.

"Why did you read my letter?"

"What letter?"

"You know damn well what letter." I grabbed her arm and yanked her from the flow of runners. "Tell me."

"Okay, okay, don't have a fit. I was looking for an envelope. And the letter was sitting right there, so I read it."

Sitting right there, my eye. "Who else did you tell?"

Her gaze slid away from mine. "No one."

My fingers indented the flesh of her upper arm. "Who did you tell?"

Still not looking at me, she said, "I was really worried because of Daddy and what he'd say if we didn't go, or went without you—because you're the stroke, and it's too late for someone else to take your place, and I knew we needed you to win a medal." She inhaled and rushed on. "I was afraid you'd go all moral and resign. And even if you wanted to pay, I didn't think you had the money." She smiled. "Daddy *always* knows what to do, so I told him."

I blocked her attempt to move away. "Who else did you tell?"

"Carol."

"And why did you think *you* had to tell Carol?"

She looked at me as if I'd asked a ridiculous question. "Carol needed to know as soon as possible. If we had to persuade you, she'd want time to prepare her arguments."

I released her arm.

"What are you going to do?"

"You'll have to wait and see, won't you?" I launched myself up the path.

After the run and before I showered, I called the hospital, asked for Wilhemina Groenveldt's room and was told she was in intensive care, and no information was being released. At least she was still alive.

In the shower, as the warm water sluiced over me, I knew I

didn't want to join my team for lunch. But I had to eat. When you work as hard as we do, you load up on the calories. In the cafeteria, I picked up three wrapped sandwiches, two bottles of orange juice and a chocolate doughnut and took the bag back to the residence, where I dumped it on the desk and switched on the radio.

"The police, who are investigating an incident at the Bide-a-While cabins on Highway 5, are requesting that anyone in the vicinity between midnight and five this morning contact them immediately."

An *incident*. What did that mean? Someone else had been involved, and that would make it…*attempted murder*! But had the attempt been connected to the letter? If it was, who could have done it? Not Marshall. He would have consulted a battery of high-priced lawyers and found the information the Children's Aid had given me. Not Carol. She wanted the eights to win, but it wouldn't change her life if they didn't. Not Bobbie. Her father dominated her life—she'd do anything to please him—but I doubted if "anything" included murder. There had to be some other reason: if Wilhemina had threatened me, she'd probably done much worse things to other people.

During our second rowing session I dipped, pulled, lifted, turned the oars and dipped again as I reviewed the facts.

Out of the boat I detoured to the public phone in the hall of the gym and made two calls—the first to Constable Stern, the second to the hospital.

Inside the gym, we headed for various pieces of exercise equipment. I picked an elliptical trainer which faced Carol's office. I was tired and wanted to click on "a walk in the park", but if Carol happened by while the electronic printer flashed that info, I'd be in trouble. Reluctantly, I entered "a mountain hike", set the level of difficulty at "max" and the time at sixty minutes. The machine and I began working our way up an imaginary mountain.

Fifteen minutes later, a plump, middle-aged man in a tan suit marched through the gym to the office.

Less than five minutes later Marshall Johnson followed the same course.

The machine said I still had thirty-seven minutes to go when Carol emerged, looked at her sweating crew and motioned for me and Bobbie to join her. The mountain would have to wait.

The man in the tan suit, who introduced himself as Detective Roston, sat behind Carol's desk and faced me as I entered. Carol perched to his right and Bobbie sat in front of him. Marshall stood beside Bobbie's chair. I took the empty seat beside Carol.

"Miss Marks, I've told these people that early this morning at the Bide-A-While cabins someone tried to asphyxiate Wilhemina Groenveldt." Detective Roston paused and allowed his gaze to sweep the room. "Someone wanted her dead. We believe it was because of a letter she wrote to you which these three knew about."

"I certainly can't believe anyone would think I was involved in this sordid affair," Marshall said as he straightened, puffed out his chest and appeared to expand. "As I've already said, I knew nothing about this woman, and I see no reason why I should be here." Fully inflated, he continued, "I'm sure Spike Vinca..." He paused to make sure the detective got his message: that he knew the police chief, James Vinca, well enough to use his nickname. "I'm sure Spike would like to hear about police harassment."

"I'm sure he wouldn't, sir," Roston said. "If you object,

we'll get a warrant and have you come downtown."

"Well, for the moment that won't be necessary." Marshall gave a tight-lipped smile. "I certainly don't want to impede police work."

"The three of you also should know that Anna Marks investigated the threat and knew it was without foundation. Because she received a new legal identity the moment her adoption became final, her actual birth place had no bearing on her status as a Canadian."

Bobbie's eyes widened. Her father frowned and jingled coins in his pocket. Carol, who must have been holding her breath, released it in a long sigh.

Roston's lips turned down, and he appeared to have smelled something nasty. "Now, isn't that a surprise for the three of you?"

No one spoke.

"And I have another little surprise. Last night a teething baby woke the young woman staying in Cabin Four. When she looked out the window, she saw a car with the engine running parked near Cabin Ten. And," he avoided looking at me, "an early morning visitor to Wilhemina Groenveldt's cabin had the presence of mind to drag her outside and apply artificial respiration. This same woman informed us that when she arrived at the scene she witnessed a car speeding away."

Carol slid down on her chair. Marshall's frown deepened to a scowl. Bobbie's eyebrows lifted, and her eyes shifted repeatedly from me to Carol to the detective and back again.

"What do you drive and were you at the motel last night?" Roston asked Carol.

She didn't answer immediately. Instead, she crossed her arms on her chest and slumped down. "A silver Windstar van and no, I wasn't there."

Roston's gaze circled the room. I had a feeling he was enjoying this interrogation. He focused on me. "What make of car do you drive, and were you at the cabins last night?"

"An old blue Honda Civic. I was there at five a.m."

Bobbie burst into tears.

"Get a grip," Marshall ordered.

Bobbie fished in her pocket for a tissue and blew her nose.

"And you sir, what do you drive and were you at the Bide-a-While cabins last night?"

"I drive several vehicles: a black Mercedes SUV, a Lincoln and a Porsche. At the moment I'm driving the Lincoln. The Porsche is in for servicing. Furthermore, I don't even know where the Bide-a-While cabins are. And, not that it's any of your business, but I spent the evening at a fundraiser for the Alliance Party. Of course, I wasn't there." He levelled his gaze at the detective. "Perhaps it's time for me to call my lawyers."

Detective Roston's lips curled upward. No one would have described the expression as a smile. "If you wish, sir." He pushed the phone across the desk.

Marshall made an abortive move to reach for it and pulled back. "Later," he murmured.

Roston looked at Bobbie. "And you?"

The white knuckles of her clenched hands betrayed her anxiety. "A Porsche." She stared at her hands and mumbled, "I wasn't there."

"I think you were." Roston's voice dropped, and he sounded almost tender. "I'd like your car keys and permission to search your trunk. I think I'll find a hose—a hose you used to pump carbon monoxide into Cabin Ten with the intention of killing Wilhemina Groenveldt."

Marshall's head lifted and his eyes narrowed. "This is outrageous. It's harassment."

"I did it for you, Daddy." Bobbie said and began to cry again.

As the significance of Bobbie's words registered, Marshall's self-confidence collapsed. He reached over and gripped his daughter's shoulder hard enough to make her wince. "You little fool," he hissed.

Detective Roston charged Bobbie with attempted murder. Her back hunched and her face ashen, she made one last try, "I really did do it for you, Daddy," she said as Roston led her away.

Marshall stomped after them muttering about lawyers. Carol came over, put her arm around my shoulder and hugged me before she left. When the office was empty, I moved behind the desk and phoned the hospital.

An officious voice admitted that Wilhemina Groenveldt's prognosis had improved. The letter flashed into my mind. "I did you a FAVOUR... It's time to return the FAVOUR." Whatever the future held for Wilhemina Groenveldt and me, we would begin as equals. I had returned the favour—any debt I might have owed her had been paid.

JOAN BOSWELL *fantasizes about rowing on Canada's Olympic team while writing, painting and attempting to outwit her flat coated retriever. Her short stories have been published in several periodicals and five anthologies. In June 2000 she won the $10,000* Toronto Star *Short Story Contest.*

A BRISK SITDOWN

Here lies Joe "Couch-Potato" Howard,
A push-up, sit-up, jogging coward
Who never went to the local gym
That kept wife Janis so nice and slim.

Janis caught Joe with a neighbour's wife
And Joe—in panic—exorcised his life.
Joe jumped through the window one second before
He remembered they lived on the sixteenth floor.

JOY HEWITT MANN

A MATTER OF THE HEART

DAY'S LEE

"Our reputation is ruined!" Mrs. Tan's heavy body sank into the worn sofa cushions. She clutched wet tissues in one hand and a package of fresh ones in the other. Granny listened sympathetically. Dressed in a rose print blouse and navy pants, her petite body was almost lost in the armchair's pink and blue floral pattern. Her face, still clear and smooth at the age of sixty-six, registered shock. But Jenny Leung knew she was not surprised to hear the Widow Woo was involved.

"Mr. Lau, the owner of the Phoenix Noodle Company, has accused my husband of fraud!" sobbed Mrs. Tan. "He claims we owe him two hundred dollars, but we have not ordered anything from him for over a month."

"Not a lot of money," Granny murmured, "but enough to cast suspicion."

"And it was only a month ago, during a mah jong game at the community business social, when my good husband discovered the Widow Woo had extra tiles hidden in her pocket." Mrs. Tan's voice wavered.

"Isn't Mrs. Woo the bookkeeper for the Phoenix Noodle Company?" Jenny asked.

Granny nodded.

Mrs. Tan wailed louder.

Jenny poured tea and listened to Mrs. Tan's hysterical intonations as she told her tale in Cantonese. Jenny was glad she had decided to come that Saturday morning for her grandmother's lesson on how to make pork buns. Mrs. Tan's stories of the goings-on in Chinatown were better than fiction. The aroma of freshly baked buns and roast pork were filling the house as Mrs. Tan rang the doorbell.

Mrs. Tan inclined her head and accepted the teacup from Jenny with both hands, but refused her offer of a bun.

"She did it. That woman is poison!" The distraught woman exclaimed between sips of the fragrant brew. She hiccuped and patted her ample bosom.

"Mrs. Woo is a bad gossip," Granny said. "People will learn to ignore her."

"It is her weapon of choice," sobbed Mrs. Tan. She dabbed her brown eyes with a tissue and placed it on top of the little pile accumulating on her side of the coffee table. "It leaves no visible marks, but in her hands, gossip is as deadly as a sharp knife."

"It is just talk." Granny was always the voice of common sense.

"But she does more than talk," Mrs. Tan gulped. A lone tear followed the worn path around her plump cheeks, down to the corner of her mouth and splattered on her green polyester dress. "Nobody can prove it, but wherever there is trouble she is close by." Anger gleamed in her eyes. "She arrived from Toronto only a year ago and has already proven herself a meddler of the worst kind. And what decent woman her age wears so much make-up?"

"Her lies are evidence of her character," said Granny.

"And what she did to Mrs. Yu is unforgivable!"

"What happened to Mrs. Yu?" Jenny asked.

"She had an affair with another man," Granny said. "A tae

kwon do master. He frequented the restaurant where Mrs. Yu worked as a cashier."

"Isn't her husband almost twenty-five years older?" Jenny said.

"Yes," Granny said. "Mrs. Yu arrived from China forty years ago as a mail-order-bride. She and her husband had a son and a daughter, both of whom became accountants. A few months ago, Mr. Yu caught his wife having lunch in a restaurant far from Chinatown with the tae kwon do master."

"It was only lunch," said Jenny.

The older women shook their heads. "The person who 'happened' to accompany Mr. Yu there was the Widow Woo," Mrs. Tan said in outrage.

"It was unfortunate," Granny added, "that the rumour was true. Mr. Yu had a stroke when he saw them."

"And the Widow Woo will gloat to everyone how she was right about them while she ruins our family business!" wailed Mrs. Tan, frantically pulling at a fresh tissue from the package.

"Mrs. Yu finally found love after all these years?" Jenny sighed.

"Mr. Yu survived the stroke, but he now needs constant care." Granny continued. "Their daughter, Wendy, had a nasty row with Mrs. Woo and blamed her for her father's condition. And because of the shame brought onto her family, Mrs. Yu separated from her lover, who eventually moved to Vancouver."

"Customers are checking their change and studying their receipts." Mrs. Tan dabbed at the fresh stream of tears. "There is no more trust." She shook her head vigorously, but not a strand of her hair, permed and dyed jet black, moved.

"People will forget once they hear the next scandal," Granny said.

"The very reason why I came here today." There was a new

determination in Mrs. Tan's voice. "To warn you."

Granny's eyes widened and her back stiffened as she leaned towards her friend. "Warn me? About what?"

"About Mrs. Woo. She is talking about you."

"Me? I am an old woman," Jenny's grandmother protested. "What can she do to me? I have nothing she wants."

"I don't know, but she has been seen talking to your husband whenever he goes to Chinatown," Mrs. Tan said in a conspiratorial whisper. "Did he tell you?"

Granny's lips tightened. She sat up straight and looked down at her hands on her lap. "Of course he did," she replied.

According to the gossip mill and Mrs. Tan, the Widow had met Grandfather several times—a couple of times in Chinatown and a couple of times on the street.

"She is only talking to him." Granny didn't look entirely certain.

"She is planning something," Mrs. Tan warned.

"A woman who needs to attack others does so because she is weak and unhappy." Granny waggled a bony finger in the air. "She was not fortunate enough to have had a good marriage arranged for her."

"Many women were not fortunate," argued Mrs. Tan, "but they didn't ruin others because of their own misfortune."

"But they are not weak," Granny replied.

"She's evil," Jenny blurted out.

"You are young," chided her grandmother. "Even though you are in university, you do not yet fully understand the ways of the world."

"You are as young as your grandmother was at your age," Mrs. Tan said with a light laugh. "And you look like her too, but she never had such long hair!"

A half-hour later, Mrs. Tan was ready to leave. Granny

insisted on giving her friend some home-made pork buns and shuffled off to the kitchen to wrap them in foil paper. Jenny was stacking the dishes on a tray when Mrs. Tan grabbed her arm.

"You must look after your grandmother," she hissed into Jenny's ear. "You are right. The Widow Woo is evil."

"But what does she want from my grandmother?"

"Not your grandmother, silly girl," Mrs. Tan said impatiently. "Your grandfather. Did you not know they were almost betrothed to each other?"

The news jolted Jenny like an electric current.

"That woman's spiteful spirit feeds by preying on innocent people." A light spray of spittle accentuated the force of Mrs. Tan's words. "Believe me when I tell you it will be on the Widow's conscience if something happens to your grandmother because of her."

Granny came back with the pork buns wrapped and tucked into a plastic grocery bag. Mrs. Tan accepted the bag with gratitude. Jenny walked their visitor to the front door.

"*Jiély*," Mrs. Tan addressed Jenny by her Chinese name. "You must come and practise tai chi with our little group next week. You will find it very informative."

Jenny smiled and accepted the invitation. When their visitor left, she closed the oak door and slumped against it.

Maybe Mrs. Tan was overreacting. Gossip hurt, but it never killed anyone. Grandfather was now seventy years old, retired, and bored. His main activity these days was reminiscing about the past. Maybe she could get him to talk about Mrs. Woo.

An hour later, Grandfather returned from his visit to Chinatown.

"*Jiély*," he said, entering the living room. The strands of white hair covering his balding head had been restyled by the wind. He wore the white polo shirt and khaki pants her parents had bought him for his birthday. The shirt fit snugly around his waistline but sagged at the shoulders. "*Nay sic phan mah*? Have you eaten?"

"*Sic joh, a goong.* I already ate, grandfather," she responded.

"You learned how to make pork buns today." He sniffed the air and smacked his lips. "Let's see how good a student you are."

"Want to eat outside?" Putting down the newspaper she'd been reading, she rose from the sofa. Granny was napping in her room, but Jenny wanted to be sure she wouldn't overhear their discussion. "I'll bring some for you."

By the time Jenny appeared on the front balcony carrying a tray with a plate of buns, a pot of tea and two tea cups, her grandfather was reclined comfortably on a patio chair.

Jenny placed the tray on a small plastic table. He picked up a pork bun, took a large bite and made a low guttural sound of satisfaction. She perched on a small lawn chair with the tray between them; they sat in companionable silence for a few minutes, watching passers-by and listening to the sounds of summer erupting from Fletcher's Field across the street.

The park was glorious in the summer. Its paths were alive with people strolling, bicycling or in-line skating. The playground and the wading pool were busy with small children. The open area was where Granny's tai chi group met twice a week.

How was she going to bring up the topic of his near-engagement to Mrs. Woo?

"What did Mrs. Tan want to see your grandmother about?"

"How did you know she was here?" Jenny asked in surprise.

"I saw her at the Lucky Grocery Store." He paused and shook his head. "Such a bad thing to happen to them."

"Yeah," Jenny said. "She thinks Mrs. Woo is causing all their trouble."

He grunted in response.

"Do you think she is?"

"She could be." He sighed. "That woman is so much trouble."

"How bad can she be?"

"She is as charming as a poisonous snake!"

"How long have you known her?"

A few seconds passed before he answered. "I knew her in China." He grimaced at the memory. "When she was young, she was beautiful, but not nice."

It was difficult to picture how the Widow's hardened face might have looked in her youth. Now her styled coiffure and make-up created the illusion of beauty over mean eyes, a flat nose and a hard mouth. Jenny leaned forward, encouraging him to tell his story.

"She wanted to marry me so she could come to Canada." He brought the teacup to his lips and slurped the hot liquid. "Her parents offered a big dowry, but my parents had already arranged for me to marry your grandmother." He shrugged. "It was my duty as the eldest son to marry. One day, a friend and I sneaked to the village where your grandmother lived. I saw her from a distance."

"Did you talk to her?"

"No." He shook his head. "Not allowed to. I was not supposed to see her face until the wedding day. But when I saw her, I knew she was the one to marry."

She'd never heard him say anything so sentimental. "What did Mrs. Woo do?" Jenny asked, suppressing a smile.

"Oh! She was so mad. Screaming. Crying. Yelling." He paused. "I never understood why she behaved like that." He picked up his teacup, drained it and held it out to Jenny. "Pour me some more."

Jenny picked up the pot and filled the cup. The Widow

could either be nursing a hatred for Grandfather or carrying a torch for him.

He closed his eyes to take a nap. Age had not eroded the features of the man who had immigrated to Canada decades ago. He had the same sparkle of kindness in his dark brown eyes and the same smile of contentment on his lips as in his wedding picture. Considering how happy her grandparents were, Jenny wouldn't be surprised if the Widow Woo nursed a grudge.

• • •

As she had promised Mrs. Tan, Jenny arrived at Fletcher's Field promptly at eight the following Tuesday morning. The group was already assembled at the south end of the park. Jenny was surprised to see Grandfather. He was not inclined to exercise and only came if Granny nagged him. After she greeted her grandparents and Mrs. Tan, Granny introduced her to the other women: Wendy, a slim, pretty woman in her late twenties who, Jenny remembered, was Mrs. Yu's daughter, and Mrs. Hong, a grim-faced woman who was about Granny's age. They arranged themselves into two parallel lines and began the form.

Raise Hands.

Strum the Lute.

Grasp the bird's tail.

A male jogger stopped and joined them. So did a woman out for a stroll with her German Shepherd.

White Crane Spreads Wings.

Brush Knee Twist.

Practising the form in the park under the clear morning sky was meditative. The cool morning air flowed over Jenny's bare arms. Concentrating on the movements erased her worries about finding a summer job. From the corner of her eye, Jenny noticed another person join them. She turned to smile at the newcomer.

A pair of dark eyes gleamed and bright red lips painted with insincerity smiled back.

The Widow Woo.

Goose pimples rose on Jenny's skin. Her smile wavered. She glanced towards her grandparents to see if they had seen the Widow. If they had, they didn't show it.

Step Forward, Parry and Punch.

Fifteen minutes later, after they had finished the last movement, the Widow stepped up to Grandfather.

Like a dandelion in a garden of roses on a breezy day, she bowed her head. "Mr. Leung, how pleasant to see you here," she said with a practised smile. "Ah, Old Lady Leung, I am glad to see you are well. You must enjoy the day while you are able."

"I will be enjoying many more days, as I am in perfect health," Granny answered.

"Mr. Leung, please do not hesitate to call me if you find yourself alone. After all, old friends should comfort each other." Without another word, the Widow walked away. Wendy Yu spat on the ground behind her heels.

"Aiee-ya!" Mrs. Tan exclaimed. "How dare she! You should have kicked her out, Mr. Leung."

"This is a public park." Grandfather clenched his jaw.

Granny walked away while the others argued and headed towards her house. Jenny caught up to her.

"Why is she causing us trouble?" Granny's thin body shook with anger.

A ball of hate churned in Jenny's stomach as she silently accompanied her grandmother back home.

• • •

Mr. Tan wielded the butcher's knife in his right hand and, with quick accurate strokes, sliced half a roast duck lying on the butcher's block into bite-sized portions. He scooped the slices up onto the blade, neatly plopped them into an aluminum foil container, and sealed it. "Very good duck," he said with a faint smile. "Very fresh." He wiped his hands on the stained apron tied around his waist.

It was apparent his battle with the Widow and the Phoenix Noodle Company was taking its toll. Jenny had always thought his smooth round face, hairless head and short stocky body resembled a happy Buddha. But now, creases and lines accentuated his forehead and his eyes; his smile lacked its usual sparkle.

Jenny's mother had given her a list of groceries and asked her to shop at the Lucky Grocery Store as a show of support for Granny's friends. Mrs. Tan rang up the purchases and began stuffing white plastic bags with bottles and boxes of oriental condiments, tea, tofu, fresh bok choy and the aluminum container of duck. Jenny handed her the money and pocketed the change without a glance.

"Mrs. Woo came back to tai chi on Thursday. Can you believe it?" Mrs. Tan lowered her voice so the other customers wandering up and down the aisles would not overhear. "That woman knows she is not welcome in our group, but still she comes." Mrs. Tan's shoulders heaved. "This time, she told your grandmother exercise cannot protect a person. Healthy and fit people are not immortal."

An invisible weight pressed against Jenny's chest. "Was she threatening my grandmother?"

Mrs. Tan's face was grim. "She chooses her words carefully. I believe she meant to make your grandmother uncomfortable.

Hopefully, it was nothing more." She moved away to serve another customer.

De la Gauchetière Street was crowded with Saturday morning shoppers. The street, which had been converted into a bricked pedestrian mall years ago, was lined with sidewalk merchants selling inexpensive toys, slippers, incense and other dry goods. Jenny stepped into the flow of the crowd and headed east to St. Laurent Street.

She saw her grandfather first. He stood on the corner gesticulating wildly at a petite woman who held herself rigidly against the storm of his anger. It was the Widow Woo. Jenny's curiosity propelled her towards them. Neither of them noticed her.

"I am not ruining your life," the Widow said icily. "It was you who ruined mine."

"You cannot hold me responsible!" Jenny's grandfather bared his lips and forced the words out from between his clenched teeth.

Anger clouded the Widow's face. "You could have saved me. Instead, I was forced to marry an unmerciful man."

"*Jiély?*" Jenny's grandfather had noticed her. "What are you doing here?"

The Widow smirked. "Ah! The truth is out, Mr. Leung." With a proud tilt of her head, she left.

• • •

Granny's favourite shopping day was Sunday, when she always bumped into friends in Chinatown. Jenny couldn't shake the conversation she had heard the day before and volunteered to accompany her. If Granny ran into the Widow, Jenny wanted to be there.

The sidewalks along St. Laurent Street were crowded with open crates of exotic vegetables and fruits. Shoppers jammed the narrowed sidewalks. The street was a confusion of double-parked trucks unloading more crates and cars looking for a parking spot. The buzz among Granny's friends was about more than who had the freshest fruit. The shocking news was that Mrs. Yu had committed suicide because her ex-lover had met and married a woman in Vancouver.

Jenny balanced herself with the grocery bags she carried in each hand and hopped over some mangoes that had fallen out of a crate to the sidewalk. Scanning the shoppers for Granny, Jenny spotted her examining fruit on a stand in front of the next store and headed towards her. Suddenly there was a crash of boxes and cries of astonishment.

People quickly collected around the store entrance. Pushing through the crowd, Jenny saw someone lying on the sidewalk amidst cracked crates.

"Granny!" she exclaimed when she broke through the throng, dropped the bags onto the ground and knelt beside her grandmother who was cradling her left arm.

"She was pushed!" someone cried out.

Jenny scrambled to her feet and scanned the crowd.

With a furtive glance over her shoulder, the Widow Woo hurried away from the scene.

• • •

Jenny couldn't prove the Widow had pushed Granny, but she intended to confront Mrs. Woo at the next tai chi practice. Grandfather had had a fit when she told him she'd seen the Widow walking away. She'd been afraid he'd have a heart attack right there in the hospital emergency room. His face became beet red and he clenched his fists and pounded his knees. She had never seen him act like that; she'd also never feared for her grandmother's safety before.

The next Tuesday morning, she arrived at Fletcher's Field a few minutes after eight. As she walked up Duluth Street, which bordered one end of the park, she saw everyone at the usual spot, except for Granny. who had been ordered to stay home and rest. Jenny drew closer and realized they were standing around someone lying on the ground.

Grandfather! Her heart pounded as she raced across the street.

The sight of him safe and sound brought tears of relief to her eyes. He stood comforting Wendy. When Jenny halted breathlessly beside them, she discovered they were hovering over Mrs. Woo.

"What happened?" Jenny asked in bewilderment. Wendy's hands covered her face, muffling sobs. Her grandfather stared in shock at the still figure on the ground.

"Mrs. Woo had a heart attack. Mrs. Tan has gone to the house to call for an ambulance." He closed his eyes and bowed his head. "But I think it is too late."

• • •

After the ambulance had removed the body, the group abandoned practice for the day. Jenny returned to her grandparents' house with Mrs. Tan. The four of them settled in the living room where Mrs. Tan plumped cushions for Granny.

"Mrs. Woo died of a heart attack?" Jenny stated in disbelief.

Her grandfather nodded. "It happened when Wendy struck her."

"Are you saying Wendy killed her?" Shocked, Jenny looked

from her grandfather to Mrs. Tan. "Why would she?"

"Ah!" exclaimed Mrs. Tan, easing herself onto the sofa next to Granny. "Revenge. If not for the Widow's interference, Wendy's mother would still be alive and her father would not be an invalid."

"But how did she do it?" Jenny recalled there had been no weapon and no blood.

"We had started the form," her grandfather explained, "and they both stood behind everyone else. We heard them scuffle. I saw Wendy strike Mrs. Woo's chest. Hard. Mrs. Woo collapsed." Grandfather looked thoughtful. "Maybe she didn't mean to kill her."

"Did anyone tell the ambulance attendants?" Jenny asked.

"We couldn't say for certain that Wendy killed her," Mrs. Tan replied. "So we told them what we thought was true. Mrs. Woo died because she had a bad heart."

DAY'S LEE *lives in Montreal and buys pork buns in Chinatown. This former tai chi student gave up martial arts for action behind the keyboard. Her fast-fingered exercise has resulted in the publication of several short stories.*

THE BRIEF LIFE OF ALICE HARTLEY

LIZ PALMER

"Excuse me?" Alice tapped gently on the counter in Richardson Falls police station.

Constable Blain looked up from the comics on the back of *The Falls Fare*. "Miss Hartley." It came out as a groan. "What can we do for you today?"

"I'd like to report a murder."

Constable Blain folded his paper and laid it on the desk. "Where did it happen this time?"

"Up by the new development." Alice mumbled, not meeting his eyes.

"The road construction site?"

Alice nodded.

The constable stood up and came to the counter. "Do you know there are laws against wasting police time, Miss Hartley? If there were as many bodies as you've reported, it wouldn't be a road they're building, it would be a bloody cemetery." He took a deep breath. Alice thought if she hadn't been a cripple, he would be shouting at her by now. "I don't have the manpower to send people off on wild goose chases, Miss Hartley."

"But I saw the body. A woman. I couldn't tell who she was because she was lying face down. Grey hair, red sweater, grey skirt and one shoe…"

154

"Here. Hold on." Constable Blain slipped round the end of the counter and steadied her. "You've gone pale. Come and sit down." He helped her limp to a chair. "I'll get you a coffee."

Alice waited, hands clenched, fighting down the bile which threatened to rise into her throat. She could still picture the stockinged, shoeless foot.

A minute later, Constable Blain came into the waiting room, a styrofoam cup in hand. "Why didn't you telephone? It's too far for you to come." He handed her the coffee.

"You know it's a party line." Alice heard the quaver in her voice. "And the police should be first to know."

"Don't you worry about that." He reassured her in the false tone some people use for children. "Just for the record, where were you when you saw the body?"

"In my living room." Her hand trembled, and the tea slopped over the rim of the cup onto her white glove. She winced as the hot liquid hit her skin. "It entered into my head shortly before lunch this morning."

•   •   •

One shoe. One shoe. Limping towards the bus stop, the words pounded in Alice's head, keeping time with her steps. She felt sick with dread. She could not wait to reach the safety of her house.

The tree-lined lane to the old farmhouse curved sharply away from the main road. Her churchgoing clients, not wanting to be seen visiting a psychic, had been grateful for this feature. Today, stepping down from the bus, Alice wished the lane were shorter, wished she had left her bike at the corner. She must not hurry; it would be out of character. One mistake was already one too many.

"Jean Mayhew ate some stew, fell asleep and lost her shoe." The rhyme sprang, ready-made into her mind. Alice sniggered, then pressed a hand to her mouth. She was becoming hysterical, a sure path to disaster.

"Discipline, discipline." Edie-Rose's voice whispered from the past, and Alice, breathing slowly, heeded the words.

Unlocking the house, she slipped in, pushed the door shut with her shoulder and slotted the chain into place. She stood for a moment in the dark of the windowless hall, thinking back. She was sure no one had seen Jean arrive. She had come at dusk, walking along the abandoned logging road which ran behind the farmhouse. Alice sighed, took off her heavy-rimmed glasses and tucked them into her skirt pocket. She went into the lace-curtained parlour and sat down on the sofa. Folding her gloved hands on her lap, she closed her eyes and concentrated on the events of the previous evening.

• • •

"Miss Hartley. I'm here." Jean Mayhew called from outside the kitchen door.

Alice let her in. "Miss Mayhew. You will join me for a little supper first, won't you?" She watched Jean's eyes glance first at the scrubbed wooden table set for two, then alight eagerly on the Tarot cards waiting on the pine dresser.

"I hadn't really—"

"Please," Alice interrupted. "I missed lunch and I can't concentrate when I'm hungry." She pulled a chair out for Jean and went over to the stove. "I hope you like beef casserole." Lifting the dish from the oven she carried it to the table. "There. Fresh bread and butter, and a glass of wine."

Jean Mayhew didn't argue, but then Alice hadn't expected

her to. Clients never wittingly upset Alice in case it affected her ability to see their future.

Obviously eager to start the session, Jean ate quickly, pausing only to praise the meal. Alice deliberately slowed herself. She needed Jean to drink more wine.

By the time Alice laid down her fork, Jean had finished her second glass and looked ready for more. Three would be too many. "I'm done," Alice said quickly. "Another spoonful for you?"

"No, no. Quite delicious. Let me help." Jean stood up and carried the plates and glasses to the sink. She stopped and leaned against the counter. "I...I feel a little funny, Miss Hartley."

Alice rose and limped over to her. "Perhaps you drank the wine too quickly. Take my arm." She led Jean back to the table. "Sit down. I'll fetch the cards."

"Perhaps I shouldn't." Jean shook her head. "It was a mistake coming here. Reverend Stevenson would be so disappointed in me." She started to rise.

Alice put a hand on her shoulder. "I don't really need to use the cards, Miss Mayhew." She put them down on the table. "I can see both your past and your future without them."

Jean sank back into the chair, staring up at Alice. "What do you mean?" Her eyes held a look of uncertainty.

"I'll tell you a story, and you'll see what I mean." Alice returned to her chair and looked across the table. "There once lived a little girl and her widowed mother. Elizabeth was spoiled and liked to show off, but she wasn't a bad child. When she was eleven, her mother married a divorced man with a fourteen-year-old daughter. This girl, Leslie, hadn't had such a soft life. Rejected by her mother, she had come to live with her father in Westing not long before he remarried."

Jean's hands clutched the edge of the table.

"I see you recognize the story, Miss Mayhew. Everyone in Westing knew about it. Some thought Ruth Sullivan foolish to marry Eric Mills. She with all that money and he a salesman with a troublesome teenager. Others thought it would be good for Elizabeth to have a father. No one consulted Elizabeth Sullivan or Leslie Mills.

"Elizabeth learned a lot from Leslie. How to shoplift. How to lie convincingly. She experimented with marijuana and she got to know the local criminals. She didn't become addicted to drugs, but she did become a moody, difficult teenager."

"Terrible girl. Thought she was so clever." Jean's words slurred.

"Yes. You didn't like her, I know. What did she used to call you? Miss Make Spew." Alice laughed. "You weren't alone in your opinion. Most adults found her a pain then, while Leslie…Leslie settled down, grew out of her difficult ways. She became soft-spoken and polite. People thought well of her—except those whom she had blackmailed. No, Jean. May I call you Jean? Don't try to stand. Your legs won't hold you." Alice reached across the table and patted Jean's hand.

Jean jerked away. "The wine! You put something in it." She tried again to push herself up from the table. "Let me go."

Alice watched her struggle. "I'm sorry, but I've been wanting to tell you this story for a long time. Sit still and listen." She leaned forward. "What secret did Leslie discover about you, Westing's respected librarian?" She waited for an answer. "Not going to tell me? You were lucky Elizabeth and Leslie had that fight the day you went to confront Leslie, weren't you? All the world heard Elizabeth yelling 'I'll fix you for good' when she slammed out of Leslie's place." Alice got up and filled a glass with water. "I'm not used to so much talking."

Jean didn't move. Blue veins stood out against the pallor of her skin.

"Back to the story. Naturally, when the body of Leslie was discovered and Miss Mayhew, staunch pillar of the church, claimed to have seen Elizabeth leaving the house at the crucial time, everyone believed her. Especially since you described seeing Elizabeth's prized possession, her black racing bike, leaning against the hedge. No one believed Elizabeth when she said she'd been asleep in bed. Elizabeth Sullivan in bed before eleven! The police laughed."

Putting her head on one side, Alice studied Jean. "You killed three people that day," she said softly. "Leslie, Elizabeth and her mother."

"No." Jean swallowed, then licked her lips. "No. Only Leslie. Had to kill her."

"I can understand you killing Leslie. Blackmail's despicable. But why blame Elizabeth? Did you think being rude to you, the librarian, warranted a lifetime in jail? Imagine the different path her life might have taken if you had helped her. You had the chance. Remember that? It was before she became so unmanageable."

If Alice closed her eyes she could see Elizabeth, bright with enthusiasm, skipping up the steps to the old brick library, dark braids bouncing against her back. See her at the desk. "Hi, Miss Mayhew. I need some books on speed cycling. I want to race." See that brightness fade at the look of distaste on the librarian's face. "That's not the sort of thing your mother would like, Elizabeth. Nice girls play tennis and go horseback riding. Anyway, bicycle racing is only for men."

Alice picked up the cards again. "Racing would have given her a goal, and losing would have been good for her."

Jean raised her head. "She always wanted to win. Show

everyone how clever she was." Jean spoke like someone whose mouth had been frozen by the dentist. "Anyway, it didn't stop her. She failed Grade Ten because she skipped classes to ride her bike."

"That's true. She loved the freedom, the speed and the feel of the wind in her hair. Did you ever wonder what it felt like to be nineteen and have that freedom taken away? To be sentenced to twenty-five years? Be deprived of a chance to marry and have a family? Would it surprise you to learn Elizabeth became a model prisoner and holds two degrees? It was hard at first, of course..." Alice's thoughts veered to her turbulent early years in prison and to her saviour, Edie-Rose.

Edie-Rose, staring at her with compassionate brown eyes set in a scarred face.

"Ain't no use fighting the system, little girl," she'd said. "We're all here for a reason. Maybe you didn't commit no murder, but if'n you'd been a nice p'lite girl no one would've fingered you." She'd stroked the bruises on Elizabeth's arms. "You make a plan for what you're gonna do when you get out. Me, I'm gonna do murder, and ain't no one gonna guess who done it."

It had been the goad Elizabeth needed. How to take revenge and get away with it? Under the wing of Edie-Rose, her life in prison had changed. Inmates didn't dare touch her. She was Edie-Rose's protégé. Never a lover, although some thought they were. Edie-Rose had become her mentor, teacher and comforter.

Twenty years they had worked together on plans for the perfect murder. Along with courses in French language and literature, Elizabeth had soaked up Edie-Rose's knowledge of the underworld. In the mornings, Elizabeth studied French verbs. In the whispered quiet of the night she learned where to get false identities and the art of simple disguises. They'd created "Alice" together. No one, Edie-Rose had asserted, really looks at a cripple.

Edie-Rose had favoured a Ford pick-up for a get-away vehicle, but she never got the chance to use it. She had died of a heart attack three weeks before her release. Elizabeth owed it to her to succeed.

But right now she was Alice. She spread the cards face down on the table and looked directly into Jean's dulled eyes. "Ruth Sullivan always believed her daughter innocent. It broke up her marriage, and she spent all those lonely years waiting for Elizabeth's release. But Elizabeth always kept track of you. Elizabeth wanted to know where to find you. Ruth died at sixty-six. The year after Elizabeth came out. It doesn't seem right you should live longer than she did."

Alice chose a card. "It's time to read your future." She turned the card over. "A skeleton in black armour astride a white horse, Miss Mayhew. The Death card." But Jean Mayhew wasn't listening. She sat with her head slumped against her chest.

Alice studied her own feelings. Edie-Rose had thought getting back at those who had destroyed them would exorcise the anger and the hatred boiling within them. Looking at Jean, Alice felt no sense of triumph, only the realization that this was something she had to finish in order to start her own life.

She fetched the wheelchair from the hall. Spreading open a plastic bag from the mattress she'd bought, she laid it on the chair. Manhandling Jean's sleeping form into the chair wasn't easy, but she and Edie-Rose had practised this manoeuvre using a prison chair. Getting rid of the body couldn't be planned; it depended on the circumstances. Alice wished she could tell Edie-Rose how cleverly she'd arranged it.

Leaning down, she zipped the bag up as far as Jean's waist

and tucked a blanket around her. If anyone were to see them, Jean would look like a sleeping woman. Alice would close it completely before she slid Jean into the big sewage pipe laid to service the new development.

• • •

Leaving the parlour, Alice went to the kitchen. She knew the shoe wasn't there. She'd scrubbed the place after she got back from the construction site. There would be no trace of Jean Mayhew and no fingerprints from Elizabeth Sullivan.

It must have fallen off, gotten caught between the plastic bag and the footrest and dropped somewhere en route. It wasn't on Jean's foot when Alice had pushed her into the pipe. She could picture the body perfectly as it lay face down in the clear plastic bag, could remember thinking Jean would have a peaceful death, suffocating long before the sleeping draught wore off. Why hadn't she registered the missing shoe then?

Alice looked out of the window. Daylight was fading. She could at least check that it hadn't fallen somewhere between the house and the old logging road at the back.

Head down, searching through grass grown long in the wet spring, Alice suddenly heard voices coming from the front of the house. She had time to reach the shed, duck under the cobwebs and scoot behind the door before the voices got closer.

"She may be out doing a reading, Andy." Alice recognized Constable Blain's voice.

"Reading?" That must be Andy.

"Yes. She tells fortunes. Has done ever since she rented this house. Makes a good place for the church ladies who don't want to be seen." Constable Blain laughed. "Keeps the place spotless, doesn't she?"

Alice imagined them standing, faces pressed against the window.

"Odd how she went white when she described the body. She hasn't done that before. That's why I want to see her face when I ask her what the shoe looked like."

Goose bumps rose on Alice's arms. She listened intently.

"Yeah. You often see old sneakers lying about, but a woman's brown leather shoe…how would that suddenly appear on a road construction site?" Andy asked. "Any missing women reported?"

"Not yet."

"What's the background of this Hartley woman anyway?"

"That is something I'm about to look into." The voices fading. "I'll run a check before I return."

God, how stupid she'd been. Why hadn't she listened to Edie-Rose? "Girl, you got a talent for bringing attention to yourself. Keep quiet, and ain't no cop gonna think 'bout you." And what had she done? Been in and out of the police station all year.

Jean was supposed to have gone on holiday today, so she wouldn't be missed yet. And they were unlikely to come across the body. That section of the road had been covered with six feet of fill before she'd reported the murder. But as soon as they started looking into Alice Hartley's background, they would discover she didn't have one. She waited in the shed until she heard the car turn onto the main road.

In the house, Alice climbed the stairs to her room. Going to the closet she knelt down, moved her winter boots and pulled out a cardboard box. From it she took a black nylon fanny-pack and a pair of black leather running shoes. She didn't need to look into the fanny-pack; it had been ready from the moment she arrived. Now she would stow it with her get-away vehicle. Then she would clean the house and be ready to leave in the morning. She had no fear that Blain would discover her non-existence before then. Alice Hartley had no police record, and all bureaucrats would have gone home by now.

The phone rang, and Alice paused. Should she answer it? It could be Blain. Better to talk on the phone than have him come round. She went down to the parlour and lifted the receiver.

"Is that Miss Hartley? Jack Lee here."

"Hello, Mr. Lee." Why would he be calling? A warden of the Anglican Church wasn't likely to be wanting his cards read. "How can I help you?"

"I'm worried about Jean Mayhew."

Alice froze. No words would come out of her mouth.

"Hello? Are you there?"

Trying to gather her wits, Alice managed to make a response.

"Did Jean come and see you yesterday?" Mr. Lee asked. "She said she was going to."

Damn her. She wasn't supposed to tell anyone.

"No, no. She never arrived. I think she's gone on holiday." Alice knew she sounded flustered.

"There was a problem. She postponed it until this evening. I was supposed to drive her to the station, but she isn't home."

"Perhaps she forgot and took a cab."

"Her luggage is in the hall. I could see it through the window." He paused, then "You're sure she didn't come?"

"Could she have fallen when walking over? Oh, Mr. Lee," Alice's voice trembled, "I did have a dreadful vision this morning. I went to the police, but I don't think they believed me."

"I'm going to call them now." He hung up, taking Alice by surprise.

"You are not going to cheat me, Jean Mayhew." Alice said. Quickly, she returned to the bedroom and looked around. Not much to do here. She ran into the bathroom. Spraying liquid soap onto her facecloth she wiped taps, toothpaste tube, toothbrush, the sink counter and the toilet seat. Then she unclipped the plastic shower curtain. A wash would remove any fingerprints. The machine was in the mudroom next to the kitchen. Alice sped downstairs and stuffed the curtain in. She could hear Edie-Rose's voice clearly. "Still wearing your gloves, girl? Good. Now the Pledge, jus' in case youse forgot sometimes."

Up the stairs, Pledge in hand, spraying and wiping as she went. First the banisters, then into the bedroom spraying all the fronts, handles, tops. Mentally ticking off the list she and Edie-Rose had memorized, she went around methodically cleaning all surfaces she could have touched without her gloves. The kitchen she had done in the early hours, and in the parlour and entrance hall they would find only the previous tenant's prints. Alice had never been in them without gloves.

Back in the mudroom, Alice removed the dust cover from her bicycle. Her "get-away vehicle". Edie-Rose had laughed at the idea, but Alice felt convinced people didn't notice bikes. Plus it had the advantage of allowing her to wear a helmet.

I'm going to make it, Edie-Rose, she vowed silently. She'd practised this next move many times, fantasizing great get-aways. Night after night she'd cycled down the paths in the dark, headlight hooded, relishing the freedom, toning her muscles. She knew every bump and grating on her escape route, but she'd never really expected to have to leave in a hurry.

Into the empty pannier on the bike went the wig, the blouse with the special padding to make her back look crooked, the glasses, watch and skirt. On top of them she placed Alice's shoes. Wearing a built up shoe had been a brilliant idea. It meant she didn't have to remember to limp, it happened naturally. From the pannier on the other side came jeans, black ribbed sweater and fleece vest. Taking some baby-wipes she cleaned the beige make-up from her face, checking herself in the mirror behind the door. The dirty wipes went into the pannier too. Running shoes, helmet and fanny-pack completed the change. Only the white gloves stayed.

Folding the dust cover, she placed it on top of her spare clothes in the pannier. It might be useful if she had to sleep in the rough. Then Alice wheeled the bike out of the house, locking the door behind her. She stood and double-checked everything in her mind. There should be nothing to connect Elizabeth Sullivan to Alice Hartley.

A siren sounded in the distance. Time to go.

She patted her fanny-pack. Alice Hartley was dead. Michelle Roubillard was born. French passport, wallet, sunglasses and snapshots of family in France. All the things a tourist might be expected to carry. She smiled to herself. She had received an excellent education in prison.

Michelle tucked the white gloves into her pocket and cycled down the lane to the bike path that ran parallel to the highway. Richardson Falls boasted of its network of trails, and Michelle knew them all. She travelled two hundred yards then took the fork leading away from the road. As she turned, an ambulance flashed by with a police car right behind it. So the siren hadn't been for her. An accident would occupy Blain for a while. She could imagine his language when he eventually arrived at the farmhouse and found it empty.

The kilometres flew by. Michelle settled into a steady rhythm. She had a long way to go before morning. Thoughts floated in her mind. She'd planned well. Apart from losing Jean's shoe, she'd made no mistakes. Not bad, considering she'd been playing "Alice" too long for her to wait. Maybe she ought to have heeded Edie-Rose and been unobtrusive. But it wasn't in her nature.

Wheels humming, Michelle picked up speed. She wanted to be across the Ottawa River into Quebec before morning. Not until the lights of Kanata lit the sky did she remember she hadn't switched on the washing machine.

LIZ PALMER *of Chelsea, Quebec, has recently discovered kayaking. Dividing her time between various volunteer activities, writing and this new addiction is proving difficult. She is currently searching for a waterproof laptop that floats.*

TEE'D OFF

MARY KEENAN

I t's just bizarre to think that because of the murder, I'll be able to do whatever I feel like when I grow up. Well, the murder and being good at sports.

In my high school, being good at sports makes you kind of like a god. The popular kids here are the jocks and jockettes, and they're so competitive, they'll ignore all sorts of things that would get a kid beaten up someplace else if that kid can help them win all the big games. With me, they mostly ignore the fact that I think sports are stupid, especially when they're pointless. I mean, what's the good of a lot of girls running from one end of a field to another, chasing a big white ball and getting all out of breath? It's like mom on her treadmill. She never actually gets anywhere. I'm not saying exercise is stupid, but I'd rather do it for a good reason. Like when my cousin Judy and I play golf so we can talk about stuff for a few hours without our folks listening in. I really like that about golf.

Anyway, because I'm good at sports, Coach Flannigan kept me late after swim class that day, trying to talk me into trying out for some special synchronized swim team he'd heard about. Totally pointless. I couldn't get out of that pool fast enough. And I really didn't, either, because when I got into the change room all the other girls had staked out a place to strip out of their swimsuits, and the only privacy stall was taken.

The whole female bonding thing is super-overrated in my opinion. Especially with the jockettes, who spend all their time together either coming up with some sports strategy, figuring out the theme for our big grad party this spring or talking about Dex Monaghan being hot for them.

"He asked me about my lipstick today," Heather Lane was bragging when I came in from the fast shower I had taken with my suit still on. No way was I showing off my tush to this crowd, at least not for a week. "He leaned real close and asked me if it tasted good."

Kelly Baxter, a pretty good hitter on the softball team, one-upped her as always. "He asked me about my underwear. Wanted to know whether I go for red nylon or black lace."

The jockettes all started swooning, so I rolled my eyes and turned around and smacked into one of the dopeheads who must've thought she could see my tush through my bathing suit if she just stared hard enough.

"What did you get, Allie? A butterfly?"

"Please. Butterflies are so yesterday."

The dopehead girls want me to join their clique just as much as the jockettes do, and for pretty much the same reason. They figure my being fit and coordinated makes me their poster girl for all the perfect body, perfect mind crap they puff out the window with every drag on the weed they smoke to prove they've cornered the market on inner peace. They are so lame. I think it was their lameness that made me tell them I'd gotten a multi-coloured tattoo on my tush, just to see how many of them would pull a lemming and get an even more daring tattoo in a more private spot. I'd bet Dex that at least a dozen would show up at Eddie's Tattoo Shop by next Tuesday and turn my hypothetical act of bravado into a total cliché.

Anyway, having the dopeheads staring at my tush made me even more interested in getting out of my swimsuit and into my jeans so I could go home and have a long bath out of Mom's way. And, judging by the purple toenails on the feet sticking out of the bottom of our only stall, Caitlin was still in there, which was bad news for me. She always did hog that stall. Looked like I'd be changing in the toilets.

Then I had to look closer, because I couldn't figure out why there'd be all that thick red stuff on the floor around her feet. Caitlin's red cotton swimsuit was too old to bleed out colour like that. Not to mention that this stuff didn't look like water. I didn't like it. I knocked on the stall door and asked if she was okay. She didn't answer. I pushed it open and looked at Caitlin sort of wedged on the bench inside, and what I saw wasn't very nice. Teenaged girls shouldn't have big knives sticking out of their chests.

"You." I pointed at Heather Lane, who was the closest to being dressed. "Go to the office right now and get somebody to call the police."

After that, you can imagine what happened. School was closed for a couple of days, and all the kids went around kind of shocked, and some social workers came out to talk to us about our feelings. And of course, right away the police were turning up, asking a lot of questions about Caitlin. Please.

"Caitlin didn't kill herself," I told the cop who interviewed me, Detective Stewart. He's a tall weedy guy with a big nose, kind of like a picture of a monk I saw once, except the monk had more hair.

"I didn't say she did, Allison. But now that you mention it, there was some fresh graffiti on the inside of the stall, and it suggested that Caitlin had been doing bad things with one of the boys." I got the feeling that if I pushed, he'd start coming up with some more super hilarious ways to protect my virgin ears, but I had other things to do.

"You think she carried a knife around in her gym bag so that if her reputation got ruined one day she could just end it all right there, huh? Which boy?"

Stewart coughed. "It said 'Dex'. I understand there is a Dex Monaghan in this school?"

"Sure, and there's a Serious State of Denial in this school, too. Dex is the best athlete this town has ever had, so practically all the kids here pretend not to know he's gay. I mean, the guys need him to win their games for them, so they just act like he's joking when he makes passes at them, which he almost never does because the guys here are so lame. And the girls don't understand why a guy would want to do it with another guy anyway, so they keep thinking he just needs to meet the right girl. If he'd fooled around with Caitlin, she would have been totally in with the jockettes. They'd want to know how she got him."

"I see." Stewart looked totally confused. He probably wasn't old enough to have any teenagers of his own.

"I'll make this simple for you, Detective Stewart. Caitlin Anderson was a fringe girl. Even if she was going to kill herself, she would never have done it at school." Stewart didn't seem to be getting it. "Look, just last month she tried to get in with the jockettes by bringing a bunch of marbles to school from her mother's glassblowing studio. Thought she could get them to sit down on the ground like fourth-graders and shoot marbles for fun. Social suicide." Bad choice of words, Allie.

Detective Stewart must have thought so too, because he got all soothing on me. "All we're trying to do is figure out how Caitlin ended up in that stall. So far, the only thing we know for certain is that she'd been a little down this year."

"Of course she was down. She was an unpopular fringe girl, and her parents just split up. But there's no way she'd decide to off herself, and then do it with a knife wearing her oldest swimsuit while she's in a crummy change room stall surrounded by a lot of people who didn't like her.

"Here's how I see it. When swim class is in last period, Caitlin had permission to get out of the pool ten minutes early so she could make her piano lesson. Today Coach Flannigan kept me back to talk about some new team thing, and I was super-bored about it and I was watching the door to the change rooms. I can tell you that all the other girls went through it in clumps. Nobody in our swim class could have stabbed Caitlin without all of the girls being in on it, and that just wouldn't happen, because most of the class is made up of two cliques, and they'd never side together on anything. But I figure there were maybe five minutes when somebody could have gone into the change room from the hallway, stabbed Caitlin, and gone back out before anybody noticed."

I didn't expect the guy to give me a medal, but I sure didn't expect him to flash me a look like I'd handed him a squawking turkey in church or something. Then he stood up to let me know I was dismissed, which I thought was pretty rude considering.

"Thank you, Allison, this is very helpful. As I said, we're looking into many possibilities." Yeah, I'll just bet he was. The way I saw it, the cops were so busy figuring out why the local jewellery stores kept getting robbed, they practically had to write off a kid like Caitlin as some crazy teenager.

Boy, I was ticked. I mean, it was bad enough that Caitlin died in the first place, but to have to sit there while Detective Stewart got snotty and told me he was wasting time on possibilities? That really burned me.

It burned Dex, too. I saw him the night before school opened again, in Walters', our local department store, mostly because he saw me first.

"Can you do me a favour, Allie, and take this stuff through the cash for me?"

Geez. I still don't get how Dex can say he's all comfy about being gay and then go and ask me to buy his silk undies for him when he decides to get experimental. Hasn't he figured out yet that anybody who single-handedly beats the Panthers five games in a row can pretty much do anything he wants in this town? I vetoed the yucky stuff he'd picked out and took him back to the ladies' department. He shouldn't have been asking the jockettes for fashion advice.

"I am so cheesed about Caitlin," I told him while we looked for a leopard print thong in his size. I'd just told him about the stupid police thinking she might have done the depressed diva dive. "What did you do to get your name lined up with hers on that change room stall, anyway?"

"Nothing. Well, I helped her with her math homework a few times. Last time was the day before she died." He looked really sad, and I knew how he felt. We were probably the only two kids in school who'd even bothered to get to know Caitlin.

"Who could have seen you together? Where did you study?"

"In the library, after last period."

Well, that ruled out most of the planet. The library at our school isn't exactly a zoo in normal hours, and once classes are over for the day, it's deserted.

"Okay, so maybe whoever killed Caitlin just picked you because you're popular and wrote your names on the inside of the stall door after stabbing her."

"Was there enough time?" Dex is so practical. "If I'd done it, I would have been outta there right after doing my thing with the knife."

"Okay, maybe the killer went early, wrote the graffiti inside the privacy stall, then waited for Caitlin to come in from the pool. Everybody knows she always used that stall to change."

"Everybody? You mean the other kids, right?"

"Who did you think I meant?"

"Nobody gets a spare at the end of the day, Allie. All the other kids would have been in a class, not sneaking into the change room with a knife."

"You mean, you think one of the staff did it?"

I was still thinking about what Dex said at school the next day, but I was super confused. Why would one of the staff want to kill Caitlin Anderson? Or any of us, for that matter? And how many of the staff would know about Caitlin always using the privacy stall? It's not like that was a hot gossip item. Whoever it was must have known her pretty well. Maybe she'd been having an affair with a teacher? It happens, but I couldn't imagine even Caitlin being dopey enough to want to sleep with any of the ones at our school. They're all so geeky, like Mr. Dorbinette, who's a birdwatcher, for God's sake. Still, I figured it wouldn't hurt to find out who'd been roaming the halls that afternoon.

"I didn't hear about your special project, Allison. How nice." Mrs. O'Reilly is the cutest school secretary ever, I swear. She looks like one of those sweet little garden gnomes, but without the hat.

"Oh, it's really interesting, Mrs. O'Reilly. I get to draw a map of the school and then plot out where people go all day long, and figure out which rooms get used the most, and when, and stuff like that."

"It's unusual to get such a complex assignment this late in your final year though, isn't it?" Mrs. O'Reilly went through the school schedules and waddled over to the copier, and I tried not to feel guilty about lying to her.

"It's a makeup thing. You know, I've missed a lot of class time lately."

"Oh, yes." She gave me the gnome smile that scrunched up her eyes, and she pinched my cheek. "Our little athlete!"

Of course I didn't go over the lists in the hallway where a homicidal teacher or attendance cop might find me. I mean, I was skipping gym. I did it in the yearbook room, which was mostly deserted now that everything had gone to the printer, except for when some jockette decided to use it as extra locker space. It took me right up to the end of the last period, but I finally figured out that the only teachers not in a class when Caitlin was killed were Miss Rumsey and Mr. Clark, and everybody knew those two had taken off early that day for a long weekend in Vegas. We all figured they'd do a quickie wedding there, but it turned out they didn't even get engaged.

I was writing down which teachers were close enough to the change room to kill Caitlin on a bathroom break when Sarah Ann Felding came in and yanked a jean jacket off the coat rack in the corner.

"Oh, hi, Allie!" She was acting all bubbly at me, but she looked like she was cheesed underneath, as usual. She's one of those jockette girls who carries around grudges like they're fashion accessories. I didn't really care, since I'd just remembered she had English class in her last period, with geeky Mr. Dorbinette, whose classroom is just up the stairs from the pool and the girls' change room.

"What are you doing here?" She was accusing me of something, God knows what. I thought I'd play her for a minute before I pumped her for information about birdwatcher boy.

"I'm so upset, I just had to have a few minutes to myself." I put on a teary pout. "You won't tell anyone, will you?"

Sarah Ann got that breathless look she gets when she thinks there's good dirt coming, and she whipped a chair out from the table and sat down on it. "Of course I won't tell. Is it about Dex? Did he dump you?"

"Dump me?" I had no idea what she was talking about, but I knew she'd fill me in if I gave her half a chance.

"Yeah. I saw you guys in Walters' last night. Looked like you two were getting ready to, you know, hook up."

The lingerie. She thought he was choosing stuff he wanted me to wear. Gross! I had to put my face down so she wouldn't see me laugh. "It was so…heartbreaking," I choked out after a minute. "We were just about to…you know…and I found out he was really fantasizing about my being…another girl!"

I peeked up and saw Sarah Ann looking like her head was going to explode. "Who?"

"You!" I just choked out the word, threw my head down on my arms and really let myself go. I figured she'd see my shoulders shaking and assume I was crying my eyes out. It was crappy of me, but I'd had a bad week.

When she started patting my back, I brought my head back up and made a big fuss about drying my eyes. I knew the only way I'd keep her attention now would be to spill some more stuff about Dex lusting after her. I launched into this story about his telling me that he'd tried to get her attention the other day in English class when Dorbinette went out of the room, but that Sarah Ann hadn't noticed, and then everybody found out about Caitlin, and he hadn't had another chance to make his move yet.

"But Dorbinette was out of the room for ages that day!"

Sarah Ann's eyes went all sticky-outie. "How could I have missed Dex like that?"

"Maybe it only seemed like a long time to you. Dex told me he hardly had a chance."

"No way. Dorbinette was gone for nearly twenty minutes. He said he wasn't feeling well and gave us an open book test. He was in the john forever."

The look on her face was funny, and I really did laugh, which meant I had to cover by getting all bitter and jealous. "And you just did your test like a good girl instead of noticing Dex trying to make you be bad."

"Well, I'm not going to make him wait any lo—" she hesitated, looking at my flushed face.

"It's okay," I said like I was being all noble and giving up the last rocky road bar on earth to a kid who'd never had one. Then I squeaked out "It's you he wants" and threw my head back down onto my arms. This time she didn't bother patting my back, and when I looked up she was gone. Well, Dex was more than paying his dues for getting me a reputation as a lingerie-buying slut down at Walters'.

Now I had more stuff to chew on. Like, if Dorbinette killed Caitlin, how come? I looked at my watch and decided I might as well check out Dorbinette's classroom for a clue. He'd probably be on his way home by now.

On my way to Dorbinette's end of the building, I passed Dex looking all wild and sweaty, like he'd been running. "You're in big trouble, Allie," he said as he speedwalked toward me.

"Aw, you know you love it," I told him when we passed each other, and he slapped my tattoo-free tush.

Sarah Ann nearly knocked me down as I turned the corner to the change rooms, where Detective Stewart was standing with some other cops. Even though they'd had a whole weekend, plus another day when school was closed for the kids to have a grief break after Caitlin's so-called suicide, it looked like the cops still hadn't finished doing their detecting. There was yellow police tape over the door to the girls' change room and everything.

"Hey, Detective Stewart," I said when he saw me. "Taking a pretty close look, huh?"

"Just making sure, Allison," he told me in that way-too-soothing voice of his. Aren't cops supposed to be authoritative? Maybe he was trying to go easy on me, what with me being the one to find Caitlin and all. Please.

"Sure you're making sure. You know I'm right, don't you?"

He didn't say yes or no, but he did tell me to come to him if I had any more information.

"I might," I told him. "I mean, I will if I do, and I might. I'm not sure yet. I have to check something, and then I'll come back, okay?"

I don't think he liked that, but one of the other cops came over then, so I headed up the stairs.

Dorbinette's classroom was empty, all right. I went in and over to the window to check the parking lot in case his car was still there, and it was, but since he was just opening the driver's door, I figured I was okay to check his desk. Just as I was stepping back, though, I noticed a woman come out from the trees behind Dorbinette's car and start talking to him. She looked like she was being sneaky. I squinted to see if I knew who she was, but the sun was too bright, and she was too far off. I decided I should go through the guy's desk fast, while whoever it was kept him busy.

Even while I did it, I figured it was probably really stupid to bother looking. I mean, if they'd been having an affair and he killed her to keep it a secret, Dorbinette wouldn't have kept nude photos of him and Caitlin in his desk at school. Would he? After I had checked all four drawers, I figured I was right about that if nothing else. He just kept ordinary things like his birdwatching binoculars and a calculator and a lot of rulers. But then I had a smart idea. If he did have something that he wanted to keep a secret, something most people would look for at his house, then it'd make sense for him to hide it at school. My mom does that all the time with her diamond rings when she goes out without them. She finds a place no thief would ever check, like underneath her treadmill, and she puts them there.

So I got under Dorbinette's old oak desk. The only interesting thing was this gap at the back, between the drawers and the front part of the desk that all the kids see. I ran my hand up into the gap on either side and sure enough, I found a purple flannel drawstring bag taped to the back of the upper right drawer.

After I'd gotten up from under the desk and dusted myself off, I looked back toward the window and remembered the binoculars. Now that I knew he was hiding something for sure, I figured it was worth checking to see if that lady was still out there talking to him. I took the binoculars over and looked out and saw that she was Caitlin's mother. I was just thinking how weird that was when Dorbinette looked up at the window.

I jumped back right away. Not that he would have recognized me behind those big black goggles, but I guess anybody standing at the window of his classroom with the binoculars from his desk drawer might make a guilty guy a bit mad. Then I looked down at myself and realized I was wearing my lime green flowered shirt, which a guilty guy might remember if he went looking for the kid who was messing around with his desk and watching him talk to some woman in the parking lot who was acting like she knew him as a lot more than just the English teacher of her dead daughter.

I crammed the binoculars back into the desk drawer and got out of there fast. I mean, I really flew down the stairs to the first floor, but Stewart and all his buddies were gone already. While I tried to decide what to do next, I weighed that drawstring bag in my hand, wondering what was in it, and stupid me, I checked it first instead of going straight to the office where Dorbinette couldn't bother me without looking pretty suspicious.

It was so weird. The bag was full of marbles. Big ones mostly, with amazing colours and stuff in the centre, sort of like the kind Caitlin's mother had shown us how to make when our art class had a field trip to her glassblowing studio, but nicer. More sparkly, somehow. I'd just dropped them back into the bag and pulled the drawstring when I saw Dorbinette coming down the hall toward me. He didn't exactly look thrilled.

I had limited options at that point. He was blocking the easiest route to the office, and with the change rooms taped off, I could either go into the gym or through a plate glass window into the courtyard. I picked the gym.

One good thing about all the sports they make me play at this school is that I didn't need to turn on the lights to find my way around. Dorbinette knows the layout too, because he directs our school plays. But he didn't know that a bunch of us had already set up the gym for a big obstacle course competition.

I heard him fall in kind of a breathy, squishy way, which probably meant he was still at the inner tubes before I was over the low jumps, and it sounded like he'd fallen twice more by the time I swerved around the big plastic tunnels you're supposed to crawl through. Then I dove out the doors that lead to the playing field at the back of the school.

I thought I was so smart. I'd scaled smaller fences than the one that divided the field from the school parking lot, where I could see Stewart and the other cops talking around their cars as I ran. Then I looked up and saw that the school board had been busy putting up a taller fence with barbed wire along the top. How could I have missed that? They'd been talking about better security forever, but they hadn't done anything about it. There was no way I could climb that thing, not with a guy like Dorbinette on my tail. I screamed really loud, but Stewart didn't seem to hear me. I guess he was too far away. I'm a fast runner, but without any exits from the field except back into the gym, which you can't get back into without a key anyway, Dorbinette would be chasing me around in circles for a long time before somebody noticed and did something about it. If he ever got out of the gym, that is. Last I'd heard from him he was cursing about his head. I hoped he'd hurt it bad.

That was when I had my bright idea, the one that made me think I'm pretty smart after all. I ran to the equipment shed, zipped open the combination lock, and hauled out Coach Flannigan's golf clubs. I figured his five iron was my best option, given the distance I was dealing with. And then I just dropped those marbles down in a row and shot them, one after another, over the fence and into the parking lot. Turns out marbles break up pretty good when you smack them like that, but I made my point. I got Stewart's attention by dropping a marble right into his cap when he took it off to wipe his head. By the time Dorbinette staggered out into the field about fifty yards away from me, the cops had him covered.

Detective Stewart was pretty happy with me. Turned out Dorbinette had been behind all those jewellery store hits, and he'd been hiding a lot of diamonds and stuff in Caitlin's mother's marbles until he could sell them to somebody else. Mrs. Anderson kept saying that she didn't know he was a criminal and that she wouldn't have kicked out her husband if she'd realized Dorbinette was just using her to hide stolen goods, sneaking down to her studio when she was asleep. I figure she's got to be pretty stupid if she really didn't notice what he was up to. But either way, Caitlin must have caught him, and he'd killed her at the school after marking up that stall door so people wouldn't go snooping around back at the Andersons' house.

Coach Flannigan was even happier. I guess some of those shots I made with his five iron were super-amazing, and not just because I didn't bean any of those cops with a broken marble. He made some calls, and I did some tryouts. It turns out I'm one of the best new golfers anybody's seen in years and years. So now I'm going to be rich and get to do whatever I want, because a bunch of companies want to give me tons of money to wear their clothes whenever I play golf. And I'll probably get to do the LPGA tour next year, too. Pretty good, huh?

MARY KEENAN *is a Toronto-based freelance writer whose first novel was shortlisted in the annual St. Martin's Press/Malice Domestic contest for Best First Traditional Mystery. Her short story, "The Bedbug's Bite", won first place in a contest run by A&E Television on its www.mysteries.com website.*

STRAIGHT LIE

Was the ball that killed the golf pro
An accidental shot?
The detective who was on the case
Felt that it was not.

The suspect pleaded innocence:
"Sir, I just play for fun."
The thing that really cinched the case?
His second hole-in-one.

JOY HEWITT MANN

ALTHOUGH, ON THE OTHER HAND...

PAT WILSON AND KRIS WOOD

I settled my stole firmly around my shoulders and turned to see how he was doing. As usual, he'd gotten his stole wound up in his cincture. "Father Donald," I said, "let me do that."

I knew it would be easier to disentangle the snarled fringes and knots myself, rather than watch Father Donald fumble ineffectually with the mess. You'd think after twenty years in the ministry, he would have figured out how to put the stuff on right the first time. I remembered to duck as his right arm shot out from the shoulder, stiffened, held and then snapped back to his sides.

The first time, I'd gotten a black eye, but after six weeks of his exercise regime, I'd learned to be wary. At any moment, he was likely to squat, stretch, twist or flex without warning. Father Donald was a large man, and woe betide any poor, unsuspecting lay reader who got in his way. Frankly, I wished that Molly Thubron had never given him the book. It went with him everywhere, and even now lay open on the vestry table, *Flex-er-Cise: Twenty Weeks to a New Physique.* I sighed. Six down, fourteen to go. It was going to be a long summer.

"Oh, shoot. I got it tangled again, didn't I? I don't know what I'd do without you, not that I couldn't do anything, but it's easier, well not easier, but takes less time, although on the other hand, time isn't really an issue, although some people get annoyed when the service doesn't start on time, not everyone though, some come in late themselves, though they probably have a good reason, although my sister Dorothy always says there's no good reason for being late for church…"

I tuned Father Donald out with the ease of long practice. Five years as his lay reader and I knew that, at the most, only one of every forty words was worth taking note of. His other arm suddenly shot out, held and snapped back. I took the opportunity to slip the green chasuble over his head and roll the collar down smoothly.

"There," I said. "You're ready to go."

"Okey-dokey." He squatted down. "Uh…could you give me a hand?" I heaved him back up. Maybe he wasn't getting fit with his new regime, but the weight training sure was paying off on my biceps.

"Where's my trusty server?" It was a question he asked every week with just the same note of anxiety.

Little Mindy Horton, prudently positioned behind the door well out of the way of Father Donald's gyrations, waved the processional cross and said: "Right here. You want me to start out now?"

"Just a minute, Mindy." Another small trick I'd learned. "Father Donald. Here is your hymn book, prayer book, announcements sheet, sermon papers, Gospel folder." I knew better than to give them to him any sooner than this moment. "All right, Mindy. We're ready to roll."

I opened the vestry door, and Mindy started out. I followed, Father Donald close on my heels. The notes of the opening hymn, "Onward Christian Soldiers", trickled reedily from the electric organ, under the quavering fingers of Edith, our fill-in organist. I'll be glad when Boris is back, I thought. His annual holiday in Portugal always meant we had to endure three weeks of Edith's fumblings. She wasn't a bad pianist, if only we had a piano in the church. As it was, she was terrified of the electronic Hammond organ and never played above a whisper.

Mindy and I settled into our accustomed places, and I waited for the service to unfold as it always did, although with Father Donald in charge, it tended to be a little more fluid than perhaps the church fathers had intended. I watched him tuck in a couple of knee-bends as he stood behind the lectern. I wondered how it looked to the congregation as his head appeared and disappeared several times over the top edge. I opened my prayer book and turned to page 185.

However, our beloved rector had something else in mind. "Before we begin, well we've really begun, but before we get into the service, although on the other hand, I've already started, I have a really important announcement to make, well maybe not that important, but fairly important, at least it will be to some people, in fact, probably to all of you, and certainly to me…" His voice dropped to a low, serious note we seldom heard. I saw his sister Dorothy, ensconced in her usual seat, last pew, right hand side, sit up and cast a gimlet eye on him. Uh-oh, I thought. She doesn't know anything about this.

Father Donald turned his head sideways, held it, then rotated to the other side. He snapped back and continued: "An extremely serious matter has surfaced. I don't want to go into right now, although I probably should, but then, we really don't have time, not if we're going to get out of here by twelve, and I know how you feel, although not all of you, but most of you have homes to go to, not that everyone doesn't have a home…" He executed a full neck roll. As his head returned to the frontal position, his eyes locked on Dorothy's.

Even from my seat at the back of the choir stalls, I could

smell the brimstone. Get on with it, man, I silently urged him, before she explodes. I'd seen Dorothy in action before. She ran a tight ship, whether it was the A.C.W., the Altar Guild or Father Donald. Even his current exercise craze was her idea. "It's time he pulled himself together," she'd told me, "took off some of that flab, toned up, showed a little discipline." This from a woman who easily weighed 250 pounds.

"So, in light of what I've found out, discovered really, although I wasn't looking for anything, I'm calling a special Parish Council meeting for Monday night at seven in the rectory." Dorothy's glare could have felled an ox at a hundred yards. Father Donald backpedalled rapidly, "Er, that is, not the rectory, but the church basement. Yes, that would be a better place, wouldn't it? Although, on the other hand, not that you aren't all welcome at the rectory, you understand, but with Dorothy's spring-cleaning and all…" I saw her massive bulk lift slightly from her pew. So did Father Donald. He hurried on. "It's to do with our monies, and you know how important that is, especially to our treasurer although, not as important as some things perhaps, as our Lord tells us 'where a man's heart is, there also is his treasure'," and I saw it coming. One of his awful jokes. "And we all know where our treasurer's heart is. It's in that brand, spanking new boat of his, right, Morley?" Everyone laughed and nodded in agreement, but I saw Morley Leet turn deathly pale. Oblivious to everything, Father Donald launched into the service. "Page 185 in your prayer books," he announced.

The service rolled on without incident except for a slight hitch when Edith hit the Samba button on the organ by mistake, and the second hymn, "Sweet Hour of Prayer", was underlaid with a distinct "oom cha cha, oom cha cha". Father Donald took the opportunity to twist and roll from the waist in time to the music, seemingly unaware of the inappropriate beat.

We all settled into the service groove, but when the time came for Morley Leet to pick up the offering plate, he had disappeared. Finally, Dorothy leaned forward and tapped George Anderson on the head with her hymn book. He got the hint and stumbled forward.

As Father Donald collected the full plate from George's hands, I saw Morley Leet come in and stand at the back of the church. I wondered if he wasn't feeling well again, since he'd looked so pale earlier. We all knew that Morley Leet suffered from "the nerves", the same malady as Father Donald's sister had. I could understand Dorothy's malady, living with her brother as she did, but what Morley had to be nervous about, I couldn't imagine.

Father Donald beamed broadly at George and said, "Well, looks like we got a new money man. Everyone wants to be treasurer, eh? Must be a pretty well-paid job." He laughed at his own small joke, lifted the collection plate up and down several times as if he were bench-pressing a hundred pounds, mumbled the prayer and dropped it carelessly on the side table. I lunged for the plate and steadied it just as it was about to slip off the edge. I did this every week.

I took a deep breath and settled back. It was time for the sermon. I had a little game I always played with myself. It helped pass the time. I counted every instance when Father Donald said "although", then qualified his previous statement. So far, the record stood at twenty-one, but I had hopes for something I could call Guinness about.

The past few weeks, I'd been off my count. Watching Father Donald under cover of the larger pulpit doing various flex-er-cises was distracting to say the least. From my vantage point, every bend and curl was easily seen.

"My text for today's meditation," he began, using his best sermon voice, deep and resonant and slightly British, "is Matthew, Chapter 21, Verse 13, 'my house shall be called a house of prayer, but you are making it a hideout for thieves'." I saw Morley Leet duck back out. He must be sick, I decided. Or smart.

There were only eleven "althoughs" today—not a record, but satisfying, nevertheless, and I might have missed a couple when he began to jerk and swing his hips from side to side, not seen by the congregation, but all too clear to me.

At the end of the service, a smattering of "amens" followed us down the aisle. As Father Donald passed Dorothy, she leaned out of her pew and smacked him sharply on the leg with her purse. "Coffee," she hissed.

"Whaaa?" Father Donald halted suddenly. I glanced back. We'd lost him again. The procession straggled to a halt.

"Coffee Sunday!" she whispered urgently. "You forgot to mention it!"

"Oh! Oh! Shoot! Wait, just a minute. Hold the phone! I forgot. It's coffee Sunday. Come on downstairs—coffee's on. Although, not just coffee. There's tea, too, although if you don't like coffee or tea, I don't know what you'll do. You could have water, although on the other hand, we know our water's not that good. Well, good enough, I guess. For coffee, anyway." Dorothy smacked him again. He pulled himself together and joined us at the door.

Later in the vestry as I disrobed, I noticed that the collection plate which Mindy had brought in was still on the table.

"Where's Morley Leet?" I asked her. "He hasn't picked up the offerings."

"I think I saw him going downstairs. Shall I go and get him?"

"Never mind. I'll take it down to him." I scooped the money into an old envelope and shoved it in my pocket. "Let's go and take our lives into our hands with a cup of St. Grimbald's coffee." Only the fact that it had been perking for the last two hours made it drinkable at all. Father Donald wasn't kidding about our water.

Mindy and I left the vestry, marched through the now-deserted pews and gathered up Father Donald, who was still at the back of the church. Together we descended the steep stairs into the dank, dark nether regions under the church which the wardens and the A.C.W. had ineffectually tried to render habitable. The usual miasma of mildew and old hymn books was mercifully overpowered by the sharp, heady tang of coffee.

We used Father Donald as a battering ram to take us through the throng to the counter. It wasn't difficult, since he'd already caught sight of Carol Morgan's butter tarts and was moving in on them like a elephant who'd spotted a bag of peanuts. Unfortunately, Dorothy was on an intercept course, and at the last moment, she scooped up the plate of tarts, shot him a triumphant glance and disappeared into the kitchen.

"Shoot!" Father Donald visibly sagged under the disappointment.

"Here you are, Father Donald. A double-double. Just the way you like it." Someone handed him a cup of coffee. Before he could take a sip, the cup was snatched from under his nose.

"I've got *your* coffee here. Sweetener and just a little skim milk." Dorothy took the offending cup and handed it to Edith, who was waiting in line next to the coffee urn. "Here," she said, "you can have this one."

"Shoot!" Father Donald sipped glumly, bending gently at the knees as he did so.

I remembered the offering envelope in my pocket and

looked around for Morley Leet. "Have you seen Morley?" I asked Dorothy. "I've got the offering to give to him."

"He was here a minute ago. Probably stepped outside for a cigarette. Filthy habit." Dorothy sniffed.

"I'll drop it off on my way home. I go right by his house." I grimaced as I sipped my own coffee. Even three spoonfuls of sugar couldn't disguise the bitter undertaste.

"Now, Donald," demanded Dorothy in her no-nonsense, take-no-prisoners voice. "What's this about an emergency meeting tomorrow night?"

Father Donald froze in mid knee-bend. He shot her a glance like a deer caught in the headlights of an oncoming Mack sixteen-wheeler. "Don't get excited, Dottie. You know what the doctor said. Perhaps you'd better take one of your pills," he suggested hopefully. He'd privately told me that the pills were a godsend—one of them and she was gentle as a lamb, two and she was out like a light.

"No." Even I cringed at her tone and tried to edge surreptitiously away. "I expect Charles would like to know, too. Wouldn't you, Charles?" The Mack truck had changed course and was bearing down on me.

"Umm, sure, I guess."

"Well, I wanted to tell you. I would have told you, although I didn't want to say anything until I was sure, well not sure, but at least pretty sure, although there was no reason not to be sure. Anyway, it's hush-hush, well not really, I just can't say anything right now. Although, I could say something, but it wouldn't be any use because I can't tell you everything, not that I know everything, although I think I probably know more than most do about it, well, not more, because as I said to the Bishop... Oh! Shoot! Never mind what I said, not that I said anything, but you're just going to have to wait until tomorrow night, well not night, evening really, although the meeting is pretty late. I'm sworn to secrecy and that's all there is to it." He took a large gulp of his coffee and smiled smugly.

Dorothy and I looked at each other blankly. I wondered if she'd made any sense of it all. I tried to sort out the "facts". Earlier, he'd mentioned an important discovery to do with money and now, a confidential discussion with the Bishop. That could cover anything from the Guild Ladies Luncheon to grand larceny. I decided we were never going to get anything out of Father Donald today, so I left him to the tender ministrations of his now seething sister and headed out to find Morley Leet.

• • •

Bessie Leet answered my knock. "He's upstairs, lying down," she said. "He came in from church, looking terrible. Couldn't eat a bite of lunch. Said he didn't feel well." She shot a worried glance up at the ceiling. "I hope he's all right. He's been real edgy these past few weeks. I think he's worrying about that new boat of his. I wisht he never got it. How we're going to pay for it, I'll never know. Him with just his pension. I told him to take one of them nerve pills the doctor gave him. That usually settles him down."

I handed her the envelope. "Perhaps he shouldn't bother with the meeting tomorrow night," I said. "I'm sure Father Donald will understand if he can't make it."

"Well, I think this treasuring stuff is all too much for him. His nerves can't take it. Going to resign at the end of this term, so he says. He only done it because his family's always been the treasurers at St. Grimbald's." She opened a kitchen drawer already stuffed full of receipts, envelopes and various ledgers.

I could see several bankbooks on top. "I'll just put this into his treasurer's drawer. He'll see to it when he's up later." She crammed the envelope in and pushed the drawer shut. I headed home for lunch and a much-needed cup of my own Special Blend coffee, black with no sugar.

•　•　•

Early Monday afternoon, while I was in the midst of a particularly difficult chapter that just wouldn't write itself, I got a frantic phone call from Father Donald. It took me several minutes to make out what he was saying. He was even less coherent than usual, if that were possible.

"My dear Charles. It's just awful, well more than awful, a tragedy. Poor Edith, what a loss, although Boris will be back for next Sunday, but a loss in the broadest possible sense, perhaps 'broad' isn't a good choice of words, Edith is such a lady, I mean was such a lady, oh dear, I can hardly believe she's left us."

I wondered if she'd finally got the message and resigned. Organ one; Edith nothing.

"Left us?' I managed to insert.

"Yes, gone, passed, asleep, away, finished, ended, kaput, no more…dead!"

"Edith's dead?"

"It's just awful. An overdose, although they're not saying that, not that they're saying anything, at least, not to me, but I can read between the lines, well, not read, but listen…uh, where was I?"

"You mean she committed suicide?"

"No, no!" His voice was horrified. "She wouldn't do that, I mean, her playing wasn't that bad, at least, nobody complained, not to me, anyway. You didn't hear anything, did you? People upset perhaps?"

I saw a quagmire of non-sequitors opening before us and quickly reined in Father Donald's thoughts. "You said an overdose?"

"Yes…that's what they told Benjamin. And he told them she never took anything stronger than echinacea, although I suppose you could overdose on echinacea, at least I'm sure if you took enough of them, although I've never heard of it happening, but people keep taking these plants and herbs and things when there are perfectly good drugs on the market, well, not drugs, but you know, medicine, real medicine, and anyway, Benjamin said she was perfectly fine when she left for church…"

I jumped in as he paused for breath. "When did she die?"

"Probably yesterday afternoon, although it might have been later, she was having an afternoon nap though, so I suppose technically that would make it in the afternoon, although I often nap much later myself, especially if I have an afternoon service. Benjamin said she was terribly sleepy when she got in from church, went to lie down and never got up again. He let her sleep and didn't realize she was dead until this morning. I'm so upset. I'm going to need your help with the meeting this evening. Could you come over?"

I was on my way in minutes, not so much to help Father Donald but to get some coherent information from Dorothy.

●   ●   ●

If they say that a clean office is the sign of a sick mind, then Father Donald's mind was in outstandingly good health. I cleared a pile of old bulletins off the nearest chair, pushed aside a litter of used Lenten folders on the desk and put down the cup of tea that Dorothy had handed me as I came through. She looked grimmer than usual and indicated with a shake of her head that she didn't want to talk about it. Not that I blamed her. It would only set him off again.

Father Donald was standing in front of the filing cabinets, doing deep knee bends as he pulled and pushed the two top drawers rhythmically in and out. I wondered if the author of *Flex-er-Cise* had anything like this in mind when he penned his little volume. I doubted it.

Before we could begin our work, the doorbell rang and Dorothy appeared with Sergeant Bernie Bickerton of the local RCMP detachment. "The sergeant wants a word with you, Donald." I started to get up.

"No, no," said Father Donald. "Stay, Charles. This won't take a minute. Yes, Sergeant, what can I do for you, not that I can do anything, of course, but I suppose I must be able to do something, or you wouldn't be here."

I saw the familiar dazed look in Sergeant Bickerton's eyes. "Er, umm. Yes, well, the thing is, we want to corroborate that Mrs. Edith Francis was at the service yesterday morning at St. Grimbald's?"

"Why yes, and a lovely job she did, too, especially her rendition of 'Sweet Hour of Prayer', most unusual, but quite touching." Father Donald pulled up his shoulders to his ears and dropped them rapidly three times. Then he rotated them clockwise and anti-clockwise.

Sergeant Bickerton stared, fascinated. "Got a crick in your neck, Father?" he asked.

"No, no. It's my flex-er-cises. You should try them." Father Donald shifted to his neck rolls.

Sergeant Bickerton nodded. "Yes, well, very interesting. Now, was Mrs. Francis also at the coffee hour following the service?"

"Indeed she was. Never missed it, well almost never, although she did forgo once or twice when Mr. Francis arrived early to pick her up, but otherwise, always there. She will be sadly missed."

Sergeant Bickerton gamely plowed on. I could see why he was a sergeant. "And did you happen to notice what she ate or drank?"

"Well, there were some of Carol Morgan's butter tarts. I'm sure she would have had some of those, except, now that I think of it, I don't think they were there when she came down, not that they'd all been eaten up, although they often are, right off the bat, everyone wants one, the most delicious butter tarts anywhere, well, perhaps not anywhere, but certainly at St. Grimbald's, in fact, I often tell Carol she should start a butter tart business, although not a business, more of a home kitchen thing…" He trailed off, unconsciously licking his lips in remembrance of butter tarts past. "Although," he rallied, "they were gone because Dorothy had taken them back to the kitchen."

"She didn't offer them to Mrs. Francis?"

"Good grief, no! Dorothy wouldn't give Edith *anything*! They were mortal enemies, well not mortal any more, more like immortal I guess, what with Edith being gone and all. But they never got on, never since Dorothy discovered that it was Edith who told the regional president of the A.C.W. that Dorothy…Oh! Shoot! It's a secret. Dorothy said she'd have my…well, let's just say it wouldn't be pleasant, if I told anyone. Can't say a thing, not a thing, silence of the confessional and all that, not that she confessed, at least not to me, but then she wouldn't, would she, confess that is. 'Vengeance is mine' is Dorothy's personal motto. No, no, I can't say another word." With this, he made the motion of locking his mouth shut, turning the key and throwing it away.

"So they didn't get on?" Sergeant Bickerton leaned forward intently. "Was Ms. Peasgood in the kitchen then?"

"Who? Ms. Peasgood? Oh my sister, of course, I always think of her as just 'Dottie'. Yes. She was in the kitchen." He sat on the edge of the desk and lifted both legs up, held them rigid and slowly lowered them back down. His face mottled a bright purple. Steady, I thought, or we'll be having two funerals at St. Grimbald's this week.

"And did you see Mrs. Edith Francis drink anything?"

Father Donald looked off into space. I could almost see when the light bulb went on. "Why yes! I did! She drank the cup of coffee Dorothy gave her."

Sergeant Bickerton was instantly alert. "So, you're saying that Ms. Peasgood *did* give Mrs. Francis something, after all?" he asked in a voice of steel. "I think I should have a little talk with Ms. Peasgood myself."

"Oh, dear, must you? She gets upset so easily. It's her nerves, you know—very delicate. Always have been, although not when she was younger of course, not that she's all that old now, but still, the pills have made a great difference, although she'd rather not have anyone know that she takes them, in fact please don't mention I told you, she'll kill me, I'm sure. She's capable of almost anything when she gets in a temper…"

After that, I watched it go steadily downhill. The upshot was that Dorothy was asked to go into the station with Sergeant Bickerton to give a statement, and Father Donald insisted on going along to give her moral support. Frankly, I feared he'd given her far too much support all ready. I, of course, was asked to take the Parish Council meeting in his absence.

• • •

I arrived several minutes late, but contrary to their usual practice, everyone was already there. Even Morley Leet made it, although I thought he still looked a bit shaky. It seemed appropriate that I break the news about Edith so that we could begin with a moment of silence for our dear departed substitute organist.

"I have some very sad and serious news," I began. "Today, we have lost a vital part of St. Grimbald's, someone who is near and dear to each and every one of us, someone whom we will all sorely miss, someone who unselfishly contributed so much towards the spiritual worship in our congregation. I know you all feel as saddened as I do by this tragic loss." I paused dramatically, thinking I'd done pretty well by poor old Edith, and wondered if I'd be called upon for the funeral eulogy. Before I could continue, Morley Leet stood up.

"I'd like to say a few words," he said. I was surprised, since I hadn't realized he was especially fond of Edith.

"I'd like to have it put on the record that I have always admired the steadfast leadership and deep spiritual qualities that were brought to this parish by Father Donald. I'm sure I speak for us all when I say that he was a good rector and an all-around good human being." He wiped a tear from his eye, sat down and looked solemnly around him.

Before I could say anything, the door banged open and Father Donald bounded into the room. "I'm back! Well I wasn't really away, just gone for awhile, but I was with you all in spirit. So how's the meeting going, Charles—have you told them my good news?"

Morley Leet stood up. His chair fell with a crash backwards onto the cement floor. He thrust an arm towards Father Donald. "You! You're, you're…" and he fainted dead away.

Suddenly, I flashed back to yesterday's coffee hour, and I

could see the arm thrusting the cup of coffee into the Father Donald's hands. I could hear the voice, "Here you are, Father Donald. A double-double. Just the way you like it." It had been Morley Leet. The drugged coffee was not only deliberate, but it had been meant for Father Donald. And Edith was dead because of Dorothy's vigilance, not vengeance.

"Shoot! I knew Morley Leet was going to love my news about the money, but I never expected him to be this excited, well maybe not excited, although he is pretty overcome." Father Donald rushed to Morley's side and slapped him, not too gently on the cheeks. Morley sat up and looked groggily at Father Donald.

"I guess ten thousand is a lot of money, Morley, enough to make any treasurer faint," Father Donald told him.

"Ten thousand! I never took *that* much! Just enough to put a down payment on the boat!"

"No, no! You've got it all wrong. The Bishop has given us a grant of $10,000 for a new well and septic system. I don't think we can help you with your boat, although, perhaps you could get some kind of grant from the government, they're always handing out money for fishermen, although you don't fish do you, or at least not professionally, although on the other hand…"

It was time for me to intervene. "Excuse me, Father Donald, but Morley Leet and I have some business with Sergeant Bickerton, don't we, Morley? I'll just leave you to carry on with the meeting." I got a firm grip on Morley's arm and hustled him into the kitchen, where I could lock the door while I made the phone call. Behind me, I could hear Father Donald's voice.

"Shoot! What a shame! Charles has let the cat out of the bag, and I wanted to be the one to tell you the good news, well not really news now since you already know, and not really good since I suppose he told you about poor Edith, well, not poor in spirit, but poor in, well, not poor at all, especially where she's gone. At least I presume that's where she's gone, although, on the other hand…"

PAT WILSON AND KRIS WOOD *have been friends for over 30 years, although they've seldom lived near each other. Instead, they've run businesses, written stories and collaborated on many projects through e-mail, fax and phone. Pat is an international speaker. Kris is a gerontologist. Both are published authors. Now they are next-door neighbours living in Nova Scotia. The characters in this story will be appearing in a full-length mystery novel that the pair are currently preparing.*

SEIGNEUR POISSON

R. J. HARLICK

----

*M*audite neige!" Jacques cursed as he fought through another deep snow drift. Those stupid old fools to go fishing in such weather.

With his eyes half shut against the stinging snow, he scanned the frozen lake, hoping to see his grandfather and great-uncle. The sooner he found Pépère and Mononcle Hippolyte, the sooner he could get back to his tape of last night's hockey game.

"Impossible to see in this soup," he muttered at the wall of swirling white. He pulled his hood tighter.

Wondering how far he'd come, he looked back to the shore and groaned when he saw the red blur of the barn, its light the only sign of life in this vacuum. *Sacrifice!* He'd only come a short distance. But then again, it meant the beer he'd abandoned was still within easy reach.

It would serve those two crazies right if he left them to handle things on their own. After all, it was their pig-headedness that had forced him out in this blizzard.

He wavered for a second. He could almost feel the smooth beer running down his throat. Then with a deep drag on his cigarette, he turned back into the storm's fury. He had no choice; he had to find those stupid old men.

It was difficult going. And the blasted snowshoes didn't make it easier. He heaved one foot out of the snow and slapped it onto the shifting surface in front of him. It disappeared under a foot of powder. He picked up his back leg and swung it around.

"*Tabarnac!*" he yelled when his leg, minus a snowshoe, plunged into the snow. He'd kill that old man when he found him. He jammed his boot back into the binding and cursed forward.

When he'd discovered that his new high-tech snowshoes were gone from the barn, leaving only the ancient bear-paws, Jacques had blamed his grandfather for taking them. Now he figured it was really his uncle's fault. Hippolyte had put Pépère up to it, which wasn't surprising. Ever since his younger brother had arrived, Pépère was doing things he'd never dare do before.

Like today. It was only because of Hippolyte's goading that Pépère had risked ice fishing in such weather. After eighty years, his grandfather knew better than to go out on the snow covered lake in a blizzard, when you couldn't tell sky from ground. Sure, it wasn't snowing when the two of them had set out this morning, but Pépère knew those clouds on the other side of the lake meant it would be snowing like stink by midday, that's for sure. He'd even said as much, but Hippolyte wasn't having any of it.

"*Eh ben!* You gone soft behind the ears, old one?" Hippolyte challenged in his hoarse smoker's voice. "Afraid of a little snow? *Maudit crisse*, you are truly an old man." His grandfather didn't even bother to reply, just stomped out of the room.

Next thing Jacques knew, the two burly shapes, loaded down with tip-ups, buckets and other ice fishing equipment, were lumbering down the hill to the flat plain of the lake. Each was the bookend to the other. Although there were ten years separating the two brothers, the passage of time had made them twins, short and stocky with thick spare tires around their middle, that even heavy duffel coats couldn't hide.

And of course they both had the nose, the Tremblay nose that Jacques too had inherited. No one could miss it for the amount of space it occupied on the high cheek-boned Tremblay face. And from the side profile it jutted straight out with a sharp downward turn like the beak of some giant bird, which was why people around here called the Tremblays the Crow's Beaks.

Unfortunately, a nose of this size had one distinct disadvantage in this weather. It froze. Jacques rubbed the numb tip with his icy mitt. He tried to see if there was any sign yet of the two fishermen and was blasted once again by the wall of blinding snow.

"Pépère, you there?" he shouted, praying they'd had the sense to fish in this part of the lake and not where they usually went. But the only response was the muffled rasping of the snow against his hood.

A quick backward glance brought on a faint lick of fear. The shoreline had vanished. He was cut off. And his track, the last reference to home, was fast disappearing.

He thought of the advice his grandfather had pounded into him since he was a child. "In a whiteout, stay put, *mon p'tit*. Don't move, you'll get lost, maybe even fall into a hole in the ice."

Yeah, well, a fat lot of good that advice would do him now. He might as well fall into a hole rather than return home without his grandfather.

"I don't trust that God-cursed Hippolyte," Maman had

shouted from the kitchen. "No saying what he'll get up to in this tempest. Turn that TV off now and go find your Pépère."

And when Jacques hesitated, she shouted "And if something happens to him, you'll answer to God."

So what choice did he have? Besides, he knew she was right; he didn't trust Hippolyte either. With a last drag on his cigarette, Jacques turned back into the driving snow.

For sure, his grandfather and uncle were fishing in the bay at the other end of the lake, next to English Bait Point. Since the big storms always blew from that shore, he figured if he walked straight into the wind he'd eventually stumble into them.

There was a curious thing about this particular fishing spot. Before his uncle came to live with them, the old man had avoided it like it was the devil's curse. Instead, his grandfather fished winter and summer near Indian Rock, convinced the biggest walleye hung out in the surrounding deep water. In fact, he fished there so often people had renamed the giant slab of granite "Crow's Beak Rock".

It had taken some convincing by Hippolyte to get his brother to go against habit and of course his fears: Pépère clung to the belief that even one step on the neighbouring water was a step towards death. Hippolyte had argued hotly and loudly that his brother was a silly old fool to believe in such superstitious nonsense. It had happened so long ago that it was only crazy old men like his brother who still believed that death would come to those who walked over the dead man's bones. Besides, everyone knew that the bones had long since been re-buried in the Protestant cemetery at Mont Georges.

At first, Pépère wouldn't budge. As far as he was concerned, Indian Rock had been good to him. Indian Rock was where he was going to fish come hell or high water. Hippolyte could go fishing where he damn well pleased, but he'd go alone. At least that was what his grandfather had said, until his uncle came home with the biggest, meanest looking walleye Jacques had ever seen. Next time Hippolyte went ice fishing, he didn't go alone.

"*Tabarnac!*" yelled Jacques, as his boot slipped out of the ancient bindings again. He struggled to retrieve the snowshoe and promptly lost his balance, landing nose first in the snow. Sputtering in frustration, he fought with the icy powder until he gained enough purchase to push himself onto his feet.

They deserve to freeze to death, he thought as he kicked his boot back into the binding. He jerked the strap tight. It broke. He tied the broken end of the strap to the webbing. It broke again. In a fit of anger he flung the snowshoes away.

Sacrifice! He was screwed. But he couldn't turn back.

He lit up another cigarette and struggled through the deep snow. It felt like he was moving a ton of bricks with each forward step. *Tabarnac!* He'd never reach his grandfather in time. A sudden squall sent him reeling backwards. But he braced himself, and, bending into the wind, ploughed onward.

It was curious how Hippolyte had just turned up out of the forest one hot day last summer. Why, Jacques didn't even know he had a great-uncle by the name of Hippolyte until the gnarled old man was standing in the doorway, swatting black flies and demanding to see his brother. Even his grandfather seemed a bit puzzled by the stranger in the crumpled suit, clutching the tattered suitcase. But as recognition dawned—for you couldn't mistake the Crow's Beak nose—Pépère's face cracked first into a suspicious scowl then into a weak welcoming smile. "Hippolyte? *C'est vrai?* It is really you? Unbelievable. We thought you were dead, that's for sure."

And so Hippolyte came to live with them, but not without considerable opposition from Jacques' mother. As far as she was concerned, looking after one old man was enough; two would make it impossible, particularly since the newest arrival probably hadn't lifted a finger to do any work in his entire life. She searched through the family for another home for Hippolyte.

Of his eleven brothers and sisters, only three had the courtesy to reply. Sister Claudette, the youngest, pleaded that a convent was no suitable place for an old man. Father Jean-Paul, the second eldest, said he had no room in the presbytery. And Madeline, the bluntest of all, said that not even for an audience with the Pope himself was she having a crazy live with her.

For that, as it turned out, was the problem with Mononcle Hippolyte. It was also why Jacques and his mother didn't know about this youngest boy of the Crow's Beaks, the one the family had hoped and prayed was long since dead.

Fifty years ago, Hippolyte had been locked away in an asylum for something so dreadful that the family had given part of their land to the church to atone for his sin. They were so ashamed, they'd even asked the priest to excommunicate their son and erase his name from the parish records.

It had taken much pestering by Jacques to discover what Hippolyte had done. At first his grandfather had refused to discuss it, saying it was best left alone. Even his uncle didn't want to talk about anything other than fishing and the weather.

Then one night after a bit too much *piquette*, the moonshine Pépère bought from Papa Drouin, the two brothers finally divulged what had really happened. Hippolyte had killed a man, an Anglo to be exact, which made Jacques wonder why his family had been so upset. After all, fifty years ago, killing a man, especially an Anglophone from Ontario, was no big deal. And still wasn't, as far as Jacques was concerned. But it turned out the family's shame came not from the murder but from what Hippolyte did to the body afterwards.

All that summer, Hippolyte had been trying to catch a hundred pounder. Several times he'd almost caught the enormous muskie, but each time it got away. Until one day he arrived at his secret fishing spot just in time to see the giant flapping fish being hauled into a boat by someone who had no right to be there.

At this point, Hippolyte said he didn't remember much, just sparks going off in his head, and next he knew he was hauling a big sucker of a muskie into his own boat with some strange looking bait stuck in its mouth. "Then," he said, his eyes wide in remembered wonder, "them fish started jumping out of the water like the devil himself was snapping at their tails. I figured maybe it was this funny lookin' bait, so I put another piece on the hook. I tell you, Jacques, us Tremblays lived like a monsignor that night, eh Pierre? And for the rest of the summer. We never had it so good. Why people called me Seigneur Poisson, eh, Pierre? Sir Fish, much better than Crow's Beak, that's for sure."

But the Tremblays' feasting was brought to a sudden and sickening close when hunters discovered the mutilated remains of a body hidden amongst the rocks on an isolated peninsula, the one people now called English Bait Point. It didn't take the police long to discover Hippolyte was the one who'd killed the man and chopped him into tiny bait-sized pieces.

Jacques shivered, and not from the cold. He wiggled his fingers to make sure they were still there and wiped the icicles from his nose. Exhausted from pushing through the drifts, he wasn't sure how much longer he was going to last. English Bait Point had better be straight ahead.

A few minutes later, he stumbled over a rusty metal bucket

with a broken handle. He sighed with relief. The old man's fishing pail. He was on the right track.

Feeling more optimistic, he pushed forward with renewed energy. However, the farther he moved away from the stranded bucket, the more he questioned why Pépère had thrown it away. Maybe it was useless for carrying gear, but for sure it was better sitting on an overturned pail than on snow.

This uneasiness increased when he discovered the augur. This was serious. Not even for a free jug of Papa Drouin's *piquette* would Pépère throw this new drill away. Even if he had his old homemade spud with him, he didn't have the strength any more to drill one hole with it, let alone the five he always made in the ice. But then again, Hippolyte was more than strong enough for the two of them.

Fear for his grandfather took over when Jacques uncovered the clump of pink crystals in a nearby mound of churned snow. There was no mistaking the signs. The two old men had been fighting. And one of them was hurt. That must be why Pépère had dropped his gear.

Jacques reached behind to ensure the long case was still slung over his back then picked up his pace. He prayed he wasn't too late.

A short distance later Jacques spied the looming mass of shore and hoped he'd arrived at English Bait Point. He turned to follow the shoreline in search of the cliff that marked the end of the peninsula. Once around it, he should see some sign of the two fishermen.

Jacques couldn't understand why his uncle insisted on fishing next to this reminder of his bloody crime. At first Jacques had thought maybe Hippolyte wanted to seek forgiveness from his victim's spirit. But after more pestering, it came out that throughout his long stay in the asylum

Hippolyte could think only of the gigantic muskie he'd caught beneath the cliff of English Bait Point. He was bound and determined to be Seigneur Poisson once again.

All summer and fall until the lake froze over, Hippolyte had spent the daylight hours trolling back and forth in the water around the point. But other than a few good-sized muskies, no giant had snagged his line. Surly to begin with, he'd become more so as the season progressed. Once, he had rammed the boat of another fisherman who had dared to fish in his spot.

Hippolyte had begun to experiment with bait. First, he'd tried worms, crayfish and other standard fishing lures. But when that had failed, he'd tried raw chicken. With bloody chunks of freshly killed rabbit he had some luck, so he'd started trapping them in earnest. Before long, Jacques's mother, revolted by the blood and squealing rabbits, screamed at him to stop, and when he didn't, at Pépère to do something about it.

For a time, they thought he had returned to normal bait, but one day not long before the lake froze over, Jacques had discovered his great-uncle chopping a deer haunch into tiny bait-size chunks. However, since this was on English Bait Point and well out of sight of his mother, he'd decided not to say anything, particularly when the next day Hippolyte had brought home his largest catch of the season.

Unfortunately, it was not the largest fish caught by the Crow's Beaks that season. Pépère had brought home one monster fish after another, muskie, lake trout, you name it. He had the golden touch. And with each large fish his grandfather had brought home, his uncle had become quieter and quieter, while his eyes had grown colder and colder.

Then accidents had started happening to Pépère. The first

one had occurred in the barn when a pitchfork fell out of the loft, skewering the old man to the ground. Fortunately, it had pierced the loose material of his jacket, not his chest, so he had walked away, yelling at Jacques for leaving it in such an unsafe place. But Jacques was sure he'd left it beside the manure pile.

Next, his grandfather had almost sliced his leg in two when the ax had ricocheted off the piece of firewood he was splitting. Close inspection had revealed a nail hammered into the center of the log. Pépère had put it down to just one of those things. Jacques remembered seeing his uncle with a can of nails and a hammer shortly before the accident.

Once the lake had frozen over, things calmed down for as long as the two brothers couldn't fish. When the ice was thick enough to support them, each had returned to his own special fishing spot. Except this time, it was Hippolyte who brought the big fish home. A thirty-pound walleye was followed by several others of equal size. No one dared ask what kind of bait he was using. Pépère was so infuriated he moved to English Bait Point.

And the race to become Seigneur Poisson had geared into overdrive. To this point, Pépère had only been toying with Hippolyte's obsession. Now he was determined to take the crown away from his brother. So far there was no clear-cut winner. Both brothers were bringing home monster walleyes the like of which made Jacques decide he'd never swim in the lake again. It also made Jacques begin to suspect the kind of bait his grandfather was also using.

Then last week, another accident had happened. Hippolyte had been cleaning a rifle when it accidentally fired. The bullet had knocked the toque clear off Pépère's head and he had only escaped the next bullet because he'd hidden behind the milk separator.

That was when Jacques's mother had decided enough was enough. One bullet could be labelled an accident; a second bullet was something else altogether. She had told Hippolyte to leave. Today was his last day. Tomorrow he was to go to a group home a hundred miles away run by the good Sisters.

This was the reason why Jacques had agreed to abandon Les Canadiens to come out in such weather. While normally Pépère could look after himself, Maman was right, there was no saying what the God-cursed Hippolyte would get up to today when you couldn't see sky from ground.

Through the lessening snow, Jacques could see the outline of the cliff at the end of English Bait Point. He slipped the gun case off his shoulder and unzipped it. When his mother had said "Go find Pépère", he knew he might be needing his rifle. He pulled it out of the slender case and ran his fingers along the well-oiled stock. He'd killed many a deer with this. No reason why he couldn't kill Hippolyte if he had to.

He dug into his pocket and pulled out some cartridges. He jammed them into the magazine and hammered the bolt home. He was ready.

When he reached the end of the cliffs, the snow suddenly stopped, and the sun came out. At first he was blinded by the sudden brilliance, but as his eyes adjusted, he saw what he had come to find. From one side of the bay to the other ran a familiar line of orange tip-ups; the specialized ice fishing rods his grandfather used. They reminded Jacques of a cemetery of lopsided wooden crosses, each stuck into a mound of ice at the edge of a small hole. Before the first lopsided cross sat a figure covered in snow.

Jacques was about to call out when he realized he was seeing only one fisherman. Anxiously, he searched for the other. But the bay remained as empty of other human life as the lake behind him.

Sacrifice! He was too late. It had happened.

Ignoring the cold, he removed his mitts and felt the icy steel of the trigger. It was now up to him to finish this off.

He moved cautiously towards the hunched back of the silent figure. He was halfway there when he began to wonder why the fisherman hadn't moved since he'd first seen him.

He was about thirty feet away when he noticed a dark patch at the feet of the still figure. At first he thought it was just a shadow. But when he drew closer, he realized with dread it was frozen blood, a pink crystalline mixture looking much like the snowcones he bought at the carnival.

He pointed his gun and pushed silently forward. The fisherman still didn't move. Jacques was beginning to wonder if he was still alive.

Suddenly the cross bar of the tip-up jerked down into the hole. The figure lunged forward. Next thing Jacques knew, a gigantic silver fish was flopping on top of the packed frozen snow.

"*Arrête!*" shouted Jacques, "Stop, and raise your hands high above your head." Jacques had seen enough westerns to know these were the right words.

The figure remained rigid, then the hood slowly swivelled around and pointed the long Crow's Beak nose towards Jacques.

"Come on, Mononcle, hands above your head!" Jacques jabbed his gun towards the silent figure.

Two icy mittens slowly rose.

"*Eh ben!* What have you done with Pépère?"

"Jacques! My grandson. It's me…your Pépère." The man struggled to raise himself from the overturned bucket.

"Stop right there. How do I know it's you?"

"*Mon Dieu.* What is the world coming to that a grandson doesn't know his own grandfather?" One mitten brushed back the hood while the other lifted the toque from the high cheek-boned Tremblay face.

Jacques relaxed with relief when he saw the familiar bald pate and the twinkling brown eyes, but stiffened when he saw a deep gash extending from his grandfather's eye to his mouth. A frozen trickle of blood still clung to his cheek.

"*Tabarnac!* What did that crazy man do to you?"

His grandfather removed his mitt and ran his hand over the bloody gash. "This? It is nothing. A disagreement," he replied with a slight shrug of his shoulders.

"Where is Mononcle?"

Pépère crossed himself, then pointed. "*Sainte-bénite!* There's been an accident."

Jacques followed the line of the pointing finger to a spot beyond the last tip-up, not far from where the inlet flowed into the bay. It took him a few seconds to discern what looked to be tracks spoiling the smooth surface. Then he realized they led in a direct line to a patch of black water. A frozen red toque lay at the edge of the hole.

Jacques looked back at his grandfather. "Mononcle Hippolyte?" he asked.

"*Oui.*" Pépère crossed himself again.

Jacques was tempted to look into the hole where his uncle had fallen through, but he didn't, knowing as did anyone who fished on this lake that the ice where the river flowed into the bay was never thick enough to support a man. Still, he was a bit confused by the presence of a large patch of what looked to be frozen blood close to the hole.

"*Oui.* I told him to stay put in the white-out, but Hippolyte wouldn't listen," continued Pépère. "He was sure the big fish were over there, eh?"

By his grandfather's feet lay a number of equally enormous fish, each with a perfectly round staring eye, some frozen, others limp with glistening water. Next to them, on the patch of icy pink were chunks of raw bait.

As horror slowly engulfed Jacques, Pépère beamed and said, "Now I am Seigneur Poisson, that's for sure."

R.J. HARLICK, *an escapee from the high-tech jungle, decided that solving a murder or two was more fun than chasing the elusive computer bug. When she's not inventing the perfect murder, she's roaming the forests near her country home in West Quebec. "Seigneur Poisson" is her first published short story.*

NATURAL MEDICINE

Jones scammed the health nuts every day.
Jones sold them grass and made them pay.
He sold them herbs he said were healthy:
Bought cheap, sold high, got very wealthy.

Sucked in the wife of the town M.E.,
And every year he raised her fee.
He was an expert id motivator:
"Quit now and you'll regret it later."

His clients stayed, they paid—regretted.
Nature Guru spent—was wildly fêted,
Until the day they found him dead
His throat chokeful of twelve-grain bread.

And the M.E. said—without any pauses—
"It's clear this man died from *natural* causes."

JOY HEWITT MANN

LOVE HANDLES

H. MEL MALTON

Peter loved my shape for nine of the ten years we were married.

"I love the way your little belly pooches out like that," he'd say, cupping my stomach in his big hands and jiggling it in a friendly way. He'd nuzzle underneath my chin, where the skin was beginning to take on a soft roundness, and he'd take my upper arms between his fingers and gently squeeze. "Mmmmm," he'd say, "like warm bread." It wasn't as if I was running to fat. Just spreading is all, the way you do past forty, if you're not a health Nazi. I like my food, I'll admit that. So did he.

We'd met at a gourmet dinner club. Each month a group of us would get together at someone's house and revel in the glories of food, cream sauces and fresh, tender vegetables drenched in butter. Exquisite pork tenderloin marinaded in port and thyme, robust red wines and dazzling desserts glazed in syrup. We'd fallen in love over a coulis of raspberries and praline ice cream, and our wedding feast was to die for.

Everything changed in the spring of the last year of our marriage. Something got into him, I don't know what it was. Fever, maybe, or a mid-life crisis. All of a sudden he was passing up my Dijon Chicken with apricot-basil sauce and asking for tofu instead. On his birthday in June he had a token bite of my famous Chocolate Death Cake and then pushed the rest away, saying he was full. He'd started jogging in July, and by August he had dropped fifteen pounds and was pumping iron.

"Peter," I said one night, "are you having an affair?"

"Of course not, Pumpkin," he said. He called me that, but my real name's Phyllis. "I'm just trying to improve my lifestyle so I'll live longer," he said. "I wish you'd join me." It was then that he cupped my belly with his hands, and he didn't say he loved the way it pooched out. He jiggled it, but it wasn't very friendly. "You could stand to lose some of this, you know," he said. I smacked him with my pillow and started spending more time in my garden and less time with him.

Not long after that, he started trying to get me involved in his "improved lifestyle". First, he volunteered to do the grocery shopping, a thing he had never done before. He totally ignored the list I sent him off with, and instead came back with organic vegetables, a fifty pound bag of rice, a bunch of dried peas, beans in bulk and a vegetarian cookbook.

"Give it a shot…for me," he said.

Oh, I tried. I soaked and boiled legumes until the bed sheets billowed with his new found flatulence. I concocted salads and pilafs, soy cakes and falafels and did my level best to acquire a taste for them. But secretly, late at night, when Peter was snoring and farting and perhaps, losing weight in his sleep, I would sneak down to the kitchen, take my stash of farmer's spiced sausages from the back of the freezer and fry 'em up. Sometimes I'd add some garlic glazed potatoes and top it off with a sticky homemade Chelsea bun.

I went jogging with him once, finally giving in after he promised to take me out to dinner afterwards.

"What'll I wear?" I said. He was standing at the door stretching like an Olympic triathlete, bending this way and that and breathing through his nose. His newly minted hard body was already encased in skintight running gear, like a muscular sausage. He wore a tank top with "Just Do It!" screaming across the front of it, his chest hair bristling up out of the scooped neck, a patch of moss on a hunk of granite. He'd recently booked time on one of those tanning beds. and his skin had turned an interesting orangey-bronze colour that I guess he considered attractive. I yearned for the pale soft doughboy I'd married.

"I don't know what you want to wear, for gosh sakes," Peter said. "Something loose and comfortable, if you still have anything like that." That was unkind, although it was true that I had gained a pound or two since Peter had started working out. It was almost as if every little lump of fat that Peter banished from his own body had hidden itself secretly in the walls of the house, leaped out suddenly when I wasn't looking and fastened itself onto my thighs. Not many of my clothes fit any more, and there was no way I was going to try to squeeze into a pair of shorts, no matter what kind of activity I was letting myself in for. I eventually settled on a pair of Peter's own pre-workout sweat pants and a baggy T-shirt.

"You look great," he said, half-heartedly, but I knew I looked grotesque. I laced up the new running shoes he had bought me at Fitness World, and we moved out onto the front lawn.

"Now," Peter said, "I'll just guide you through a few basic stretching exercises, okay?" I grimaced. Suddenly, I was back in Grade Six, standing in front of Miss Featherstone, our gym teacher at Mumford Public School. Miss Featherstone had weighed us, measured us and put us through our paces like a drill sergeant, getting us ready to take the province-wide Participaction tests which would yield, for some, a handsome achievement badge in bronze, silver or gold. For the also-rans, there were mingy little plastic "Good Effort" pins. I had several of them rattling around in a cardboard box somewhere, relics of a thankfully denied past. I had hated Miss Featherstone with all my childish heart. As Peter went into fitness trainer mode, showing me how easy it was to flop over like a rag doll and touch his toes (I couldn't quite see mine), I felt all those Featherstone feelings well up in my throat again.

"Come on, Phyllis, you're hardly trying," he said, annoyed because I was sort of rolling my eyes as he bent sideways like a piece of overcooked spaghetti, demonstrating a move that, for me, was a physical impossibility. "Think of your body as a set of steel cables. Strength though stretching. At least give it a shot." I gave it a shot and felt something go sproing in my neck.

"Uh, Peter," I said.

"What?"

"I think one of my steel cables just snapped."

"Nonsense," he said, coming over to me and vigorously kneading my shoulders. "You just need to loosen up is all."

By the end of the warm-up session I was ready to call it quits. I was sweating like a racehorse and aching all over. Peter's teaching technique, which he must have learned at that awful private school his parents sent him to, was horribly patronizing. Every time I managed to execute a bendy-thing, he was right in there with a "gooood work!" remark that made my hair stand on end.

"Okay, you seem to be limbered up enough now," he said, finally. "We'll just take it easy the first time out. Usually I go a couple of kilometres, up to the reservoir and back, but we'll just go a little way—enough so that you get a chance to feel the runner's high. I tell you, Pumpkin, there's nothing like it!" He leaped away like a demented hare, turning around once and running backwards to encourage me to follow.

Remember that scene in Walt Disney's *Fantasia* where the hippos do that ballet number? That was me, in my mind's eye, not dressed in a tutu, but a dancing hippo nonetheless. I swear I saw the curtains twitch at neighbouring windows as I plodded past—people peeking out to see why the china in their cabinets was rattling.

I made it halfway around the block. By that time, he had pulled far ahead, perhaps forgetting about me, or perhaps made oblivious by his "runner's high". The only runner's high I felt was the one I manufactured artificially back at the house with a couple of stale Tim Hortons donuts I found at the back of the fridge.

Peter returned, glistening with vibrant health and righteous indignation.

"What the hell happened to you?" he said.

I swiped at the sugar on my chin and smiled sweetly. "I don't think running's for me, my love," I said. "Your body may be made of steel cables, but mine's butter cake." I thought I heard him mutter something like "lard-ass" as he stumped off to the shower, but I couldn't be sure.

I put the running shoes back in their Fitness World box and took them back to the store for a refund. Luckily, Peter had kept the receipt. The shoes had cost $149.99, and there was a friendly note scrawled at the bottom of it, "Have a nice day. Lori," with a little smiley face. Well, Lori, whoever she was, would just have to give back the commission and move on, that was all. I spent the cash at Foodland, splurging on prime rib, tender new potatoes, a carton of double cream and some California strawberries.

A couple of weeks later when I pulled into the driveway after grocery shopping, Peter was waiting for me on the porch with an eager, little boy "I've got a secret" look on his face. He helped unload the car without being asked and acted like he had to pee, which was a dead giveaway. For a while, I pretended I didn't notice, but his tension was getting to me so I finally gave in.

"Okay, Peter. What is it?"

"Promise me you won't be mad," he said.

What kind of bargain is that? I wanted to ask but didn't. He had been so disappointed with the jogging fiasco, and it had taken a while to smooth his ruffled feathers, so I just nodded and let him lead me into the living room.

There, taking pride of place in front of the TV, was a contraption straight out of a medieval torture chamber, metallic and menacing.

"I bought you a present—a rowing machine," Peter said, holding tightly onto my hand as if he were worried I'd haul off and clobber him. I almost did. This "I bought you a present" line was completely transparent and not a little annoying. The running shoes had been okay, a mistake, maybe, but not a huge one. The rowing machine was another thing entirely. How would he have reacted if I had picked up an extension ladder and a couple of cans of paint for the upstairs windows at Canadian Tire and told him I'd bought him a present? Or if I'd bought him a present of nose-hair clippers or a bottle of that stuff men spray on their bald spots? Present—schmesent.

Still, being a loving and forgiving wife, I allowed Peter to strap me in and show me how the monster worked. I felt like I was at the gynecology clinic, my feet guided into stirrups and my private parts waving in the wind.

"You could do fifty reps on this while you're watching that

cooking show you like," Peter said, a smug smile on his face. "You'll hardly notice you're doing it." I rowed for a few minutes to make him happy, bellowing like a walrus for effect. "Gooood work," he said. "Now let me get in there and show you how to make it burn." I watched indulgently for a moment or two then went back to the kitchen to make lunch, salad for him and manicotti with cream sauce for me. He rowed through an entire afternoon of soap operas and eventually fell asleep strapped into the wretched thing, slumped over the fake oars like Silken Laumann after a race.

Over the next week or two, the machine acquired the status of a sort of secondary coffee table, a designation which I actively encouraged as I loaded it up with coffee cups, bowls of popcorn and magazines. Sometimes when we watched TV together, Peter would move all the stuff off it with a little sigh, clamber into the machine and row for a bit, which didn't bother me very much, since it left more room for me on the couch. Then he'd stop and offer me a turn, but I'd always say, "maybe later," which actually meant "I'd rather have bowel surgery in the woods with a stick."

I watched him like a hawk and finally, one evening, he put his empty coffee cup down on it and left it there. I knew I had won. The transformation was complete. The next morning I dragged the rowing machine into an obscure corner of the living room and returned the coffee table to its rightful place. I don't think Peter noticed, or if he did, he knew better than to comment. When I was moving it, I found another receipt scotch taped to the underside of the seat. Fitness World again. Four hundred bucks. "Enjoy!" was scribbled on the back, along with "Lori" and the smiley face. I decided I would drop in at Fitness World some time and have a friendly little chat with Lori. The machine made a fairly decent rack for clean laundry, which I ironed while watching my favourite cooking show.

The rowing machine wasn't the end of it, though. Peter kept on nagging me to get fit, lose some weight, "trim up". Like a toddler, my reaction to the constant wave of exhortation was to do the opposite. I continued to cook rich, tempting meals, filling the house with the smell of fresh bread, cinnamon, roasting meat and savoury gravy. He continued to shun my offerings and started cooking for himself, putting together nasty looking, grey hued bean soups and drab green salads like mouldy lace, no dressing.

In bed one night, after he had turned his newly muscled back on me (I had put on my special nightie and some Eau de Hanky Panky, but it didn't work), I grabbed his hand and played it over my belly. "You used to call these my love handles," I said.

"I've got nothing against love handles," Peter said. "I just care about your health, Pumpkin." Pumpkin. Suddenly, I was reminded of that old nursery rhyme: *Peter, Peter, pumpkin eater/ Had a wife and couldn't keep her/ Put her in a pumpkin shell/ And there he kept her very well.* I saw myself getting bigger and bigger, filling out the pumpkin shell that Peter had put me into with his fitness kick, and I just couldn't stand it. I cried myself to sleep.

The next day, Peter came home with another present for me.

"Here's a thing that we can do together that'll be fun, I promise." He handed over a bag with a large square box inside. Fitness World again. The receipt ($89.00 plus tax) was signed as usual by Lori, this time in purple ink. The smiley face looked vaguely erotic, and I noticed that Lori had dotted her "I" with a little heart.

"Remember how you used to figure skate?" my husband said.

"Peter, that was a long time ago. Anyway, it's summer."

"No, no. Open it." I did. Nestled in the tissue was a brand new pair of in-line skates.

"I got some for me, too. We can take it easy, you know. Just skate around the neighbourhood. C'mon. Try them on."

"We're too old for roller-skates, Peter."

"Oh, c'mon. Try them on."

He was so enthusiastic, and the skates did look kind of alluring, purple plastic with sparkles, like grape-flavoured lollipops. I stroked them. They felt smooth and cool under my fingertips. I had a sudden image of myself skimming along the road, whippet-thin and graceful. I still had dreams about my figure skating days—dreams of freedom and power.

"We could go outside right now and try them out," Peter said. He had already strapped his on. "It'll be okay. There's no traffic this late."

I was tired. I'd spent a long day in the garden, and dinner was already in the oven—a succulent garden vegetable quiche that I'd taken some trouble over and a superior white wine that I was hoping to coax Peter into tasting.

"Okay," I said. "Just a little turn in the driveway, then dinner." I crammed the receipt from the box into my pocket for safekeeping and buckled up the skates. I decided I would take the skates back to Lori later with a thinly veiled threat attached. A threat that involved the words, "punch your lights out", in a friendly kind of way.

It was wonderful at first. Roller-skating isn't like ice-skating, though. For one thing, ice has some give to it, though you'd never think it. But the other different thing is that you can't stop on asphalt the way you can on ice.

"Wait up," Peter called. He was never much of a skater, and I was getting a little carried away, I'll admit. I was just flying along the sidewalk, the wind in my hair. Pavement is a lot bumpier than arena ice, too, and the rumbling shudder of the hard rubber wheels was making my glasses dance on the bridge of my nose, so that I wasn't seeing quite as clearly as I should have. I didn't see the car backing out of the driveway until I slammed into it. I tried to stop, but little rubber wheels aren't the same as metal blades, and when I fell, a whole bunch of my personal parts snapped at once. Peter may have bought a couple of pairs of in-line skates at Fitness World, but Lori, damn her eyes, hadn't bothered to sell him the necessary wrist guards, knee pads or helmets.

•   •   •

Hospital food didn't agree with me at all. During the nine weeks that I lay in traction (strapped into another machine— an irony that was not lost on me) I dropped twenty pounds.

"You're looking just terrific," Peter said during a visit. He had brought Lori with him, because, he explained, she felt really guilty about the whole thing. He was careful to reassure me that they were just friends. They worked out together, he said, patting my hand and smiling in a slightly breathless kind of way, as if he'd been running. Lori, as I had expected, was impossibly young and sleek. She wore her gleaming mane of blonde hair in a ponytail, tied with one of those plastic bobbles you see on pre-teens. She seemed genuinely concerned, though, which was sweet of her.

"Thanks for the compliment, dear," I said to Peter, smoothing my plaster encased arm across my diminished belly. "I feel just terrific, too. We should have thought of this sooner. If I'd done this in January, I'd look like a sixteen-year-old by now." He didn't get my point. Lori did, I think. She backed away from my hospital bed, her baby blue eyes going dark suddenly as her pupils dilated.

My love handles were gone, and when I was finally discharged from hospital, I discovered that none of my old clothes fit me any more, which necessitated a couple of trips to the mall. That's where I discovered the Health Food shop and the interesting book on medicinal plants.

Peter was delighted with my newfound enthusiasm for healthy eating and gobbled up my veggie burgers and eggplant supreme. He especially liked the new green salad I'd invented, the one with a secret blend of herbs and spices. I encouraged him to invite Lori over, so I could get to know his "workout buddy" better.

"I can't believe you're being so generous. So understanding," he said, and invited her at once. Over dinner, she explained that she was serious about retail and one day she would have a Fitness World store of her own.

"Go for it," I said. "The future is yours, Lori." In the kitchen, I was very careful to keep Peter's plate separate from Lori's and my own. Although he didn't know it, my husband was on a special diet. When he started to get sick, Lori called me up and asked if I thought maybe Peter should cut down on his workouts a bit. She was really very concerned. So sweet of her. I told her he probably just needed more greens in his diet.

He died in his sleep. The doctor explained that he'd had a massive respiratory shutdown, probably owing to over-exertion. "Too much running on an empty stomach," he'd said, and I'd nodded in agreement. Nobody thought to test for aconite, or monkshood, the pretty flower I had been cultivating in the garden next to the vegetables.

At the funeral tea, I served sausage rolls wrapped with butter-heavy pastry, and smoked salmon on sour cream slathered toast. Horns of phyllo pastry, bursting with fresh berries and kirsch-laced whipped cream jostled for position with profiteroles and drizzled caramel. Everybody we knew came, and everybody said how sad it was that Peter, who was looking so good, had died so young.

Lori was there, dressed in black, her ponytail secured with a black bobble-thing.

"I just knew he was working out too much," she sobbed. "I forgot how old he was. We were having so much fun together." She was really so sweet. I patted her thin wrist and offered her an eclair. Over by the stove, Dr. Herb Foote, the fellow who hadn't thought to test for aconite, stuffed a whole cream horn into his mouth and smiled at me. He had love handles.

H. MEL MALTON *is the author of the Polly Deacon mystery series, published by RendezVous Press, including* Down in the Dumps *(1998),* Cue the Dead Guy *(1999) and* Dead Cow in Aisle Three *(2001). She has published numerous short stories, articles and poems in periodicals such as* The Malahat Review, Grain *and* Chatelaine. *She is a great believer in the healing power of rich, high-fat food and doesn't indulge in exercise if she can possibly avoid it. Her two dogs, Ego and Karma, take her for a stagger in the bush twice a day and spend the rest of their time chewing on old manuscripts.*

THERE'S A WORD FOR IT

MELANIE FOGEL

On our last Tuesday Scrabble night, Mrs. D. handed me a sealed lavender envelope and asked me to keep it, "in case." Two days later she was dead.

She was the type who always looked like she was on her way to church: lipstick, permed white hair, twin set and modestly high heels. For years we'd crossed paths in the building, at the mailboxes or in the lobby, never exchanging more than a nod hello. When we finally got into a conversation in the laundry room, she introduced herself as "Mrs. DesRochers." I countered with "Annie Sapp"—let her figure out my marital status.

"You live in the basement, don't you?" she asked as she pulled folded clothes from a baby blue plastic basket, shook them out and placed them in the washer.

I answered in the affirmative, upending my green-garbage laundry bag into the machine beside hers.

"I guess you don't get much light down here," she commented sympathetically. "Does the traffic bother you?"

"You get used to it." What the hell was she after?

When she invited me up to her place to wait while Coin-a-Matic laboured for us, I guessed she was lonely. I prefer a limited circle of acquaintances, and nosy old ladies are pretty far outside the perimeter. But I was also itchy for another dose of the computer Scrabble game I'd been playing for six straight hours, so to prove to myself I wasn't addicted, I said okay.

She lived on the third floor, overlooking the parking lot. As we approached her door, a bird started chirping. "That's Bijou," she said, smiling with a pride that could be mistaken for maternal. "He always recognizes my footsteps."

Her furniture looked like she did: old, solid, highly polished; a Turkish rug for colour and lace antimacassars that probably dated back to the days of hair oil. She greeted Bijou, a turquoise and yellow budgie who welcomed her with an enthusiasm worthy of a Pomeranian, then went into the kitchen to make tea. I took the opportunity to read her bookshelves. Mostly historical romances and royal biographies. And *The Official Scrabble® Players Dictionary*.

We spent most of the twenty-two minutes talking Scrabble. I discoursed on the delights of playing against a computer, but Mrs. D. wouldn't take the hint; she wanted a Scrabble date. She preferred afternoons, and I being a self-(i.e. rarely) employed librarian, could have said yes. But I like afternoons for the web, since it's slow in the evenings, so I lied about wanting to be home should a client call. We decided on Tuesday because it's a lousy TV night.

Mrs. D. proved an excellent opponent—better, in some ways, than my computer version, whose sound and graphics lacked the charm of her wit and hospitality. Despite the heavy old furniture, her apartment was bright and airy—a nice change from my Goodwill-eclectic pit. At first I went easy on her, but when she played *mangabey* and *flitch* back to back, the kid gloves came off.

That last Tuesday, she was distracted. Didn't bat an eye when I put *enquirer* on a triple word. During the four months we'd played, we'd rarely gotten personal, so I didn't ask what was wrong. She gave me the envelope as I was leaving, and I said "sure" without comment. Then, on Thursday, I met the super in the garbage room and he told me she'd died. "Damn!" I said, somehow resentful she hadn't consulted me. Then, "Who's going to look after her bird?"

He shrugged. "She was your friend," he accused.

Acquaintance, I corrected silently. But she had a couple of my books, as well as a key to my flat, as I had to hers, in case one of us locked herself out. "One of her relatives might take him. If she has any," I said to a face neither hopeful nor helpful. "If he doesn't starve to death first."

"Well…" He went back to emptying the blue box. He wasn't going to do anything for a tenant who couldn't tip.

I returned to my flat thinking I'd better retrieve my books before they got packed with whatever her next of kin would be taking. I could feed the bird at the same time.

• • •

The super hadn't told me about the police tape. I debated crawling under it, but that wouldn't tell me why it was there. So I called Bernie, the only cop I knew and the man who was likely handling the case, and for a change didn't have to leave a message.

"It's just a formality," he explained. "I'm sure it was natural causes."

The paper boy had found her that morning. When she hadn't responded to his knock as usual, he'd tried the knob. Bernie's scenario was that Mrs. D. had fallen, as old ladies are wont to do, and hit her head on the cast-iron radiator.

"C'mon," I said. "There's nothing by the radiator she could trip over."

"At that age, you don't need anything. A dizzy spell, your

knee buckles. She wore orthopedic shoes."

"So? She was healthy as a horse. She used to take the stairs for exercise."

"Yeah, but at that age. We see it all the time, Annie. Old people. Weak bones."

"So you're going to save money on an autopsy by chalking her up to statistical probability?"

"No, we're waiting on the autopsy. She isn't high priority."

Alone people never are, I thought.

"Actually, you might be able to help," Bernie said. "You ever been in her apartment?"

"Plenty of times."

"Good. Her door was probably unlocked all night. Get the superintendent to let you in and see if anyone took advantage."

"Me? Didn't she have one of those 'in case of emergency phone so-and-so' numbers?"

"You tell me. Apparently she's got a son someplace, but we haven't tracked him down yet."

"She never mentioned him." An estranged son wouldn't know if anything was missing anyway. Was I really the only person close enough to her to know? I told him I already had a key and asked if it was okay to touch stuff.

"We don't put tape up for decoration," Bernie said. But despite the possibility of theft, he was in no hurry to send in the forensic team. "She was old, Annie," he reminded me.

"What are you saying, Bernie? That she was senile? Because she wasn't. She beat me at Scrabble all the time."

"She was eighty-two."

That surprised me. "So what?"

"You sound like you'd rather she was murdered."

I just didn't want her dismissed. "She wasn't a dotty old lady," I said.

Bernie paused to grind his teeth or something, then said, "Take a look around, don't touch anything. And don't break the tape," he warned before hanging up.

Bernie and I had met during the investigation of my nephew Ivor's murder, which got me more involved with family affairs than I'd been in decades. We aren't friends, but he finds my thought patterns useful on occasion. He says my brain's wired differently, so I make connections he wouldn't. I once told him it's an occupational hazard of subject indexers, but only once. I don't want him calling the National Library when he needs a consultant.

I hadn't told Bernie about the envelope; it must have Freudian-slipped my mind. I hadn't even opened it, as if that act would make her death more real, even though—or because—I was pretty sure this is what she'd mean by "in case."

Because Mrs. D.'s newest piece of furniture dated from around 1952, her flat looked like a scene from a PBS *Mystery!* My eyes zoomed in on the chalk outline under the window opposite her front door, travelled to the big bloodstain by the head, then panned up to the red smear on the radiator. There was nothing in the area she could have tripped over or stumbled against—unless you count sixty-inch shears a hazardous product.

The place definitely looked different, and it wasn't just poor Bijou huddled silent in his cage like a street person in a doorway. The middle cushion of the sofa had a dent in it, something I'd only ever seen after having sat there myself. The doily on the back of the wing chair was off kilter, and the cutglass ashtray wasn't quite centred on the coffee table. I bet myself that, because of cutbacks, Bernie wouldn't dust for fingerprints unless he had good reason to.

Hands in the back pockets of my jeans to avoid

inadvertently touching anything, I went up to the birdcage and said, "Hi, Bijou." He looked at me with a baleful black eye. "Guess you miss your mom, huh?" He responded with a slow blink. The cage was uncharacteristically messy, as was the area of carpet it stood on—chaff and gravel and feathers all over the place. Something like my apartment, although not so cramped and literally shittier. The food and water containers were the kind with long tubes that you filled from the top, and my conscience eased when I saw they were far from empty.

I scanned the room from this angle. Bijou's cage stood about three feet behind the wing chair, and three feet in front of and to the side of the window over the radiator. I tested the distance. Mrs. D. might have stumbled on her way to talk to the bird, but she couldn't have hit the radiator. In the light coming from the window, I could see smears in the ashtray, as if it hadn't been properly wiped. Maybe Mrs. D. made an extra effort when she expected company, but that didn't sound like her. She'd struck me as the kind of person who ironed nightgowns.

Bijou hopped off his perch for a snack, and I noticed his water cup had things in it I couldn't, and didn't want to, identify. On the assumption the cops would skip dusting the birdcage, I removed the container to clean it, but in the kitchen, the gleaming sink and counter tops needed protection. On TV the cops always use a handkerchief; I figured the kitchen towel would do.

There was no kitchen towel.

In the bathroom, there was no bathroom towel.

Who steals towels?

•   •   •

"Not everybody ties them through the fridge door handle,"

233

Bernie told me when I called him. I hadn't realized he'd taken in so much of my flat the couple of times he'd been here.

"She had one with roses on it that was strictly decorative," I told him back. "Even that's gone." I'd confirmed that after I returned to Mrs. D.'s apartment, having cleaned and filled Bijou's water container at my place.

Bernie mulled that over a moment. "Nothing else missing?"

"Hard to say, since I couldn't touch the doors and drawers. But she must have had a visitor." I told him what I'd spotted. "Unless your people sat on the sofa or used the ashtray."

"Or she did." He sounded insulted.

"You didn't know Mrs. DesRochers."

Bernie sighed like he would have to pay for the manpower personally and told me the forensic guys would be finished by the evening at the latest.

With nothing else to do, I got on the web and looked up the care and feeding of budgies, and picked up a couple of Scrabble words in the process: *cere* and *lutino*. Then I looked up Scrabble and found a site where I could play by e-mail; but it cost money, and I wasn't all that sure a remote human would prove a better substitute for Mrs. D. than my computer game.

• • •

When you're self-unemployed, time management consists of choosing between what you ought to do and what you want to do. That Friday, I still hadn't checked to see if anything besides the towels were missing and, because budgies.org said to change the water every day, what I wanted to do was assuage my guilt. So I trekked back up to Mrs. D.'s.

About the only thing not covered in fingerprint dust was Bijou; Mrs. D. would have been horrified. It made the apartment eerily different, like a familiar place in a dream. I concentrated on the cage, the only thing seemingly unchanged by the invasion. Poor tyke looked lonely. My mother used to leave the radio on for the cat, so I hunted around for a radio.

I'd never been in Mrs. D.'s bedroom and halted at the door with a creepy feeling that my nose would end up where she wouldn't have wanted it poked. But, really, I was doing her a favour looking after Bijou like this. I told myself that twice before I went in.

A television and VCR sat atop a satinwood dresser that faced the candlewick-covered bed. She'd put masking tape over the VCR's display panel. I lifted it off. 12:00 12:00 12:00 12:00. I stuck the tape back down and thought she'd carried independence a tad too far by not asking me to help her set it.

No radio here. The kitchen? I was crossing the living room to get there when I heard the snick of a key in the lock.

The man who walked in looked even more startled than I must have. Another expression flicked across his face, too quickly for me to make out, and then he smiled like a shoe salesman. "I'll assume you have a right to be here," he said, the way shoe salesmen say "Can I help you?"

He was tall and good-looking in an overly careful way. His navy blue trench coat, beige slacks and oxblood loafers were all top-of-the-line Wal-Mart. As I studied his pale face, trying to decide if his hair were natural or Grecian Formula, I recognized the eyes and forehead. "You must be Mrs. DesRochers' son," I said.

He looked annoyed that I'd guessed his secret but nodded affirmation. "And you?"

"Just a neighbour. I'm looking after Bijou until someone claims him."

I made purposeful, kootchey-coo sounds to the bird, trying

to say "Aren't you a little late to finally visit your mother?" with my body language.

He got some kind of message, because he stood there awkwardly while I pointedly ran my finger through the featureless patina of fingerprint dust on the coffee table, tsking for the shame of how this well-preserved furniture had suffered at the hands of heartless cops. He lit a cigarette without offering me one, took a deep drag, then came up with an explanation for his presence. "I've, ah, come to collect some papers."

Lucky I wasn't facing him full on, because an image of that lavender envelope popped behind my eyes, making them blink. "Be my guest," I said to him sideways.

He pulled open some drawers but without much conviction. I knew he wanted me to leave, which is why I took my time. Finally, he ran out of patience. "She must have thrown them out," he announced, slamming the bottom drawer of the sideboard.

"What, in particular, were you looking for?" I asked sweetly. "Maybe she mentioned it to me."

"Oh, just some papers. Legal stuff…"

Not a man who thought fast on his feet. How hard would it be to rattle him? "Your mother never spoke about you, you know."

He knew. "We didn't get along," he said as if that explained everything. "She ever talk to you about where she kept important stuff?"

"Bijou was pretty important to her," I said, hoping to lay a little guilt on him. "Will you be taking him with you?"

"I got no place to keep a bird. Why don't you just flush him?"

Did the Humane Society have a Most Wanted list? "You know the police are looking for you?"

A moment's panic in his eyes, then, "Why?"

"To tell you your mother's dead, I guess."

"Oh. Ah, they already told me that."

"Good," I nodded. Why hadn't Bernie mentioned it? "I guess you got the key from them?"

"Yeah."

I had no idea where Mrs. D. normally kept her house keys. Nor did I know why I was so sure this man wasn't honest. I think it was his grooming. I've never trusted guys who look like catalogue models.

"Well," he said, hands in his trench coat pockets, "I guess I'll have to see about getting this stuff cleared out."

By way of answer, I held up my fingerprint-dust schmutzed hands and then headed for the bathroom to wash them. Maybe this sleaze was his mother's rightful heir, but I hated the idea of his having charge of things she cherished.

When I got back to the living room, he was gone.

• • •

"He's a slimeball," I told Bernie next morning after he confirmed the guy had gotten the keys from the cops just before he'd walked in on me. Police HQ is only a ten-minute stroll away.

"What did he do to you?" he asked, sounding worried.

I gave him a blow-by-blow account of my meeting with the slimeball, and in return Bernie told me his first name was François, commonly known as Frank, and he had done time for pimping and drug dealing, which explained why Mrs. D. never talked about him. He lived in Hamilton and had been home when the cops called about his mother.

"It doesn't take long to get from Ottawa to Hamilton," I said. "He could have killed her and driven all night to get back."

"We don't know that she was killed."

"What about the autopsy?"

"She had a bruise on her upper left arm."

"There you go," I said. "Someone hit her."

"Old people bruise easy, she could have bumped into something."

"How was her brain, Bernie?"

The preliminary autopsy confirmed that Mrs. D. wasn't a stumbling, senile wreck. Bernie gave me the details with gruesome minuteness. He didn't usually keep me that informed, so I figured it was his way of saying I was right. As a *quid pro quo*, I told him about the envelope.

He mumbled something that could have been *merde*. "What's in it?"

The lavender sheet lay face up on the sofa cushion beside me, the single, fountain pen-written paragraph framed by the date and the signature. "It's dated Tuesday, and she leaves fifty-three thousand, one hundred and thirty-three dollars and seventy-two cents to Guide Dogs for the Blind." She used to cut the stamps off envelopes for them, too. "And a thousand to me, and the contents of her apartment to the Salvation Army."

Bernie didn't say anything for a moment, then: "You know where she'd come up with a figure like that?"

"Her bank account?"

"She was getting the Old Age supplement."

That didn't mean anything. I knew people working three jobs who collected EI.

"I wouldn't count on spending any of that thousand," Bernie warned me.

"It's handwritten, a valid will."

"That wasn't what I meant."

"She wasn't senile," I said, real slow.

238

"Okay. By the way, did she have a cleaning lady?"

"She never said anything about one."

He had a hard time believing a woman of Mrs. D.'s age could keep an apartment that clean. "She must have spent all her time polishing."

All those evenly coated surfaces came back to me. "Are you saying there were fewer fingerprints than you'd expected?"

That's just what he was saying, and we argued some more about Mrs. D.'s ability to look after herself and her home.

"Her place was always immaculate," I said, as if her standards were normal. "I mean, she wasn't anal about it, but she didn't have a heck of a lot else to do."

"Gee, I didn't know you were so busy," Bernie wisecracked. I definitely had to keep that man out of my kitchen.

"If he knew about the money, he could have killed her so he could inherit it," I said.

"She could've just fallen, Annie."

"But not from a brain seizure or anything?"

"No." Bernie knew he'd upset me and gracefully changed the subject by asking me to drop off the will.

I looked at the lavender paper again. She'd signed it Léonie DesRochers (Mrs.). Until I'd opened it, I hadn't even known her first name. Léonie, the acute accent a bold stroke, almost a tick. She'd probably been born Francophone. I admired her Scrabble prowess even more. "He's a slimeball," I said, thinking aloud.

"Yeah. Annie, if you see him again, just walk away. And call me." He gave me his home phone number. I felt like I'd been promoted.

•   •   •

Bernie's shot at my housekeeping skills hadn't bothered me,

much. But I got to thinking about myself at Mrs. D.'s age. Would I end up one of those crones with six cats? (Highly improbable.) Blue hair? (Almost impossible.) In an apartment crammed with odd bits of my life? (Very likely.) So maybe I should clean up. Right. As soon as I did more important things, like...

Bernie's not lazy; why wouldn't he link the bruise on her arm to the crack on her head? Why wasn't he working from the assumption she'd been shoved against that radiator? On the other hand, why was I so sure that Mrs. D.'s death hadn't been old age catching up with her?

No, I didn't "rather she was murdered." Maybe I was just looking for something to occupy my idle brain; maybe I resented Bernie's insinuation that old people die so easily; maybe I didn't want to think about myself dying all alone like that. Finally, I decided the reason didn't matter as much as proving that somebody had murdered her.

Crime *see* Suspect *see* Motive. Okay, a slimeball's a pretty good suspect, and money's a pretty good motive. *If* Mrs. D.'s $54,133.72 was real, and Frank knew about it.

Presumably Mrs. D. knew about it, so why were her kitchen cabinets full of yellow-label cans? Would she have been saving it all to give to Guide Dogs for the Blind? How could we have talked so much without her telling me more about herself?

There'd been a Mr. DesRochers, but all I knew of him was that he'd been in the War. And she knew Pitman shorthand, which she'd offered to teach me. I'd never had the heart to tell her voice-recognition systems were doing to stenography what hypertext had already done to book indexing.

At that dead end, I went back to thinking about why Frank had killed his mother. I even said it out loud that way: Why did Frank DesRochers kill his mother? It's a different question from: Why did Frank DesRochers kill Mrs. D.? It got me figuring another way.

The first thing I figured was: he didn't do it on purpose. Even if he was a slimeball pimp-drug pusher, he didn't strike me as the type who would cold-bloodedly kill his mother. Besides, he didn't have the brains to plan a trip to the video store. And the way she fell made it seem likely she was pushed. He was there, they got into a fight, and he pushed her. Then he didn't ransack the place looking for whatever he wanted, because Mom's dead, and he's in a hurry to scram. But he did do a cursory search, because he knew he wouldn't find anything when he opened drawers while I was there.

It was an easy scene to envisage: They shout, he shoves, she falls. He runs to check her, finds she's dead. Maybe gets some blood on him. Uses the towels to clean his hands, wipe up fingerprints, which means he had a reason to worry about leaving fingerprints. And he searches the place. Search *see* Hidden *see* Secrets. Mrs. D. had a lot of them, including her own son. And the envelope. Which she gave to me to keep secret from Frank? So he wasn't looking for the envelope, because how could he look for something he didn't know existed? So what the hell was he looking for?

Looking for…searching for…searching…the web. But you can't search the web for answers when you don't even know the questions. Okay, try another tack. Play devil's advocate. Pull a Bernie.

Could Mrs. D. have simply lost her balance and fallen? Did that really happen to old people? I got onto Google.com, and worked out the most efficient way to enter the search criteria. *Old, people,* and *falling* were just too vague. Okay, *losing your balance. Losing balance? Balance* was the most specific word, which should always come first when you're using a search engine. I typed in "balance lost." What I got was:

Results 1-10 of about 298,000 for balance lost. Search took 0.91 seconds.

Blueberries May Restore Some Memory, Coordination and Balance Lost with Age/S
...Some Memory, Coordination and Balance Lost with Age By Judy...
www.ars.usda.gov/is/pr/1999/990910b.htm

U-M freshman not drunk, may have lost balance
...freshman not drunk, may have lost balance Detroit Free Press...
www.freerepublic.com/forum/a362c2f0e24de.htm

C&EN 6/29/98: FINANCIAL ANALYSIS: Firms lost ground on income and balance sheet
...ANALYSIS: Firms lost ground on income and balance sheets CAPITAL...
pubs.acs.org/hotartcl/cenear/980629/anal.html

Lost your bank balance?
news sensation The Ketamine look, the Fashion world has been shocked this week...
www.nwnet.co.uk/n-23/xavier.htm

Bank balances and fashion. And Bernie thinks I think weird. The next page had more bank balance references, and $54,133.72 did sound like a bank account. Finally I hit one with the phrase "Unclaimed bank balance." So far, all the pages had been American. Was there anything like that in Canada?

I typed in "unclaimed bank balance account canada" and got it on the very first citation:

Frequently Asked Questions and Answers
...an unclaimed balance back from the Bank of Canada? ...
ucbswww.bank-banque-canada.ca/faq_english.htm

The Unclaimed Bank Accounts page was straightforward. All you had to do was type in the name, and it returned:

Unclaimed Balance Information
Name: DESROCHERS, LEONIE

Payee: Address: MONTREAL (QUE) Savings Account: 8135402	Transferred to Bank of Canada: $54,133.72
Last Transaction Date: 1973/8/17	Transfer Date: 1983/12/31
Status: Unclaimed	Outstanding Balance: $54,133.72

Originating Bank: NATIONAL TRUST, 1535, RUE STE-CATHERINE, MONTREAL, QC, H3N O4O

To my way of thinking, the only way a woman who taped over the flashing 12:00 of her VCR would know about a web page for unclaimed bank balances was if someone told her. And my guess was, that someone was Frank. So when he'd walked in on me, what he'd been after was evidence that he'd told her—the Bank of Canada's phone number, or claim forms—something showing that she'd begun procedures to claim her money. Because he had killed her, and the way to avoid another jail sentence was to remove any evidence of the obvious motive.

And he was going to come back—real soon, if he hadn't already—to do a more thorough search, which meant somebody should be watching the place.

• • •

"I found the money," I told Bernie over Mrs. D.'s phone.

He put me on hold while he told someone to check it out. I used the time to finish wiping fingerprint dust off the coffee table. I'd been cleaning for an hour; it was something to do while waiting for him to call me back.

"What if he does know about it?" Bernie finally said. "He can't inherit it anyway."

"But he doesn't know that," I argued. "That's what he's been looking for: her will. He tells her about the money, asks for it, she says no and he kills her."

"But Annie, if she found out about it from him, when'd she have time to write the will?"

I look forward to the day Bernie can follow my thinking without my having to lay it before him step by step. "He sees her some time before Tuesday night, because Tuesday night's when she gave me the envelope. He'd found out about the money and asks her for it. She says, 'I'll think about it,' or something. She writes the will, gives it to me. He comes back Wednesday night, she says no, he gets mad--" I heard a key in the front door. "He's here," I whispered, hanging up and grabbing one of Mrs. D.'s novels to look like I was reading.

"Hello," I beamed when Frank walked in.

"You move in or something?"

"Just keeping Bijou company." The phone started ringing. "Somebody has to look after him."

His eyes narrowed, darting from me to the phone and back again. "I told you, I got no place to put a bird."

"Pity," I said, shriller than you should say a word like that, but the phone was pretty loud, "your mother really loved him."

We stared at each other a moment, waiting for the next ring, but it didn't come. "Look," he said, "I got stuff to do here."

"I understand," I said, standing up. His face took on a self-satisfied look, like a teacher who'd just ordered a rotten kid to do something, and the kid obeys. He even stepped aside to clear my path to the door, so he had to turn around to follow me when I headed for the kitchen.

He found me rinsing the dustcloth. "Leave it," he said. "You can go now."

"Thanks, but I'd like to finish cleaning up."

"You don't have to do that."

"Yes, I do. I have to do it because I cared about your mother, and she cared about her things."

"Well, they're my things now, so you can go."

"Are you sure?"

He stood there for at least half a minute before he finally gave me one piss-poor imitation of a skeptical laugh, and said, "She leave a will or something?"

"As a matter of fact, she did." I brushed by him as I strolled back to the living room.

"No, she didn't," he insisted, following so hot on my heels that he almost bumped into me when I stopped.

"Is that what you've been looking for?" I asked, turning to face him. "Because you won't find it here."

"Where then." More of an order than a question.

245

"Safe and sound." I started to head for the wing chair, but he snatched my arm.

"Is this what happened on Wednesday? Did she refuse to give you the money, and you got angry and grabbed her?" He looked worried but didn't let go. "And then maybe she said something to you, and you got even madder, and pushed her too hard? Is that what happened?"

"You're crazy." But he let go of me.

My arm hurt like hell, but I refused to rub it as I moved away from him. "You pushed her too hard and she fell, that's all. An accident." If there was any justice, manslaughter.

"I wasn't even here."

"They found your fingerprints. You didn't wipe them all away." I could practically see the smoke coming out his ears as his mental machinery ground. "How could your fingerprints get into this apartment when you haven't seen your mother in twenty years?"

His lips started to twitch, and he blinked in what I mistook for confusion. Then he lunged.

He moved about as fast as he thought. Aiming for my neck, he caught my shoulder, knocking me onto the sofa while he continued on momentum, right into Bijou's cage. They both hit the floor at the same time, and I caught a glimpse of him, wet and chaffy, wiping birdseed and gravel from his eyes as I ran for the door.

Which whacked me right on the side of the head.

•   •   •

I wish I could have seen it, Bernie kicking the door in, gun in two hands yelling "Freeze!" like you see on TV. But I was out cold.

It took three days for the headache to clear. Bernie called on the first to ask how I was. I don't remember what I answered, but it took him two more days to call back.

"You wouldn't think he had the brains to find something like that," he said in reference to the Bank of Canada web page.

Six-year-old kids can find web pages, but like my thought processes, I considered it wiser not to disabuse Bernie. Instead I asked if Frank's confession had been hard to come by.

"No," he replied, sounding relieved I was willing to chat. "He believed your lie about the fingerprints. We never told him different."

Frank DesRochers had called his mother several times from Hamilton, after years of no communication. Then he'd driven to Ottawa to persuade her to claim the money and give it to him—it went pretty much as I'd predicted. After he'd killed her, he'd returned to Hamilton so he could be home to receive the sad news of his mother's death.

"He said he wanted to start his own business." Bernie's tone told me how much he believed him. "Probably drugs, but he needed a stake. Fifty-four thousand would have done it."

I was thinking how fifty-four thousand isn't enough money to turn somebody's life around, let alone end it, when Bernie added, "What I don't understand is, how could you forget about that much money?"

"It probably wasn't that much when she originally banked it." I'd already done some calculating. "Don't forget, it was earning interest in the good old days of double-digit inflation. It doesn't take long at eighteen per cent. And she may have assumed it was still sitting there."

We discussed how well Bijou was settling into his new home; to my undying gratitude, one of Bernie's subordinates had taken him. Then he asked, "How're you feeling?"

"A lot better. Thanks for coming to my rescue."

He made a *pfff* noise. "You scared the shit out of me, not answering. It was stupid, confronting him like that. Especially when you think a guy's a killer."

"You mean my not answering the phone persuaded you he was a killer?"

"You always answer by the second ring," he said defensively.

"Anyway, he's not a murderer—not technically, just a manslaughterer."

"Don't sound so disappointed. What made you so sure she didn't just fall, anyway?"

I'd never been sure, I'd just disliked Bernie's version of her death. "She was my friend," I said, because it was an easy answer.

Bernie said he understood.

Author's note: All the web pages in this work of fiction are real. Because the web changes by the minute, your search on Google may return different results.

MELANIE FOGEL *is the editor of the Ellis Award-winning* Storyteller, Canada's Short Story Magazine. *Her own writing has appeared in publications as diverse as* The Canadian Journal of Contemporary Literary Stuff *and the* Ottawa Citizen. *She is also the author of two how-to books for writers.*

OLD GEEZERS

ROSE DESHAW

All the time I was washing pots in the prison at Kingston Pen, I was playing golf in my head. Tournament level shots on perfect greens. Birds chirping in a cloudless blue sky and everything effortless, the way it is in those golf videos where the pros make it look so easy.

I had a computerized golf game in my cell. Through that small, barred window I watched the weather grow warmer and made my plans. The morning after my release, I would arise with dew on my spikes, sure-grip gloves on my hands and the name of Mike Weir, that overcomer of setbacks, on my lips. I would play the perfect game. The vision grew as my parole came closer.

Unfortunately, as the loot I'd stashed had been recovered, I would only be able to afford the municipal course. It's a leftover space, nine holes amid the granite of the Canadian Shield, steep outcroppings of rock over which balls go flying like lovers over leaps. But having caddied it as a kid, I knew every inch by heart.

When that old prison gate finally slammed behind me, I gazed in the direction of the course like a dog from the pound looking towards home.

"Remember, Simmonds," the guard warned, "be careful.

Get your parole revoked, and you'll be back in here serving the rest of the sentence."

Return to prison darkness when the fairways were greening and the aroma of golfer's sweat hung pungent on the breeze? It wouldn't happen. My downfall has always been my bad temper and hanging with the wrong crowd. During the time inside I had aced the Anger Management course, remaining unprovoked when Squint Hogan swiped the Nerf ball and bed slat I used to practice my swing and when Gooseguts Malloy ratted to the warden about the holes I'd scooped out in the yard to make a putting green. On the outside I would be living with my father, as gentle a golf partner as you could wish for.

The first tiny crack in my plan appeared when Dad asked me to postpone the solitary first game to fill out a foursome with a man he knew and his nephew. "This fellow, Fairbanks, is supposed to be a real pro," he said. "It would be pretty difficult to get another player at such short notice."

Impossible would've been more like it. It didn't take me long to discover that nobody in his right mind ever played with Fairbanks twice.

●　　●　　●

We were a sober little foursome, making our way to the second tee. Fairbanks, his nephew, Fat Freddie, my father and I. Fairbanks hadn't shut up since we started. "If nature intended women to play golf, they'd be built differently. Longer arms, bigger biceps and more stable personalities," Fairbanks commented. I would have liked to have Martha Nause, the recent Du Maurier champ, hear that or give the great Marlene Stewart Streit five minutes with the man after those cracks about female players. But I decided he was just an aging buffoon, the dream customer for all those tacky golf gimmicks sold in joke stores: plastic score counters, golfer's crying towels, tee caddies and club covers with cute little golf sayings on them.

As if to provide an object lesson, feminine laughter drifted towards us. Four women in two golf carts were teeing off at the first hole. I could see a flash of their pink and yellow clothing through the trees.

"It's bad enough playing a municipal course peopled with blue-collar workers and pensioners," Fairbanks reiterated. "But I have always drawn the line at women."

My pensioner father flinched at Fairbanks's list of those imposing their unwanted selves on the world of golf. But who cared? I had robbed five banks in order to afford the leisure to golf at all. It was love at first swing when the game first caught my eye across a crowded green. Everything about it feeds my passion, including the fact that golf started in Canada fifteen years before the States. My only complaint about the game is attitudes you sometimes run into: attempts to reserve it for an upper class elite, or, as in Fairbanks's case, for men only as well.

Meanwhile, the man hadn't stopped talking. But for lack of an "off" switch, his nattering was like one of those canned lectures you stick in your ear at museums and galleries. "Since women can't be considered serious players," he was saying, "it behooves management to restrict their presence at peak times, especially weekends and holidays."

I moved to the tee and prepared to hit. "Wait," he held up a hand to stop me just as I began my swing. "I've noticed you've been topping the ball. Try moving up and shift your weight toward your heels." Following that advice, I sliced neatly into a sand trap about seventy-five yards to the left.

My blissful vision of the perfect game blipped out like a

soap bubble, and a red haze intruded between me and the rest of the world. An early warning sign of anger. Use the techniques I learned inside, I told myself. Positive self-talk. You can do it. Deep breaths. Remember to have a sense of humour...

"I adamantly opposed my club letting women into membership," the man went on as though no play had intervened.

His nephew Freddie was up next. Fairbanks advised him to maintain a proper set-up this time and watch that back swing. "Fools never learn." Fairbanks shook his head as Freddie dribbled off into the rough. Freddie's face reddened. I knew that expression. I'd seen it on the faces of men just before they knifed somebody in the shower room.

"And so I was forced to resign my membership," Fairbanks droned on, as though we cared. He stepped up to the tee like Mussolini surveying Italy, then made an abysmal shot, just like all the rotten shots I'd seen him produce since the first hole. And he was smiling and nodding as though this was another brilliant ploy in his grand scheme. Or maybe he was just delusional when it came to his own game.

I looked over at Freddie. He was rubbing his fingers over a ball he had taken from his pocket, the way you do with a gun before a knockover. Thanks to prison, I've upgraded my pickpocket skills considerably, which meant I was able to relieve him of the ball for a closer look. What he'd built was as pretty a little death trap as I was likely to see outside prison. Freddie had taken the ball apart and packed the inside with an explosive. Probably had a detonator in the other pocket. One swipe with a club and whammo! If Freddie was the amateur he appeared to be, it would open up a crater the size of an underground parking garage.

I followed him. "Drop something, buddy?" I flipped the loaded ball back his way and a look of horror crossed his face when he slapped his pocket and discovered it missing. "Don't even think of taking your uncle out while I'm around," I said.

"He deserves it," Freddie said stubbornly, his face flushing. "He's humiliated me for the last time. Today he gets it."

"Wrong, Freddie. Some OTHER day he gets it. When I'm gone." I gave him my toughest prison face, the one that made the range boss decide to loan me his TV for the length of my stay behind bars. If anything were to explode in a foursome I was in, the cops would stop investigating when they came to me, what with my record of blowing holes in any bank vault I'd ever encountered. "Now get rid of that stuff," I told him.

Leaving Freddie shaking in his spikes, I hiked over to the sand trap, pointedly ignoring Fairbanks' analysis of my stance and shoulders. After three tries with a wedge, my hook shot shanked out of the sand and hit a tree. My game had died and gone to hell.

Meanwhile, Fairbanks babbled on. "I know my former club was devastated to lose a member of my capacity in the field of golf. How often had I instructed some foursome on the art of the proper swing! I gave generously of my time on the putting green to all who ventured forth, nor did I spare analysis when spotting an errant slicer. My departure has cost them dearly, I dare say. Who now beside the pro is there to selflessly aid the individual members by pointing out the flaws in their games?"

They probably held a great big celebration, I thought, as we reached the fourth hole. Fairbanks' tinny little voice reverberated like a cheap radio in my ears. "They implored me to stay, of course. 'Oh, no, Fairbanks, we cannot lose you.' But I remained adamant. 'Allowing women equal rights and privileges with male members has ruined this club,' I said, 'and will no doubt herald the demise of any other where the issue of women's equality is raised.'"

There was a honking noise behind us. Two carts had come even with us, and the women were gesturing to play through. "Honk, honk." One of the women passengers wielded a bicycle horn in one hand and a beer in the other.

Fairbanks acted as though he had heard nothing. He stepped to the tee and began to position a scruffy old ball.

"Move it, Mac!" The women were growing restless. They leaned back in their parked carts, feet hanging out as they opened more beer and lamented the lack of proper protocol in our group. "Holdin' up the game," one of the women complained. "It sez right here on the scorecard: '*Faster golfers*', that's us, '*may play through.*'" I shrugged. Freddie was still sulking, and my father was trying to make up his mind to speak to them.

The ladies were a mixed quartet. The first and noisiest cart held two florid-faced plump women who obviously hadn't been treated to a rear view of themselves in stretch pants. The other held a slim blonde and a tiny brunette, the kind of women you'd throw your coat across a puddle for.

Fairbanks postured on the tee as though he were under camera scrutiny at the Masters. He hit. I didn't bother following the track of his ball. Another birdie, ho, hum. He was the only one paying attention to the score anyway. Then he crossed in front of the carts as though they didn't exist and bent to stow his driver.

"C'mon ladies. No sense letting this particular jerk hold us up," the brunette said. She revved her little cart engine like a dragster and took aim at Fairbanks. "Go get 'em, Cecily," one of the women yelled as they bounded forward.

"Ow, ow, ow!" Fairbanks dropped his bag and hopped around, cradling his left foot in both hands. "Did you see that? She ran over my foot! Deliberately took aim and ran over…"

"Why would she do that, Fairbanks?" my father said.

"Cecily, the brunette in the second cart, is in the process of divorcing me. She has an acrimonious nature. And did I mention extravagant? Probably playing with brand-new balls." He gestured towards the women. "Cecily knew Freddie and I were playing today. Perhaps she even managed to discover our tee-off time?" He turned to his nephew.

While he read the kid out, I moved ahead and approached Cecily, who was finishing her drive.

When I got her alone, I said, "That's the last run I want you to make at the guy. I imagine your plan is to get him jumping when he sees the cart coming till you see your chance to run him off one of the cliffs."

"Was I that obvious?" Cecily said, clenching her lovely fists. "The man's a monster, and this divorce is a nightmare. Besides, accidents happen all the time on golf courses."

"Things like heart attacks or heat strokes or getting beaned with a ball happen," I agreed. "Not murder. A golf cart's not heavy enough to kill him. I don't want anything to happen to the guy while I'm playing with him, okay?"

She put her head down and fluttered her eyelashes, but in the end she agreed with me. I wandered back to the others. Fairbanks was too caught up in lecturing my father on the length of his swing to notice where I'd been, but Freddie gave me a look that said he'd play it my way.

"Your game needs a lot of work," Fairbanks said to Dad. "Under my tutelage you stand a chance of improvement. I think the best thing would be to make ours a permanent foursome, at great cost to myself, I don't mind telling you.

Perhaps I might even be persuaded to spare a little attention to your son's game as well." He looked over at me.

The red haze behind my eyes turned crimson. My fingers yearned for his throat. Dad shook his gracious old head, but Fairbanks chose to interpret his refusal as undue modesty. "You're probably thinking you're not good enough to play with me," he said. "Which is undoubtedly true, but I have to work with what I can get." He laughed immoderately.

"Don't worry, son," my father muttered to me as we followed Fairbanks to the next hole, a tricky shot over water, "I'll take care of it." That probably meant he'd write a gentle note that Fairbanks could claim had been lost in the mail. What can I say? We were Canadians. Polite unto death. On an American course, someone would surely have shot Fairbanks by now.

We watched the occupants of the carts tee off, sending two balls apiece to watery graves. Then the rest of us followed, our hopes sinking like our balls. It was a good-sized pond with cattails, sunken logs, frogs and a duck or two.

"Take a look at this, Fairbanks," my father called, pointing to something on the ground. Since the bushes would screen the two men, I followed them.

Fairbanks bent close to the tee and my gentle father raised his driver. If I hadn't been there to grab the shaft, it would have embedded itself in the right temporal lobe of the man below us. Three attempts at cold-blooded murder in one game. Nightmare golf.

"No, Dad!" I cried. Startled, Fairbanks straightened up.

"Sorry. He was about to use the wrong club," I said. I didn't care if he believed me or not.

"Leave the guy alone," I told Dad when we were out of earshot.

"But he's getting to you, son," my father objected. "Besides, he's humiliating poor Freddie, and he's causing his wife to behave rather badly. I set up today's game to give myself another chance at forgiving him for all the times he cheated me in business when we were younger. But I realize I hate him now as much as ever."

He put his old grey head to one side and studied me. "You realize we'll never have another peaceful game to ourselves as long as Fairbanks can come around and horn in. And this is the only course we can afford."

"So you decided to do something about it," I finished up. "Better to kill him off than behave rudely. Well, take a number." I shouldered my driver as though it was a loaded gun and we moved towards the others. All that time in prison thinking about golf had not prepared me for the vindictiveness that seemed to have taken over the game while I was inside. Certainly neither Freddie nor Cecily had abandoned their plans. They were waiting like outplacement agents to downsize our foursome by one. And now my watchfulness had to include Dad, previously a complete stranger to violence.

Suppose one of them succeeded in polishing off Fairbanks before we finished? If either Freddie or Cecily knew my background they might contrive to pin the crime on me. On the other hand, I didn't dare go somewhere else to establish an alibi for fear my father might kill Fairbanks in the meantime. The thought of him going to prison wasn't something I could handle.

No, I had no choice but to stay and guard this man I despised as much as they did, even though they'd all known him much longer. Just four more holes, I told myself. If only he could keep that big mouth shut, I might have a chance. At the fifth hole his monologue had been replaced by jottings in a notebook.

"Those women aren't replacing their divots," he observed, kicking aside a piece of uprooted turf. "Nobody raked the sand trap on that last shot. And look. Litter." He gave the word a sepulchral sound, pointing a bony finger at an empty beer can, conceivably from one of the carts. I noticed he didn't pick it up.

"Management co-operates no better than the police," he complained on the sixth hole. "You'll see. This report of mine will go unenforced, despite documentation. I'm expecting each of you to sign as witnesses." Freddie rolled his eyes in a long-suffering gesture towards me. I gritted my teeth and stared straight ahead.

The women zigzagged on the seventh as if by design, sometimes ahead, sometimes behind. "How'd you ever let that big ol' stud muffin get away, Cecily?" one of the women shrieked across to the other just as Fairbanks swung on the eighth tee. "Lookit the buns on that guy," her friend hooted back. Fairbanks's shot soared straight up and down again. travelling only a few yards. There was derisive laughter from the carts.

"Would you ladies like to play through?" my father asked in a voice that said he had had enough.

The way to number nine was steep. The usually slow-moving combination of my father and Freddie surged ahead in the wake of the carts, while Fairbanks beat about in the bushes for what was presumably a lost ball. I had been falling back to shepherd the trio while watching for warning signs.

"Anger muddies the water. Calmness makes it clear." I repeated quickly to myself, but maxims weren't working any more. I stared at the smug set of Fairbanks' shoulders as he

mooched up the hill. Behind my eyes the crimson haze deepened to purple. Then a wave of adrenaline so strong I could not restrain it washed over me. Like a tornado going after a trailer park I stormed up the hill.

The ninth hole was crater-shaped, surrounded by bushes and cut off from the clubhouse by a grove of cedars. On its rim, scant inches from the cliff, Fairbanks was arrogantly tempting fate. He had set his bag down to tie his shoe. Nearby were Freddie, Cecily and my father, each a check on the other.

Without slackening my pace or caring if anyone saw, I scooped the bag up in a single motion.

"Nooooo!" Fairbanks straightened up and lunged for me.

Unflinching, I dashed the whole works, tacky mottos, snotty towel and all, over the cliff. Then I stepped aside as his beefy body grabbed for mine.

It was a ballet moment, worthy of a full orchestra and the best work of the kettledrums. In slow motion, I saw Fairbanks sail right past me and over the rocky edge of the cliff.

A sound that must've been crushed bone and human flesh splattering against ancient granite came back to us. Then there was a profound silence. "Geez," someone said behind me.

"Where are the other women?" I asked when my throat stopped choking up. Both carts were parked a short distance away.

"Peeing in the bushes. I suppose we'd better round them up and go report this," Cecily added, turning to my father. "Is there any chance my husband might've survived the fall?"

"None," he said, "Not going over head first like that. I'm sorry to say he's probably broken his neck."

"Odd sort of accident," Freddie said as we headed towards the clubhouse. "Knocking his clubs over the edge, then tripping and falling when he tried to retrieve them."

"I threw the bag over," I corrected him. Was the man blind?

"Don't be a martyr," Cecily said sharply. "My arrogant husband thought he was the god of golf. So he sets his bag down anywhere he wants. Which turns out to be the edge of the cliff. When it topples over, he topples over after it." She gave me a beseeching look. "If I hadn't had too much to drink, maybe I could've done something." She spread her hands in an appealing gesture.

"I was fiddling with my clubs," my father said. "I'm afraid I missed the whole thing, but I'll back you two up," he told Freddie and Cecily as though I was the invisible man. "I think you two must have it right."

"As long as we're clear on what happened," Freddie said to Cecily. "Do you know if he changed his will?"

"He was seeing his lawyer about it this afternoon," Cecily said. "Cutting me out and probably you as well."

•   •   •

I felt numb. Throwing the bag over hadn't been my imagination. I could still feel its old leather fastenings slipping through my fingers. However, since the sworn testimony of the other six players failed to mention me, there seemed no point in volunteering the information. The cops, who had been treated to many lectures by Fairbanks on the proper performance of their duties, weren't disposed to much investigation.

The coroner's jury brought in a verdict of accidental death, recommending tighter controls on alcohol on the fairways and that a guardrail be installed in the proper place.

．　．　．

"Thanks for coming to the funeral," Cecily said the following week. She looked me square in the eyes. "I hope you understand how grateful we all are for what you did and that you don't blame yourself for my husband's death. If a man thinks he can fly, who are we to stop him? After all, he also thought he could teach golf."

Golf is a devious game, and deviant are the men and women who make it their own. Still and all we don't make a bad foursome, Dad, Cecily, Freddie and I. Only one rule between us. No one ever gives advice on another player's game unless asked. Not to anybody, ever.

ROSE DESHAW *is a Raging Granny who plays the great game of golf on a regular basis in her head. She has written a regular column on out of print mysteries for* The Mystery Review *since that magazine began. She is on the second volume of a trilogy about an out of print bookseller in Churchill, Manitoba, who is a Raging Granny.*

RendezVous Crime
Distinctly <u>Canadian</u> Mysteries

Mary   Jane   Maffini

Speak Ill of the Dead

A dazzlingly witty mystery introducing crusty lawyer Camilla MacPhee. When a sharp-penned columnist is crucified in a hotel room, Camilla's best friend is the prime suspect. Camilla sets out to vindicate her friend, but finding the killer isn't easy, as countless celebrities skewered by Mitzi's rapier wit could have had ample motive. The investigation turns dangerous as Camilla follows a grisly killer's trail marked by more murders of humans and felines.

ISBN 0-929141-65-2, paperback, $11.95

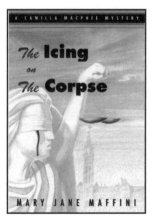

The Icing on the Corpse

It's forty below, but Camilla MacPhee is feeling the heat. When a savage serial batterer goes on the rampage looking for revenge against his girlfriend, the terrified woman turns to Camilla for help. But a sudden change of fortune causes her client to really feel the chill. Soon everyone connected with the case is either cooling their heels behind bars or trying to avoid cold storage in the morgue. Camilla's skating on thin ice looking for this killer—literally.

ISBN 0-929141-81-3, paperback, $12.95

H . Mel Malton

Down in the Dumps

The introduction of rural sleuth Polly Deacon. Polly's back-to-nature, TV-less and computerless life is violently interrupted when she finds her best friend Francy's abusive husband lying dead in the local dump with a hole in his chest. Exasperated with the ineptitude of the local police and determined to shield Francy from suspicion, Polly digs deep into the seamy underside of their small town to uncover sordid old secrets.

ISBN 0-929141-62-8, paperback, $10.95

Cue the Dead Guy

Polly is travelling as puppet and set-maker with an extremely dysfunctional children's theatre group. When the stage manager disappears with barely a trace, only Polly is convinced that he's dead. Once again, the rural area of Kuskawa is the peaceful backdrop to violent upheavals in Polly's community. The situation gets even more weird when she begins to receive cryptic threats in the form of puppet mutilations and hints of a scandalous secret in the lead actor's past.

ISBN 0-929141-66-0, paperback, $10.95

Dead Cow in Aisle Three

Polly finds herself in the unlikely job of designing a mascot for a new big-box store, despite vitriolic opposition to the new development by locals. This is nasty enough, but when allegations of corruption arise concerning the sale of the property on which the store will stand, Polly's sleuthing instincts take over. The scene starts to get ugly when people start dying—not exactly the environment that the developers desire!

ISBN 0-929141-82-2, paperback, $12.95

Lou Allin

Northern Winters Are Murder

Another freezing winter descends in seeming peace upon the Northern Ontario lake where realtor Belle Palmer lives genteelly with her dog, tropical fishes and classic film collection. But the snow-laden tranquillity is tragically disturbed when a good friend is lost in a freak snowmobile accident on an isolated lake. Or so it seems. Belle and others suspect foul play, but a motive and a criminal prove hard to find.

ISBN 0-929141-74-1, paperback, $12.95

Barbara Fradkin

Do or Die

Homicide Inspector Michael Green is obsessed with his job, a condition which has almost ruined his marriage several times. When the biggest case of his career comes up, his position, his relationships and several lives are put into danger. A young student and scion of a rich family is found stabbed in the stacks of a university library, but no one seems to have the slightest idea why. But as Green probes into the circumstances of the young man's life, a tangled web of jealousy and intrigue is revealed.

ISBN 0-929141-78-4, paperback, $11.95

---

www.rendezvouspress.com
Available from quality booksellers